BRIDES O' THE

Emerald Isle

ISBN 1-59310-631-9

Cover image © Corbis

Illustrations by Mari Goering

All scripture quotations are taken from the King James Version of the Bible.

Published by Barbour Publishing, Inc., P.O. Box 719, Uhrichsville, Ohio 44683, www.barbourbooks.com

Our mission is to publish and distribute inspirational products offering exceptional value and biblical encouragement to the masses.

Member of the
Evangelical Christian
Publishers Association

Printed in the United States of America.
5 4 3 2 1

A Letter to Our Readers

Dear Readers:

In order that we might better contribute to your reading enjoyment, we would appreciate your taking a few minutes to respond to the following questions. When completed, please return to the following: Fiction Editor, Barbour Publishing, Inc., P.O. Box 719, Uhrichsville, OH 44683.

1. Did you enjoy reading *Brides O' the Emerald Isle?*
   ❑ Very much—I would like to see more books like this.
   ❑ Moderately—I would have enjoyed it more if _____
   _____
   _____

2. What influenced your decision to purchase this book?
   (Check those that apply.)
   ❑ Cover   ❑ Back cover copy   ❑ Title   ❑ Price
   ❑ Friends   ❑ Publicity   ❑ Other

3. Which story was your favorite?
   ❑ *A Legend of Love*   ❑ *A Legend of Mercy*
   ❑ *A Legend of Peace*   ❑ *A Legend of Light*

4. Please check your age range:
   ❑ Under 18   ❑ 18–24   ❑ 25–34
   ❑ 35–45   ❑ 46–55   ❑ Over 55

5. How many hours per week do you read? _____

Name _____

Occupation _____

Address _____

City _____ State _____ Zip _____

E-mail _____

HEARTSONG PRESENTS

If you love Christian romance…

INTRODUCTION

A Legend of Love by Linda Windsor (Contemporary Ireland) Tourism director Moyra O'Cullen is thrilled to hear that travel writer Jack Andrews is coming to do an article on Ballymara's Pledging Stone—until she discovers that he intends to expose its legend that promises made at the stone in the name of the Trinity cannot be broken. Feuding all the way, they search Ballymara's past to separate history from legend. Throughout their feuds, how can they learn that, past or present, love makes all things possible?

A Legend of Peace by Vickie McDonough (1895, Ballymara, Ireland) When an American cowboy jilts Keely O'Cullen and returns to the States, Keely vows to despise good-for-nothing cowboys. After an accident at the Wild West show touring Europe, Keely's father, Ballymara's retired doctor, takes in an injured cowboy. Nick Dalton is different than Keely expects. As Nick makes peace between landowner and tenants, Keely softens. Can she trust Nick and his God, or will they both abandon her?

A Legend of Mercy by Pamela Griffin (Fourteenth century, Ballymara, Ireland) Since the orphaned Ardghal was taken into Ballymara Castle when he and Breanda were children, they have loved each other. After a shocking secret is revealed, Breanda is abducted. Ardghal and his clan are implicated, resulting in talk of war. Can Ardghal discover the truth in time to save his clan? Will his plan to reveal the true brigands help him regain favor with Lord Garland—and save Breanda?

A Legend of Light by Tamela Hancock Murray (AD 500, Southeastern Ireland) When Conn, a Christian, moves to a glen for solitude, he encounters a tribe curious about Christ. Sorcha, the daughter of a poet violently opposed to Christianity, is determined to have Conn for herself—even if she has to lie to force him into marriage. Conn must face the powerful Druids as a consequence of Sorcha's actions. When Conn's future is endangered, will Sorcha still cling to her old ways, or will love help her to see the light?

Brides O' the
Emerald Isle

An Irish Family's Past Meets the Present in Four Inspiring Tales of Legend and Love

Pamela Griffin • Vickie McDonough
Tamela Hancock Murray • Linda Windsor

BARBOUR
PUBLISHING

PRONUNCIATION GUIDE

Ardghal—AHR-dahl
Athair—AH-her, Father
Bryan—BREE-an or BRI-an
Conas tá tú?—KO-nas tah tu, How are you?
Conn—Kohn
Cormac—KUR-a-mac
cotehardie—KOd-ar-DE, a medievel gown
cuileann—KOO-leen, holly tree
Dia duit—djiah gwich, Good day.
Dia duit ar maidin—djiah gwich air MAHD-jeen, Good
　morning
eejit—EE-jit, fool
fey—fay, crazy
Fearghus—FER-a-ghus
Flann—Flahn
Killibadh—KIL-lee-bah
loch—lock, lake
Mór—Mohr
Niall—NEE-al
Niamh—NEE-av
óinseach—Own-shack, fool
Sorcha—SOO-ruh-ka or SOHR-e-khuh
tuath—tuth, a clan/tribal land or kingdom belonging to the
　tuatha people

A Legend of Love

Part 1

by Linda Windsor

Dear Reader,

A year ago, Vickie McDonough asked me if I'd like to join her, Tamela, and Pamela in an Irish anthology. With O'Reillys and Alexanders aplenty in my family and a Celtic Irish historical trilogy under my belt, my answer was a hearty yes. Little did I anticipate juggling deadlines, conferences, three businesses, and speaking and singing engagements to work in *A Legend of Love*. But I am so glad I did.

I not only grew closer to my colleagues, but God affirmed my decision, allaying my fears that I would not be able to make all my other commitments and this one as well. Once again, He showed me the truth in Philippians 1:6—*Being confident of this very thing, that he which hath begun a good work in you, will perform [it].*

To do what seemed impossible, He gave me health, mental clarity, the encouragement of my colleagues, the support of my family, who literally waited on me hand and foot that I might not have to leave my computer, and His inspiration.

May you enjoy the Lift of Laughter.

To Him all Glory,
Linda

He that loveth not knoweth not God; for God is love.
1 John 4:8

Chapter 1

Moyra Rose O'Cullen stood before the dressmaker's mirror, struck with horror. "I look like an overripe eggplant!"

She'd have expounded on her horror further, but her lip was still stiff from dental anesthesia. Of all the days for her to lose a filling. First, she had this fitting from Mars, or some such place, as maid of honor for her niece's Star Trek–themed wedding. Second, she had the most important—all right, her first—international media appointment in her new career as tourism director of Ballymara. Charged with picking up a big league travel writer coming in on the Bus Eireann from Dublin, Moyra knew a good impression could make or break the future of Ballymara's tourism.

"Always the tactful one, aren't you, Moyra?" her sister Katie observed from one of the chairs in the fitting room.

Moyra turned first one way then the other, trying her utmost to find an attractive angle. It was futile. The dark purple intergalactic garment ballooned from its fitted bodice out and around her hips like. . .well, a balloon.

"If only it flared," she observed, her *r* slurring. But some male sadist, considering himself suited to design clothing for women, had cinched it at the knee.

"I followed the pattern just as it said," the dressmaker commiserated.

"I'm schure you did, Nora." Evidently s's were a challenge to her anesthetized mouth as well.

"It's the rage, Aunt Moyra," her style-challenged niece told her. "And you've the height to carry it. You look like a runway model."

Moyra's hard glare softened, not from the blarney but because she loved her elder sister's daughter. It wasn't every day that an aunt was asked to be the bride's maid of honor. But then, as wry Katie was quick to point out, it wasn't every day the aunt wasn't married at the age of twenty-nine.

"For you, Peg," Moyra told her niece, "I'll strut about looking like I just stepped off a Star Trek set. What's the name of our mother planet again?"

"Izar."

It sounded like Gran's blood pressure medicine, Moyra thought wryly. But Peg's beaming smile was worth the sacrifice. Besides—Moyra glanced at the rack where the other bridesmaids' dresses hung—better an eggplant than a pink pig's bladder. Peg and her young beau had met at one of those Trekkie conventions, but since both were grounded enough to have finished school and become working professionals, Moyra allowed for their eccentricities.

"How's your jaw?" Katie asked, as Moyra changed into a tweed skirt and matching sweater.

Moyra worked it. "Schtiff as paddy in the grave," she moaned. "And I have"—Her v's weren't too clear either—"to be at the bus schtation by noon."

"A poor plan, if you ask me. . .and us with the wedding

only two weeks away." To hear Katie talk, one might think *World Travelogue* of New York had purposely set out to undermine Pegeen Hearn's wedding to Ned McCarthy by sending one of its writers to do a story on Ballymara and the pledging stone.

The couple planned an out-of-this-world wedding, yet vowed their love before the ancient stone that brought couples from near and far to wed in Ballymara's little church. *But then love makes fools of us all. . .or so they say.* Moyra wasn't exactly full to the brim with firsthand experience. That would require leaving the village of her heart, for she knew every eligible man within miles and had talked crops and livestock till she was blue.

"You've a heart torn between wanderlust and your roots like your da," Gran Polly told her. "Till you come to terms with one or the other, it's alone you'll be, Moyra Rose." As alone as Moyra had been when her parents died in a car crash touring Germany and Gran had taken the twelve-year-old fledgling in.

"I'd best be getting back to the Publick House," Katie announced to no one in particular. "Gran'll be needing help in the kitchen with the lunch crowd."

Gran's Publick House was the village gathering place for those so inclined to mix chat with music without the alcoholic spirits. Originally a Victorian hotel and pub that covered the entire block, it was now a small coffee shop with a dining room that saw little use, a bed and breakfast, and a home to Moyra, her widowed sister's family, and her grandmother.

Moyra shoved her arm through the sleeve of her camel wool blazer, peeking at her watch. "Ooch, I've got to push off. Grand job of it, Nora," she consoled the dressmaker. Gathering up her handbag and slinging it over her shoulder, she called back to the others as she exited the shop, "Tell Gran and Pat I'll be there in a jiff with our guest. And save us the corner wall booth."

Katie's answer followed her to the Land Rover parked by the door on the cobbled street, more dour than reassuring. "Only the best for himself, the writer."

Lips pursed—at least from what Moyra could feel on the one side—she fastened her seat belt and started the vehicle. Her sister had a dear heart but no clue how big this visit was for Ballymara. As prestigious a magazine as *World Travelogue* featuring the pledging stone and chapel was the biggest opportunity since the veneer factory outside of town had opened in the 1960s and was sure to save the dear couple who'd just bought the bankrupt Ballymara Castle.

Pierce and Mary Brennan had already spent a fortune on the bed-and-breakfast part and now worked on the hall, which was perfect for wedding receptions. Ballymara Castle was the ideal mate to Pledging Stone Chapel, where couples came from all over Ireland to be married. If Moyra could infect this Jack Andrews with the same passion she had for Ballymara and the romantic pledging stone, there was no telling what might lie in store for her beloved town.

The grass was green, the sky was bright, and the wind tried its best to strip the yellow petals from the forsythia blooming everywhere for as far as Jack Andrews's cynical eyes could see. It was spring, and he could feel the goose bumps on his flesh huddling beneath his trench coat. Between the damp chill and exhaustion, all Jack wanted was a comfortable bed with clean linens and a good day's—or was it night's?—sleep.

While the passengers in first class on the airline slept

peacefully, tucked in their lounge chairs with flannel blankets and pillows, Jack had the misfortune of sitting in the midst of a group of high school band students who were badly in need of a Ritalin dip. Not that sleep had been so easy of late, what with rumors of layoffs at the office circulating.

As a junior writer, he could see the handwriting on the wall. They'd keep that aging, pot-bellied king of florid prose and show Jack the door. Just as his ex-fiancée had—may her new husband rest in lack of peace. A sardonic smile twisted Jack's lips as the Dublin mountains, blanketed in spring violet, gave way to hillsides specked with small clumps of farm buildings.

He didn't need her or anyone else for that matter. The muse was his passion. Travel was his middle name. No roots, no ties. That's just the way he wanted it. The only catch in that dream was finding the means to afford such a life.

And that was why this assignment had to be more than good—it had to be outstanding. No nonsense about promises made over some stone in a church being unbreakable—anyone could write that. But disproving the legend, now that would put muscle in his article—BALLYMARA: QUAINT, CHARMING, AND FAKE. All he had to do was figure out how, he thought, studying the overdone brochure put out by its tourism department. The way it read, Ballymara was all but the spot of the Second Coming.

After awhile, the bus slowed, groaning as though giving birth. Jack looked up to see where the driver was taking them. Ahead was a petrol/market at a crossroad. An official-looking sign identified the route number that they were on, although under it was tacked a homemade affair defining the highway as the KILLBOG–BALLYMARA ROAD. Jack stuffed the brochure in his travel bag. Evidently this was the bus stop to Ballymara.

"Have a banner day, sor," the bus driver called after Jack as he stepped onto the rocky, unpaved parking lot.

A banner day for a duck maybe, Jack thought, managing an answering wave as rain slapped against his all-weather coat. Shoes grinding in the coarse dirt, he raced between a flatbed farm truck and a beige Land Rover for the door of the market. As he reached for the handle, a tall Maureen O'Hara clone opened the door for him.

"Fine day for ducks, isn't it?"

And the Brits waste time cloning sheep, he thought, taking in her soft green eyes and the dark auburn hair spilling in rebellious curls over the cowl of her sweater. "I think I've met my soul mate."

Confusion grazed her expression. Her smile widened, at least part of it did. And she'd put an *sh* on the end of ducks. Cloning did have some drawbacks. "I'd just thought the same thing," he explained. "About ducks."

"Oh." She laughed, confirming the song lyrics about Irish eyes smiling. Sure *'twas like a mornin' spring* to Jack's eye. "And would you by any chance be Jack Andrews?"

"I would. And you would be. . .?"

She extended her hand. "Moyra O'Cullen," she said, glancing at his wet leather travel bag. "Is that all your luggage?"

"That's it." So Mr. O'Cullen had a wife. . .a beauty with a mild speech impediment. Jack ignored a strange sense of deflation. He'd had it with women anyway.

"Would you like to dry off and have a cup of tea before we set out in the deluge?"

"How about a coffee?"

The colleen grimaced. "If you can wait fifteen minutes, I'll have you in a cozy place where the coffee's good and the food is better." She glanced at her watch. " 'Tis nigh past lunch, but anything for you, Mr. Andrews."

Whether it was the mention of coffee or the fact that Moyra O'Cullen shook him into a four-alarm alert, Jack found her proposal appealing. "Will Mr. O'Cullen be there?" he asked.

A rose pink tinged the creamy white of her complexion and darkened the sprinkle of freckles around the cutest turned-up nose he'd ever seen. "I might look an old maid, Mr. Andrews, but it's brutish to point it out."

"No—no," he stammered, wishing he could rewind his tongue. "You're a fox and a half, but my business was with a *Mr.* O'Cullen."

The prickly square of her shoulders dropped. Jack was a sucker for that '40s tailored, shoulder-padded type. Give him a classy Hepburn or the lady before him now over MTV divas any day.

"Well, I don't know how that could be," she puzzled aloud, ending with a vexed pout that nailed Jack's attention. "You see. . ." She touched the side of her mouth, self-conscious perhaps that it refused to work with her. "I'm Ballymara's director of tourism, and there's none above me save the mayor, Andrew Creagan."

Her words penetrated Jack's unexpected fascination. "None?"

"The last I heard." She shrugged on a raincoat from the rack next to the door. "Shall we be off then?"

He'd been off since he looked into those Irish eyes of hers. Jack opened the door so that Moyra could precede him. "My pleasure, *Miss* Moyra O'Cullen." The oddest thing was, he meant it.

Chapter 2

S o *you're* M. R. O'Cullen," Andrews marveled, staring at Moyra's business card in disbelief. "I've got to apologize. My secretary scribbled your name across my folder, and I thought it said *Mr.*"

"I hope you didn't have your heart set on having a man escort you around Ballymara. You're not one of those chauvinist types, are you?"

Her companion splayed his fingers, hands out in show of surrender. "Not guilty. I even did dishes for my ex-fiancée."

"Ex?" Moyra prompted. "Not that you have to answer."

"I guess I didn't wash them well enough." A smirk underscored her companion's sarcasm. "Anyway she moved on to a better dishwasher."

"Married then?"

"Yes."

This wouldn't do at all. She wasn't a busybody. "It's none of my business. My business is the pledging stone and Ballymara's tourism."

Moyra gunned the Land Rover to the top of a hillock and pulled off at a car park that overlooked the Killibadh Valley. Below, the rolling landscape was swathed in more than forty shades of green, broken only by the winding, silver blue ribbon of river and patches of bright yellow gorse. Ballymara lay nestled against a stone bridge—a cluster of slate roofs and whitewash amid treetops.

"There is Ballymara," Moyra said, more than a dreamy note in her voice. "It's never so green as on a soft. . .a *rainy* day."

She ventured a sideways peek at her strapping companion. At least he looked strapping in his long coat. It was hard to make out the color of his eyes—like an Irish sky, sometimes blue, sometimes gray, depending on its humor. That he was taller than she was another plus in the American's favor. Not that she was scoring the bloke.

"See the steeple of the chapel. . .in the trees there by the riverside. It's Chapel Park. And up there, beyond the village, if you look real hard, you can see the turret of Ballymara Castle."

Jack peered in the general direction. "If I had X-ray vision maybe. All I see is gray mist leading to gray clouds. Although that bridge down there looks like it could have been built at the same time as the castle." His demeanor veiled whether that was a good or a bad thing.

Moyra bit her lip, lest she take away from Ballymara's uncommon ability to speak for itself. She turned up the wipers on the windscreen, so that Jack Andrews could get as unobstructed a view as the rain would allow.

"I'll need to contact a local media company," he said, turning to her as if he'd seen enough of the vista. "I want pictures and some footage of the place as well."

Footage! Moyra thrummed with enthusiasm as she shifted the Land Rover into gear and pulled back onto the road. This was a better reaction than she'd hoped for.

"I'm thinking Padrac O'Connor at the *Ballymara Tribune*,"

she said as they approached the arched bridge leading into the village. "Like as not, he—" She broke off, pointing right as they circled around Chapel Park. "And there's Pledging Stone Chapel over there." The small stone chapel sat in the midst of trees that had seen its history unfold. Moyra had longed to delve into research when she was promoted from mayor's secretary to tourism director, but time had not allowed. Save the legend of the pledging stone and her ancestors of the O'Cuilinn tribe, there was little else known of the chapel and Ballymara's past.

"And it's how old?"

"It was built as it is somewhere in the twelfth century, but the history of the stone, as you know, goes back to the fifth." He had a striking face, not handsome in a pretty way but angular. Proud features, as Gran would say, sharp enough to cut oneself on.

"Look out!"

Braking, Moyra jerked the wheel and fishtailed around a shaggy goat. The remains of a rope leash dangling from its leather collar, it made its way across River Street toward the park.

"Saints preserve us! Tommy O's goat'll be the death of us all. The old *óinseach* needs a dog trotting after him, not a bloomin' goat," she fumed in a mix of shock and embarrassment from being caught with her eyes on her passenger instead of the road. After a calming breath, she turned to her passenger, who still straight-armed the dash, clutching with a white-knuckled hand. "I'm so sorry."

"No problem." Andrews followed the goat with a dumb-struck look as it trotted off, undaunted by the screech of the Land Rover's tires on the pavement. "What was it you called him?"

The start had sent her into the Irish. "A fool, I fear," she apologized. "Tommy's a dear soul, but day after day he comes into town, Jellybean following him like a pup at heel, and the moment Tommy's sitting happy as a nested hen at Corncutter's, the goat chews through his leash and shoots off to the park."

"Corncutter's?"

"The pub 'round the corner from Gran's Publick House. . . where you'll be staying." She scowled, glancing up and down the street, but no one was about in the rain. It appeared that she was the designated keeper of the goat today.

"Now what's wrong?" Jack asked.

Moyra gave him an apologetic look. Of all the days for Jellybean's shenanigans. "I'm afraid I can't leave Jellybean to the traffic. 'Twould break Tommy's heart if anything happened to him."

"*What* traffic?"

"There's people about the same as us," she pointed out. "And tour buses coming through." When they were lost, she thought with a tinge of guilt. "If you want, I can put you out at Gran's and then look up Jellybean."

"Oh no," Jack insisted. "I'd not miss a goat rescue for anything." By the look on his face, he thought he'd landed on the backside of the world.

"Hang on then," she told him, shifting into reverse to make a turnabout. Not that she needed to warn him. If he gripped the dash any harder, he'd leave prints.

A goat rescue later, Jack's tour director drove past Gran's Publick House. Three times as wide as the other stores and homes making up the hodgepodge of buildings lining High Street, it had the same slate roof, shiny from the lightening rain, and white-washed front. After pulling into a cobblestone alley that led to the hostel's back parking lot, the ever-surprising Moyra Rose O'Cullen turned to him. "Here we are at last. I imagine you're famished."

"I'm too beat to be hungry," Jack replied.

Although that little jaunt with Jellybean had spawned a bit of renewal. There was something about being on the opposite end of a makeshift leash with a disgruntled goat that got the old adrenalin going. The feisty colleen had marched straight up to the bearded muncher and replaced the frayed leash with a neon yellow towrope. Before Jack knew it, she left him holding the goat while she purchased a chain leash from the local hardware store. Now a disgruntled Jellybean was properly tethered outside the pub.

"Well you're a good sport," Moyra said, her appreciative smile brightening the dreary day. "I promise to make it up to you."

Jack squashed the possibilities that popped into his mind and grabbed his suitcase. "Glad to help."

He followed his hostess into a long, wide hall that ran straight from the back to the front door. Immediately he was struck by the stomach-stirring smells emanating from the back kitchen to the right where a black-haired version of Moyra O'Cullen hustled about arranging sandwiches on a plate.

"Katie, this is Jack Andrews, the fellow from *World Travelogue*," Moyra called to her. "Jack, my sister, Katie Hearn."

"Pleased to meet you, Mr. Andrews," she called over her shoulder, rushing over to a steaming fryer.

"You as well. . .and call me Jack." The robust scent wafting from the commercial stainless coffeemaker was tempting to the coffee-holic within—if he could keep his eyes open enough to drink it.

"Gran, we have company," Moyra sang, drawing his attention away from the sparkling, stainless and white kitchen to a comfortable but plain, family room–kitchen combination.

From a high-back rocker near the hearth, an elderly woman with a topknot of boxed blue black hair—no one would ever intentionally choose that shade—struggled to her feet. Dwarfed in a gray cardigan, Gran was a small woman with large glasses that seemed to accentuate the suspicion in her gaze.

"Don't mind her hair. My niece is studying to be a hairdresser," Moyra whispered in an aside as she drew Jack into the room. "Gran, this is Jack Andrews, the writer I told you about. Jack, this is my grandmother, Pauline O'Cullen. . .but her friends call her Polly."

Jack had the distinct feeling he would not be calling the woman Polly anytime soon.

"That is those who don't call her Gran," Moyra went on.

Jack extended his hand. "Pleased to meet you. . ."

"Gran," Moyra prompted.

"Gran. Do you mind if I call you that?" he asked, as uncomfortable as a schoolboy in the principal's office.

Ignoring his extended hand, Gran turned to put her knitting down on the chair. "Come to find your Irish roots, eh?"

"No, ma'am. My mother did that already," he said, seizing at some common ground. "I hail from the Maguires on her side."

"Jack is with the *World Travelogue*," Moyra reminded the woman gently. "To do a story about the pledging stone."

"Maguires, you say." The old woman snorted. "Never met one I liked."

Moyra flashed him an apologetic look. "He's our *guest*, Gran."

"His money's as good as the rest, I suppose." Clearly annoyed that her knitting had been interrupted, Gran took up the needles and yarn from the chair she'd just abandoned and plopped back in it with grunt. "Enjoy your stay, Jack."

Grinning, Moyra rushed him out into the hall. "I think she likes you."

"Excuse me?" If that were so, he'd dread seeing her dislike him.

"She called you by your first name," she said, leading him to the front of the public house. "You can put your case there, while we're in the loft."

"Say what?"

"The Mugger's Loft," she said. "Gran's grand idea for the combination of a coffee and tea shop."

Jack managed a crimped smile. "Moyra, if I don't get a few minute's shut-eye, I'll fall face down in my plate. Do you mind? All I need is an hour."

"I imagine you *are* knackered. 'Twould do you a world of good, no doubt. I'll show you to your room."

She bounded up the staircase ahead of him, her skirt swirling about long legs that ordinarily would set Jack's mind on anything but sleep. Ignoring the twinge of guilt over his intention to expose her little Irish Brigadoon as a joke, Jack plodded after her. If it came to a choice between his career and hers, his won hands down.

Chapter 3

Jack could have used another twelve hours rest. But when Moyra knocked on his door, he got up, pulled on a pair of jeans and cotton shirt in need of pressing, and joined her in the restaurant side of the home for a late lunch. Despite her goat rescue in the rain, she looked as fresh and radiant as the sunshine that spilled through the parting clouds and glazed the street with its light.

"Not a tea drinker, eh?" Jack observed as Moyra held a steaming cup of coffee under her nose to savor the rich, inviting scent.

She shrugged. "Sometimes I am; sometimes I'm not. But on a damp day, I prefer the bean to the leaf."

Jack leaned back, surprised as a pony-tailed young woman with the same bizarre blue-black hair color as Gran's placed a bowl of hot cream of prawn soup on the table in front of him.

"Made in honor of your visit," she announced. "Gran makes the best cream of prawn."

"This is my niece Peg," Moyra said as the girl placed a second bowl in front of her. "She's getting married in a couple of weeks."

Peg was a young fox in the clingy red top, black stretch pants, and black, high-heeled boots, although way too young for Jack's eye. "Congratulations, Peg."

Shy, she batted eyes gilded with silver glitter and painted with heavy black liner. "Thank you, sor. Love is grand."

Until the glitter wore off.

"She's a Trekkie," Moyra confided after the girl left, seconding Jack's impression that she was dressed more appropriately for a space movie set than this cozy setting.

"Ah, that explains lots. Cute girl, tho—"

Jack broke off as Moyra lowered her head in a moment of silence. *A religious fanatic*, he thought, distracted by the luminous gaze she raised afterward. He'd seen the forty shades of Irish green, and it wasn't in the landscape.

"I've been thinking about your tour," she said. "What I'd like to do is start with the stone and the chapel itself. Did you get the brochure?"

Jack put his spoon on the side of the bowl, struck that she wasn't slurring her *s* and *w* sounds anymore.

"What is it?" she asked, picking up on the change in his demeanor.

He usually wasn't so transparent. "Nothing," he answered. "It's just that your speech is different than it was this morning."

Pressing her hand against her jaw, Moyra laughed. "Bless me, I had a dental emergency this morning. I'd hoped you wouldn't notice."

"And being a cad, I had to bring it up," he said. "Sorry."

"Forgiven." She cleared her throat. "Now where were we. . . Ooch, the brochure. Did you get it?"

"Such as it was. Whoever designed it for you should give you your money back."

The moment the words were out, Jack wanted to take them back. From the startled flash in her gaze, M. R. O'Cullen was the designer. "It was my first project," she said, stiff with a mix of hurt and indignation. "We had a limited budget."

"But that's the thing. . ." Jack backed water as quickly as wit allowed. "You need to put your best foot forward." Why couldn't M. R. O'Cullen have been a short, balding man with a Guinness gut? "So tell me about the legend."

And he's back, Jack thought, admiring the glow that lifted the crestfallen look from her face. Although not for long. After all, his job was on the line. He had to write something earth-shaking, not the run of the mill florid dribble the lead travel writer put out. Of course he'd be fair. The place had its charm. . .if one had an affinity for rain and goats.

"Ballymara was once an ancient tuath belonging to my ancestors, the O'Cuilinn—" She spelled it for him. "Of course, through the years it boiled down to my current surname, but the name was taken from *cuileann*, which is Irish for holly tree."

"I read that much in the brochure."

The cream of her complexion pinkened. "Well, um, the stone was in a clearing sometimes used for fairs, where all manner of contracts were made from business deals to betrothals. The old ones considered contracts made at the stone unbreakable, but when Christianity arrived, the stone was consecrated by Conn and dedicated to God and love." With a dreamy look settling in her eyes, Moyra began to recite. *"As sure as the shamrock is green, as sure as Three are in One, our love shall be redeemed by the Father, Spirit, and Son."*

"That's it? Some holy man blesses a stone, and no pledge made at it can be broken?"

"None ever made there has been broken," she declared with the look of a child who'd been told there was no Santa. . .an angry child.

"Moyra, you're a modern woman. Surely you don't believe in that nonsense. You believe in a stone?"

"The stone has no power. It merely symbolizes the mighty power of God and love. All things are possible through Him."

"So if I pledge my love to a woman at that stone and ask her to marry me, there's no way out of it?"

The bristling beauty dropped her spoon in the remains of her soup. "Galatians," she challenged. *"Be not deceived; God is not mocked: for whatsoever a man soweth, that shall he also reap."* Gathering her purse, she looked at him as though measuring for a coffin. "I'll not sit here and have you mocking love, much less God. So when you're ready to discover the truth, I'll be at your disposal. And if scripture is too much for you to absorb, perhaps a simple Irish proverb would do you well to remember: *There's no point in keeping a dog if you are going to do your own barking.* Good day."

The following morning, Moyra needed no makeup. Face flushed with humiliation, she made her way to Pledging Stone Chapel to meet Jack Andrews, who'd left earlier to arrange for Padrac O'Connor to video the tour. No matter how much she warned the mayor that she suspected Jack Andrews was up to no good, Andrew Creagan insisted she go through with helping the man.

"Show him what he wants. Make him love Ballymara. If anyone can do the job, you can, Moyra Rose."

Armed with a prayer and a fierce determination to convince Jack Andrews that Ballymara was anything but the nonsense he'd called it, she walked up the cobbled path to the church, where a lanky, brown-haired lad with a weather-ruddied complexion set up his camera.

"*Dia duit*, Moyra Rose O'Cullen. You're looking as cheerful as a pauper's funeral," Padrac said when she reached the stone steps.

"And hello to you, lad, though I'm lost in thought, nothing more." Moyra forced a smile, hoping to keep her murderous predisposition under wraps. "I see the man found you."

"Met up with John in Mugger's Loft last night," Padrac said, referring to John McGinty, the owner of the *Ballymara Tribune*. "I'm even going to write a piece, maybe more, about this."

"Congratulations," she told him. Long past the age of most pensioners, John McGinty had kept weekly issues of the *Tribune* running but not without complaint that he was too old to do it anymore. "Next thing you know, you'll be taking John's place."

"Not likely," Padrac replied. "I'm off to the uni in Dublin come fall." He jerked his head toward the east. "Gorgeous day for shooting, innit? I already got the ruin of the round tower behind the cemetery. Straight from fairyland with the early sun's rays glistening on the dew-covered rock."

For the first time, Moyra took a moment to study the sun climbing over the eastern slopes. She caught her breath as she followed its rays into the church where the stained-glass window over the sanctuary took on the light, generating an ethereal glow about the image of Conn, first shepherd of Ballymara. Never in her twenty-nine years of attending services here had she seen it so displayed. Not exactly fairyland, but heaven, definitely.

Through the marvel of her thoughts came his words, the ones that Jack Andrews dismissed. *As sure as the shamrock is green, as sure as Three are in One, our love shall be redeemed by the Father, Spirit, and Son.*

Deep within, Moyra knew God spoke to her as only He

could. The truth would be redeemed. It wasn't up to her to convince the man. All she had to do was show Jack Andrews Ballymara's past and let it speak for itself.

"There's an old Irish proverb you'd do well to remember, son," she heard the chapel priest saying above the approaching scuff of feet on the thick carpet padding the aisles inside. "Your feet will bring you to where your heart is."

"Yeah, right, Father. Well, here's our tour director now," Andrews said, as though relieved to escape the priest's diatribe. "Have your feathers smoothed down by now, Miss O'Cullen?"

She gave Jack a watery smile, fearing the frosty gray blue of his gaze a sign of things to come for her beloved village.

"Good day to you, Moyra Rose," Father Mackenna greeted her. "I've been filling young Jack in on some of the church history. There are three accounts that I know of—the ancient record in Dublin, the letters at the Ballymara castle, and the one explaining our unusual shepherd with the lariat being in the Heritage Center at the Wicklow Gaol. If I'm not mistaken, the roping shepherd married your great, great—and maybe another great—grandmother."

"Yeah, I'll want to check those out," Jack said, dismissing the priest abruptly. "I already had Padrac video the inside of the church," Jack informed Moyra, "so all we need is a clip of you and me at the door. We can dub dialogue on the rest."

Moyra did a mental brake. "You and me? But I hadn't planned on being in your video. I—I'm here for historical input only." She pressed her hands to her cheeks, where desperation and embarrassment kindled flaming hot. "I didn't put on my face, my makeup that is. Cameras make one—"

"It's natural light, Moyra Rose," Padrac, who clearly had read no beauty magazines, assured her. "You'll look just fine."

Jack placed his hands on her shoulder, guiding her to the spot under the pledging stone arch. "I thought we'd open with the stone and then move on. Just one shot," he cajoled, crooking a finger under her chin, "and show the folks how those Irish eyes can smile."

The compliment glanced off her panic-stricken consciousness. Putting on a mannequin smile, Moyra braced for the roll of the film. Microphone in hand, Jack Andrews stood at her side and gave Padrac the cue.

"It's a fine day here in Ballymara, Ireland, where *World Travelogue* has sent me, your host Jack Andrews, to investigate the history of Ballymara's Pledging Stone Chapel. Joining me is Ballymara tourism director, *Miss* Moyra O'Cullen—"

As if her family didn't do it enough, why did he have to broadcast to the world that she was still single? Glory to God he didn't know her age.

"Who can trace her ancestry back to the fifth century and the origin of the stone. Moyra, on behalf of *World Travelogue*, thank you for offering to show us your little village and share its rich heritage."

"You're welcome, Jack." She sounded like a wind-up doll.

"Now as Moyra has told me, the basis for the legend behind the pledging stone is that no contract or promise made at the stone can be broken. Is that right?"

Moyra nodded as though her head was strapped to a backboard. "That's right, Jack." Surely the camera would see her heart fit to break out beneath her sweater. "Couples come from all over Ireland," she blurted out at his nudge, "to marry beneath this arch containing the stone. And up the hill. . ." As she pointed, she realized the futility. The viewers couldn't see beyond the camera view fixed on her. "Is Ballymara Castle, the perfect place for a reception after the nuptials." This was horrible, absolutely horrible.

"And no vow or contract made at this sight has ever been broken?"

Moyra steeled her voice. "None that we know of. You see, here in Ballymara, we take our proverbs to heart and this one in particular: 'The only cure for love is marriage.'" Satisfaction flushed through her veins at her genius. Love-struck couples would flock from all over the world to Ballymara after this.

"Then let's put legend to the test, shall we?"

Moyra's triumphant smile faded as Jack folded her hand between his. "Moyra Rose O'Cullen, *as sure as the shamrock is green. . .*"

What on earth was he doing?

"As sure as Three are in One. . ."

Moyra's lips moved, but her voice locked in her throat.

"Our love shall be redeemed. . ."

What love? This was insanity.

"By the Father, the Spirit, and Son."

As Jack lifted Moyra's hand to his lips, her jaw dropped. She had been snookered in front of soon-to-be millions of viewers.

"And there you have it, folks," Jack said, turning back to the camera. "A twenty-first-century test to an age-old belief."

"I'd as soon marry Tommy O'Toole's goat!" Too late, Moyra covered her mouth, taken aback by her own vehemence. There went her job and any hope of another.

"And there you have it, folks," Jack said, positively gleeful over his coup. "Reality television has hit Ballymara to see if the pledging stone is for real or if it's just another Blarney stone in disguise. I'm Jack Andrews for *World Travelogue*. Look for the rest of this fractured fairytale in the next issue." He shoved the microphone in Moyra's face. "Say good night, Moyra Rose."

Ire boiling in her veins at his mockery—nay, his blasphemy—Moyra seized the mike and nailed him with a lethal glare. "We've a saying in Ireland for your likes, Jack Andrews. 'May the cat eat your bones and the devil eat the cat!' "

Throwing the mike at his feet, she marched down the steps, head held high as the queen herself. If her career was to be beheaded, better she do it herself and make it a clean cut.

Chapter 4

I can't do it," Moyra shouted into her cell phone at her employer. "I won't."

Mayor Creagan had already hung up, but it felt good to speak her mind, regardless. *Do whatever it takes to make Jack Andrews change his mind about his article,* he had said. Tears of frustration and wounded pride stinging her eyes, she snapped the phone shut and shoved it into her purse. Easy for her employer, she begrudged. *He* wasn't to be humiliated in front of the world.

A quiet knock on the window of the Land Rover gave her a start. Jerking around, she saw Father Mackenna smiling at her through the window.

Clicking on the vehicle switch, Moyra rolled down the electric window. "Aye, Father, what is it now?"

"I was just telling young Jack back there that I've got a copy of Keely O'Cullen-Dalton's journal. Have you ever read it, lass?"

"My family roots have been more immediate, Father," Moyra admitted. Like helping out at the family business while getting her education and working as secretary to Andrew Creagan. "Did you ever see such a foul deed?"

"I'm thinkin' Jack might learn a thing or two as he follows

this little vale's faith back to time when." Mackenna backed away and straightened with a groan. "Give it over to God, Moyra Rose."

"If I were God, sure I know where I'd send him."

The priest laughed. "Good thing for us, you're not, lass. But what I'm trying to say, follow me round to the parish house, and I'll give you the copy of the journal that my sister sent me. Works in the gaol, you know."

Moyra let out a breath of relief. The last thing she felt like doing was driving Jack Andrews about today. "Bless you, Father. And I'll make two copies, one for myself, since it's regarding my family, and one for the American." Her face suggested the word left a bad taste in her mouth. "But hop in, and I'll give you a ride to the parish house."

" 'Tis just around the block, lass. I'll meet you there in a wink. And remember," he added, a priestly benevolence lighting on his face, "there's more flies to be caught with honey than vinegar."

Wishing she could drown Jack Andrews in either one, Moyra shifted the Land Rover into gear, a slim thread of hope holding together her shattered dream of the world falling in love with Ballymara.

Lord, the Word says all things are possible. I want You to know, I'm counting on that. Father Mackenna's warning to use honey over vinegar buzzed about in her brain, annoying as a fly. *And, not that Jack deserves it, mind You, but please help me keep a civil tongue.*

Jack followed John McGinty into the Mugger's Loft later that afternoon after hearing the small, bent, silver-haired editor of the *Ballymara Tribune* lament over having no heirs or viable prospects for taking over his weekly newspaper. As if Jack really would consider editing a rag sheet in a place where the biggest news was the dropping price of cattle.

After McGinty introduced him to the town veterinarian and his two strapping companions—star members of Ballymara's local football team, akin to American soccer players—Jack and the editor sat down for coffee next to a window.

"You know, this place looks more like a pub than a coffeehouse," Jack observed as a school bus passed by. *Good thing Jellybean was off the street,* he thought. *Traffic had picked—*

He caught himself. Twenty-four hours in Ballymara, and he was thinking of a goat.

"Funny that," McGinty replied. "It was a pub when Gran's husband ran it: the bar here and the rooms upstairs. "But when he died—" The editor heaved the sigh of one who'd lost a good friend. "Gran converted it to this coffeehouse. 'Sure, Jaysus drank wine,'" he said, mimicking a frail female voice, "'but He had bad water. Ballymara don't.'"

Had he stumbled on some Irish Brigadoon?

"Jack, you ever play football?" one of the lads at the vet's table called out, the ruddy-cheeked one with a mop of short, curly blond hair.

"I've kicked a soccer ball a time or two."

"We're short a man for the game next week," the brown-haired lad shouted across the room. "Have a care to join us?"

"I'm not very good," Jack admitted. He hadn't played soccer, which was close to Irish football, since high school, but he'd made state All Stars as a defensive player.

"Neither are they," the vet, an older fellow with an elongated face that reminded Jack of a horse, snorted. "But they have fun."

"Go on," McGinty encouraged. "All work and no play makes Jack the dull lad."

"Practice is Saturday afternoon in the park," Tim the Curly informed him. "We'll see you then?"

What was he going to do, bury himself in boring records the whole visit and not get a taste of the place? Jack grinned. "I'll be there. . .but take it easy on me."

"Go way. I'd like to see this," Peg exclaimed from behind the counter where she'd been cooing like a turtledove with a man who looked like he'd just stepped off the Starship Enterprise. Ned, the fiancé, no doubt. "I'll bring a large flask of coffee."

"You're on," the players cheered.

At that moment, Moyra O'Cullen walked into the room with a demeanor that suggested her grandmother's last breath was at stake and an icy gaze telling Jack that he was to be next.

"Here's your copy of the journal Father Mackenna told you about." She slammed it on the table. "I'll be reading mine on my own."

"But Moyra Rose," McGinty chided, "however can you save the pledging stone if you and Jack don't spend some quality time together."

High color singed her cheeks. "You're an *eejit*, John, if you think this test is anything more than a cruel, cruel joke."

Despite her withering look, Jack sipped his coffee as though it had taste and he didn't feel like shrinking away in guilt. "It's no joke, Moyra. If that stone has any power at all, then somehow we'll overcome this little spat—"

Her eyes nearly doubled in size. "Little spat, is it? Why I—" She clamped her mouth to, like a lid on a boiling kettle.

"Heads up, lads, we've a donnybrook brewin'," one of the

football players announced from across the room.

"Give 'im the works, Moyra Rose," the vet cheered.

Jack remained calm, placing his hand on the photocopy. "Thank you for getting this for me so quickly, Moyra. Maybe we can get together later to discuss it," he proposed, putting his neck on the chopping block.

Her rose red lips quirked and twisted, but Moyra stood down from her warrior maiden stance. "You're welcome," she managed, seizing her bottom lip as if afraid it might get away from her. "Later."

Spinning on practical-heeled shoes like a top, she stalked out of the room with long, stiff strides.

"Now that's a first," Peg observed from the counter, no small wonder in her voice. "I thought she'd skin you and hang you up to dry."

The corner of Jack's mouth tipped up. So did he. And some part of him was disappointed that she'd not even tried. Jack flipped over a page of the photocopy, wondering about the American cowboy whom the priest had told him about. Jack knew what brought this Nick Dalton to Ballymara, but what had made him stay?

A Legend of Peace

by Vickie McDonough

Acknowledgments

I want to thank my Lord, who decided I should be a writer and surprised me with the idea. I couldn't do it without His help and inspiration.

A special thanks to Linda Windsor for her willingness to take time out of her hectic schedule and work with us on this anthology. Her knowledge of Ireland's history and culture was invaluable.

Thanks to my family for putting up with me as my deadline drew near.

And a special thanks to you readers for buying this book. I hope you enjoy it.

Blessed are the peacemakers:
for they shall be called the children of God.
MATTHEW 5:9

Chapter 1

Ballymara, Ireland, 1895

I ndians! We're under attack!"

Keely O'Cullen jumped at the stagecoach driver's frantic cry, digging her fingertips into the seat's burgundy leather padding. Her heart pounded an anxious rhythm that matched the beat of the galloping hooves of the horses pulling the coach.

The stage swerved to the right, slamming Keely's body against the side and sending a painful jolt from elbow to shoulder. Grit from a cloud of dust entering the compartment settled over her, covering her lips as she blinked against the stinging in her eyes.

With her eyes shut tight, Darby Doyle, Keely's best friend, sat across from her, screaming like a banshee.

Da and his obsession to experience all things western will be the death of Darby and me.

What was supposed to have been a pleasant evening's ride—her first ride in a stagecoach—had suddenly turned into a nightmare.

The eerie whooping outside the stage, made by darkskinned savages with painted faces, sent shivers of fear coursing down Keely's spine. One warrior stared her right in the eye before he zinged off an arrow that flew over the coach. A split second later, the shotgun rider tumbled from the top of the stage, past the window, and thudded to the ground.

Good riddance. One less shifty American cowboy.

A measure of remorse washed over Keely for the unkind thought, but she had too much on her mind to think about that now. Grabbing the window frame, she braced her foot against Darby's seat to keep from being thrown to the ground as the coach lurched back and forth. She glanced at her father, who sat next to her, a look of sheer delight brightening his face. Maybe now she could quit worrying about his recent illness. The man seemed his old self tonight, and it warmed Keely's heart. Although, even with his fixation for all things American, how Taig O'Cullen could find pleasure in a bumpy stagecoach ride during an Indian attack was beyond her comprehension.

Another hooting Indian charged past on his powerful steed. Heat warmed Keely's cheeks as she noticed his bronze-muscled chest. Having never seen a man's bare torso before, she averted her eyes and focused on his long hair. The Indian's black mane glistened like a raven's wing. A colorful headband encircled his head, and two feathers dangling from a braided cord fluttered in the wind. There was something majestic about his savage beauty. A hair-raising war cry burst from his lips. Suddenly, a rifle shot cracked the air. The Indian's body jerked, and he plummeted to the ground in a cloud of dust.

Though the lives of everyone in the stagecoach were in danger, Keely couldn't help feeling remorse for the downed warrior. At almost the same second the brave's body hit the ground, a cowboy dressed in buckskins and wielding a pistol jumped his gray spotted horse over the fallen warrior. She covered a gasp with her hand.

As the stagecoach circled around and slowed down, Keely watched the cowboy riding just outside her window. With the attack over and the stagecoach safe, he holstered his pistol. The man must have felt her stare, because he turned his head and captured her gaze with his dark eyes. His slow, confident smile sent wee leprechauns dancing a jig in her stomach. Too handsome for Keely's liking, he reached up and tipped his western hat at her.

Scowling, she lifted her chin and turned away. In the past she'd made the mistake of letting a cowboy pique her interest, and he'd proven distrusting and full of himself, but she wouldn't make the same mistake twice. She put her hands to her cheeks, hoping the man couldn't see the blush she knew was there. Outside the other window, more Stetsoned ruffians *yee-hawed* and tossed up their hats in celebration of their victory.

"Wasn't that the grandest thing ye've ever done in yer whole life?" Darby said, her voice hoarse from her constant screaming. Hazel eyes sparkling, she straightened her spectacles and dusted off her dress with one hand.

"Aye, 'twas for sure," Keely's father replied, his eyes beaming like a child on his birthday.

Only it wasn't his birthday, it was Keely's—her twentieth—and attending an American Wild West show was not her idea of celebrating. She could understand her father thinking it was a grand thing to ride in a dusty old stagecoach that slung them back and forth during a mock Indian attack, but had Darby been blinded by the showy shenanigans, too? When her father pleaded with her to accompany him on this jolting jaunt, Keely had asked Darby to join them in the hopes of having at least one sane companion along. But alas, it wasn't to be.

Keely brushed the top layer of dust off her skirt. Having had as much of the Wild West show as she could stand, all she wanted was to go home, wash off the layers of dust and grime, and eat the roasted lamb meal that Alana, the O'Cullen family cook, was preparing for her birthday. If only the show was already over.

Keely shifted in her seat, trying to ease the pain in her backside.

"Did ye not enjoy it even a wee bit, Keely?"

She stared at her friend as if she were daft. "Oh, aye, 'tis a grand thing to be bumped around all over Ireland, covered in dirt, scared half out of me wits." Keely gave Darby a mock smile and brushed the dust off her chest, earning a sneeze for her efforts.

"But weren't those Indians fierce and the cowboys who saved us so gallant?"

"Aye, the Indians were truly majestic, but the Americans—well, you know they can't be trusted." Keely stuck her nose in the air, daring her friend to disagree.

"Keely O'Cullen." Darby straightened in her seat and gave her a motherly glare. "Don't ye dare be judgin' all Americans by the one fey cowboy who left ye standing at the altar."

"Not all Americans—just cowboys. After all, Indians are Americans, too. And I don't need a reprimand on my birthday, thank you kindly."

"Keely." Her father laid his hand on her arm. "Darby's not scolding you; she's just trying to get you to be reasonable. You can't be blaming all cowboys just because Dusty King was an *eejit* who went back to America instead of staying in Ireland and marrying you like he promised." His smile didn't cool the resentment in Keely's heart. She'd been the fool, taken in by Dusty's charming ways and intriguing accent.

She stared out the window at the crowd of cheering countrymen, jumping up and down and waving their caps in the wooden stands to her right. As the stagecoach swayed to a stop, the fallen Indians climbed to their feet and gathered up their weapons. One ran after his horse. Several bowed to the clapping crowd. Even the stagecoach's shotgun rider stood and dusted off his pants.

'Twas a difficult way to earn a living in her opinion— falling off the top of a moving stage. Were these people daft? Or just the wanderlust types like Dusty, who'd broken her heart when he dumped her and left for America while she was planning their wedding. He hadn't even been man enough to face her, leaving only a wee note behind. And if that hadn't been enough, her own brother had followed him. Connor O'Cullen had the same obsession with the United States that her father had. Praise be to God her father had too many responsibilities then, as Ballymara's only doctor to make the journey, or they'd probably be living in Texas or some other such savage place by now.

No, a cowboy had ruined her life. And as far as she was concerned, cowboys were no better than sheep droppings.

"Care to get out, ma'am?"

Keely stiffened at the deep, rich voice. The slow-smiling buckskin-clad cowboy stood at the open stagecoach door with his hand extended.

That's what I get for lollygagging. Letting him catch me off guard like this.

Studying his face, she couldn't deny the man's good looks. His tanned complexion was only a shade or two lighter than the bronze Indian's, while his dark eyes twinkled with all manner of unspoken blarney. Keely dreaded touching him, but she had to get out and wasn't quite sure her trembling legs would hold her if she tried to exit alone.

With no other choice, Keely put her hand in the cowboy's and stood. Awareness bolted up her arm with lightning speed. Confusion flickered for a moment in the cowboy's brown eyes, but it vanished with the flash of a grin. Confounded, Keely forced the matter from her thoughts.

Just get out of the coach.

"If ye're going to be standing there all day, Keely, then I'm getting out the other door. 'Tis hot in here now that we've quit movin'," Darby complained, at the same time the door on the other side of the stage creaked open.

Ignoring her friend's snide remark, Keely lifted her skirt, moved onto the small wooden step, then down to the ground. But when she attempted to withdraw her hand from his, the cowboy refused to let go.

With a flourish, he removed his hat, bowed, and kissed the top of her fingers, rendering Keely speechless. She had to tilt her head back to see his face as he straightened. He was head and shoulders taller than she. And that black western hat made him seem even bigger.

"I'm Nick Dalton, ma'am. On behalf of Bill Cooper's Wild West Show, I'm proud to wish the prettiest filly in Ballymara a happy birthday."

Oh, he was a convincing actor; she'd give him that. Keely didn't want to consider what his attention was doing to her insides—or maybe her stomach was simply in a tizzy because of her wild ride. Courtesy required a response, though she wanted nothing more than to escape Nick Dalton's disrupting presence.

She pasted a half smile on her face. "Thank you, kind sir."

If Dalton was surprised by her curtness, he didn't show it. With the formalities over, instead of releasing her hand at her polite tug, he tucked it in the crook of his arm and turned her toward the arena exit.

"A gentleman always sees a lady to her seat." His mouth quirked with an annoying hint of triumph, as though he'd somehow won the subtle tug of war.

Gentleman, indeed. If he were truly a gentleman, he'd recognize that she didn't care to be manhandled and would let her go. They crossed the arena and passed through a deep rut in the dirt made by the stage, forcing Keely to lift her foot. Stumbling on the hem of her long dress, she tightened her grip on Nick's arm.

"You okay?" he asked, holding her against his solid side to steady her.

Heat rushed to her cheeks as she regained her footing. Giving him a stiff nod without looking up, she wiggled her hand to free it. Taking the hint, Dalton loosened his grip, but stubborn as the mule that plowed the O'Cullen's garden, he didn't let go.

"I can carry you if walking is too difficult in all these ruts."

Keely flashed him the scalding glare that had sent other people retreating. He met it with a raised eyebrow and—she could swear—a chuckle. Not the least intimidated, he nestled her arm against him again, determined to play out whatever role she was sure her father had put him up to.

Infuriating man!

About to give him a good tongue lashing as they crossed the edge of the dirt arena and reached the open gate, Keely felt the eyes of the crowd upon her and swallowed the man's well deserved reprimand. She had embarrassed her father on many occasions with her hasty tongue and equally quick temper, but she wouldn't today. Not here in front of most of Ballymara. God was dealing with her about her temper, and this time she would yield.

She pointed out her seat, hoping to be rid of her unsolicited escort before her senses scattered from the manly scent of horse, leather, and dust invading her nostrils. The oak-strong, callused hand finally released hers once she was seated. With yet another elegant bow, his gaze met hers, dancing as he spoke in a voice so smooth it could soothe more than a fickle cow. "Once again, happy birthday, Miss O'Cullen."

Instead of leaving, he put his hands on her shoulders and leaned even closer. Keely pressed herself against the back of the bench until it bit into her back. What more did the man want?

"The stagecoach ride was a birthday gift from your father and Bill Cooper. Here's a little present from me."

Bewildered, Keely glanced around, looking for a present. She hadn't noticed a gift when he was escorting her to her seat. She looked up just in time to see him lean closer. His eyes twinkled again with mischief, and before she could react, Dalton planted a soft, warm kiss on her cheek, setting off hoots and cheers all around them.

In a daze, Keely watched Nick Dalton back away, bow to the crowd, and, putting one hand on the arena fence, casually hop over it. Proud as a ram on a fine spring morn, he sauntered away.

Angry thoughts swarmed in Keely's brain like a cloud of mad hornets. How dare he take such liberties—and in front of the whole town!

" 'Twould seem Keely's snagged another cowboy," someone

in the crowd jeered, evoking raucous laughter behind her.

"Aye, she can't seem to be rid of those Americans."

Wounded by the thoughtless references to Dusty and her heartbreak, Keely scooted down in her seat, unshed tears blurring her vision. Would this horrible afternoon ever end? Never in her life had she dreamed her twentieth birthday would be her worst.

Darby strolled toward her on the arm of the Indian who had fascinated Keely earlier. Keely squelched the envious feelings surging up. Why couldn't she have been escorted by the intriguing Indian rather than by that arrogant cowboy? Studying the man up close, she hated to admit he wasn't as fine-looking as Nick—not that it mattered. She crossed her arms as Darby sat next to her and the Indian strode off.

"Ye're father said to tell ye that he'll return shortly. He said something about talking to Bill Cooper. Imagine knowing the owner of this fine show." Darby's gaze twinkled with excitement. "I thank ye kindly for inviting me on that exciting ride. 'Twill be the highlight of my life."

Keely resisted the urge to roll her eyes. Darby always had a flair for being dramatic.

Back in the arena, targets of various types had been set up in a row for the sharpshooters. Colorful paper bull's-eyes attached to round hoops fluttered in the wind. A wagon wheel sported what looked like small ceramic plates attached to the end of each spoke.

A herald of music by the show's small band drew Keely's attention to the opposite end of the arena. With a rifle butt on his thigh and weapon pointing up in the air, Nick Dalton charged in on his dappled gray steed.

"Presenting Dead-Aim Dalton, the surest gun in the West!"

the announcer on the podium cried through his megaphone.

Keely uttered an unladylike snort. Dead-Aim Dalton indeed. With all the orneriness dancing in the man's eyes, he'd be lucky to hit even one target.

Nick's horse galloped around the arena. Never slowing his mount, he took aim and fired. Again and again, the ceramic targets exploded into tiny shreds, and the paper disks shattered.

All too soon, his shooting exhibition was over. Keely stewed in a mingle of surprise and disappointment. The brute hadn't missed a single shot, and the folks in the crowd were making fools of themselves with their accolades, as though they'd never seen a sharpshooter before. Nick Dalton was hardly special. . .or was he?

She didn't want to admit that she thought it might be the latter.

As the show progressed for another half hour, Keely caught herself searching for Nick. He was the first man since Dusty had deserted her who had her looking twice. It wasn't his show of gallantry or his ability to annoy her. She'd passed many a man who did one, the other, or both without a second glance. But the moment she'd put her hand in his, something had come to life inside—something better left dead than be revived by the likes of Nick Dalton.

Ignoring a trio of Indians in colorful beaded garments dancing to the sound of eerie chants and rhythmic drums, Keely's gaze traveled to the silent but impressive silhouette of Ballymara's castle, up on the hill behind the arena. Near the castle, on lower ground at the river's edge, sat the ancient chapel where she attended church. The words of the pledge that young lovers had recited together for centuries meandered across her mind:

As sure as the shamrock is green,
As sure as Three are in One,
Our love shall be redeemed
By the Father, Spirit, and Son.

Only a man who felt the same about the pledge etched in the stone archway entrance of the chapel had a place in her heart. But did such a man exist? A man who would pledge his love to her at the ancient landmark as her mother and father had done years ago? Dusty had scoffed at the tradition of young couples promising to God at the pledging stone to love each other through eternity, not realizing that it wasn't the stone but the spiritual union it stood for that was important. And like as not, Nick Dalton would think the same as Dusty.

Keely sighed. 'Twas best she put him out of her mind for good. Come morn he'd be leaving town with the rest of Bill Cooper's Wild West Show as it continued its European tour.

She lifted her eyes again to study Ballymara's castle, which stood watch over the town like a stone sentinel. For centuries the O'Cullen clan had owned and lived in it, but about a hundred years ago, her great-grandfather had donated the castle property to the town. For decades it sat crumbling and decaying, but in recent years the town had rallied to repair it. Once renovations were complete, Ballymara would realize a decent income from charging tourists a fee to tour the castle and to use it for special events.

Even though her own ancestors had lived in the old fortress, Keely couldn't imagine staying in the cold, drafty place. A surge of gratitude washed over her that her family had come to live in the O'Cullen's large estate home on Wicklow's rolling green hills, about a half mile from Ballymara, after the castle had been ceded to the village. Since then, her family had made a decent living from raising and selling sheep and collecting rents from all the tenants who leased their land.

"Would you look at that?" Darby's excited voice drew her attention back to the arena.

In the center of the ring, three cowboys did brilliant rope tricks. On the outer circle, two cowboys and a cowgirl were performing frightening riding feats. Dust flew behind a galloping horse as its rider, a young girl, hung upside down with her foot in a loop on her saddle horn, her blond braids almost dragging on the ground. Another rider on a gray horse flipped and turned as his mount continued to gallop around the arena, its thundering hoofbeats drowned out by the cheering crowd.

Keely's heart nearly stopped upon recognizing the daring rider as Nick. The man was going to kill himself doing a handstand in his saddle, his horse at full kilter, and nary a soul guiding the animal.

Her mouth went as dry as the dust stirred up by Nick's mount. While she may not like Nick Dalton in the least, she didn't want to see him killed before her very eyes.

"Keely. Look!" Darby called.

She glanced to her right where Darby pointed. Keely's heart all but stopped when she recognized a familiar black and white blur. To her horror, Corky, her ornery border collie, charged in the arena gate, heading straight for Nick's horse.

But I tied that daft dog to our wagon meself after he followed us to the show!

Keely jumped to her feet, her warning caught in her throat. Skirts hiked, she raced down the bleacher steps and through the gate and into the arena, where Corky insanely nipped at the hooves of Nick's horse.

The frightened dapple gray balked and bolted straight toward Keely, who stood frozen to the spot as the steed charged toward her. Feet high in the air, Nick spread his legs in a V to maintain his balance. Just as the snorting trick horse reached Keely, it swerved to the left, slinging Nick, arms flailing, to the right—directly into the wooden arena fence. He hit head first, the splintering wood breaking the stunned silence of the crowd. Almost in slow motion, the fence bucked Nick to the ground where he landed with a dull, stomach-turning *thud*.

Chapter 2

Nick battled the dark, swirling fog that held him captive as the wagon he lay in bounced along, jerking him fully awake. The last time he'd felt this bad was the one and only time he'd gotten drunk—but he didn't want to remember the night of his father's cruel betrayal. He just wanted to figure out what had caused the thunder in his pounding head, not to mention the fire in his left shoulder.

As he reached up to touch his throbbing head, a soft, warm hand on his forearm stopped him. "Now, don't you be touching that bandage. 'Tis a concussion you have." The prim, nononsense voice sounded familiar.

He blinked his eyes, forcing them open. The bright light from the afternoon sun peeking through the clouds above sent javelins of pain shooting through his head. Nick tried to move his left arm, but discovered it bound tightly against his body. For a split second he panicked. Had this alluring female and her band of renegades captured him and tied him up? And where was Storm Cloud? Had some yahoo stolen the horse he'd raised from a colt?

Moving his tongue around in his mouth to work up some spit, he pressed it against the roof of his mouth, and let out an ear-splitting whistle that wreaked havoc on his aching head. The woman at his side jumped, kneeing him in the thigh.

"Sure now, you've just scared me half out of me wits!"

Storm Cloud's answering whinny and bobbing head drew Nick's attention from his pain to where the horse trotted along, tied behind the wagon. Reassured, Nick relaxed and lay back, hoping if he stayed still the vice grip of pain that continued to squeeze his head would fall off. But lying still on the hard bed of the wagon as it jostled and creaked over every stone in Ireland was impossible. With every part of his body aching, focusing on what caused his injury was as futile as drowning a fish. "Ohh, I must be getting old."

"Do not resent growing older, for many are denied the privilege," the woman beside him stated in a matter-of-fact tone.

"This has to be what it feels like to die."

"You're not dying yet, though you mightily asked for it."

The woman's quick response smacked of a scolding. She sounded like someone's mother. Nick ventured a second look, his vision clearing enough to recognize the lovely but haughty birthday girl who'd ridden in the stage with her father. What was her name? Keely O'Something. An image of her standing in the arena in front of his horse just as Storm bolted took shape in his mind. He could almost hear the splinter of the wooden fence as his body struck it. The memory loosed a thundercloud in his head, and Nick yielded to the growing darkness. Anything to be free of the pain.

Leaning back against the side of the bouncing wagon, Keely crossed her arms and closed her eyes. Her father was the town doctor—albeit temporarily, until the regular doctor returned from his holiday in Scotland. Surely someone else could have taken this horse-brained buffoon in. Da simply wasn't up to it in her mind.

Ever since her father had had that horrible argument with her brother, Connor, and Connor had left for the States to join up with the smooth-talking American who'd broken her heart, Taig O'Cullen had battled with melancholy and diminishing health. When a young doctor had come to town, her father up and quit his practice, walking away from the career he loved.

The Wild West show had been one of the few events he had attended in the past year. He mostly tended the sheep and small herd of cattle on their estate. Though Keely loved having her father home, she grieved over the void left in his heart at the loss of his only son. Now that time had finally doused the fire of her hurt and anger over losing both her fiancé and brother, she'd come to forgive Connor, even miss him. If only he'd come to his senses and return home.

The cowboy beside her moaned, drawing her back to the quandary at hand. Nick Dalton could have moved on with the show, but her father was adamant that the cowboy needed to be under a doctor's care. Maybe the old man hoped having him around would ease the loss of Connor. It was a temporary reprieve at best, because once he was on his feet again, Nick Dalton would surely hit the road just like Dusty had. But what would Nick think when he discovered the show had gone on to England without him?

Keely studied the man beside her. A clean, white bandage encircled his forehead, where her father had placed nine stitches to close the long gash that Nick had received when his head collided with the fence. Straight, dark hair flopped down across the bandage, giving his face a boyish appearance. He didn't look all that old to her. In fact, he couldn't be much older than she.

She glanced at his lips then looked away, afraid someone walking down the road might catch her staring. Thankfully, Darby had ridden home with her brother, or she'd have noticed Keely's interest in the man. Of its own volition, her hand lifted to touch her cheek where Nick had kissed it. Like as not, Nick thought she was the same as other women who acted as if their only longing in life was to be kissed by him. She wanted to be angry and truly was, especially with the whole town leering on, but something about Nick's kiss touched more than her cheek. Was it just that the kiss reminded her of Dusty's better qualities?

Och! Aren't I the melancholy one? She didn't want this cowboy at her home, stirring up memories that she'd buried. She forced the thoughts of Nick's cocky smile and his kiss from her mind. 'Twould be best if she kept her distance from Nick Dalton—even if she had to do the cooking and cleaning just so Alana would be free to care for him. The sooner this American was out of her life, the better.

Food. A delicious aroma spurred Nick to force his weighted eyelids open. Someone nearby was cooking something that smelled heavenly. His stomach grumbled in response.

He pushed up on one arm then fell back against the soft bed when the room started spinning, aggravating his sleep-abated pain.

"Here now, don't you be thrashing about." Small hands pressed against his chest, holding him down. "You don't want to hurt yourself, do you?"

Too late. Ignoring the sharp pain squeezing his head, Nick forced open his eyelids again. Blinking against the dry, sawdust sensation in his eyes, he concentrated on the woman in front of him. Average in height, a pleasing figure, and thick black hair and blazing blue eyes. His heart bucked a time or two as he realized the feisty Miss O'Cullen stood beside his bed.

He pulled the sheet covering him up to his chest. What in the world was she doing in his tent?

Light in the corner of his eye drew his attention from the lovely woman beside him to a window swathed in lace curtains. He wasn't in his tent. It didn't have lacy curtains or the white plaster walls and a four-poster bed.

"Where am I?"

"You're at me father's estate, 'bout a half mile from town. You took a tumble from your horse, and me father brought you here—to our home."

He cleared his dry throat, wishing he had some water. "Why your house?"

She fussed with a roll of cloth bandages then set it down on a table cluttered with bottles of medicine and doctor's tools. "Me da's Ballymara's doctor, so 'twas natural for you to come here, even though in truth he's retired."

Nick sensed by the tilt of her brows that she wasn't too happy about his being there. Leaning back against a soft pillow, he tried to remember what had happened to him. He'd been looking at the world upside down from a handstand on Storm's back when the horse bolted for some reason, veering straight for Miss O'Cullen. But why had she been in the arena? Visitors weren't allowed there after the stagecoach scene. He couldn't shake the fact that this pretty Irish colleen had had something to do with him tumbling off his horse—something he rarely ever did. He narrowed his eyes, determined to test his theory.

"The accident—it was your fault?"

Miss O'Cullen drew herself up straight as an arrow; a look of guilt combined with indignation clouded her pretty face. "Oh, nay, 'twas caused by a daft dog that frolicked into the arena and frightened yer horse." Her gaze shifted from his to the floor, giving him the impression she wasn't telling the whole truth.

Odd, but her Irish accent was more pronounced. Maybe because she was upset?

"Excuse me, I've duties to perform elsewhere."

She spun around faster than a Texas tornado and sailed out of the room, leaving in her wake a gentle floral fragrance that tickled his senses.

As he shifted around to ease the pressure on his shoulder, he thanked the good Lord it wasn't broken, just strained. Lifting his hand to his head, he discovered a bandage circled it, just like an Indian headband.

Indians! What had happened to the show? Nick shot up like a bullet, ignoring the spinning room as he swung to the side of the bed. Hugging himself against a swell of nausea, he wobbled and swayed like a toy top, assailed by an iron fist that clawed at his head.

"Here now, what's that you're doing? You've no business getting up yet." An older man rushed to his side and thankfully steadied Nick before he keeled headfirst to the floor. "Are you all right sitting there for a moment?"

"Yeah," Nick murmured, not all that certain. He didn't dare try to nod.

"Don't move. Just sit still."

No problem there. He didn't care if he ever moved again. Elbows on his knees, he rested his throbbing head in his hands.

Beyond him he heard the clinking of glass then saw a blurry cup of water enter his line of vision.

"Here. Drink. You must be thirsty. You've been here almost two full days."

Nick took the cup, steadying his shaky hand, and sipped, trying hard not to tilt his head too far. The cool water refreshed his parched throat. He took several swigs then handed the glass back.

"I'm Dr. Taig O'Cullen."

"The retired doc?"

"Aye, 'tis true."

Nick glanced up, instantly sorry for the movement. He closed his eyes and started to lie back down, but the doctor gently grasped Nick's shoulder.

"Hold steady a wee bit. I need to be changing that dressing while you're up. 'Twould be easier for the both of us. My old back doesn't take kindly to bending too long." He chuckled as he released Nick's shoulder. "I see Keely's been filling your ears about my retirement. Rest assured, I've not forgotten a whit about doctoring."

Sighing inwardly, Nick sat still while Doc O'Cullen unwound the bandage around his head.

"You took a good fall. Banged your head and dislocated your shoulder. I had to put nine stitches in your forehead."

Nick winced when Dr. O'Cullen pulled off the bandage covering his stitches.

"Sorry. That dried blood was stuck on tight."

Studying the green and black plaid rug at his feet, Nick tried to ignore the doctor's painful prodding and poking. He lathered on some kind of salve that smelled to Nick like horse liniment.

"Looks good. No infection."

In a few minutes, the doc had his head rewrapped.

"So what about my shoulder?"

"Not much can be done for that, lad. Just keep it immobilized and don't use it for a few weeks."

Nick carefully peeked up at the doctor from the corner of his eye. "Weeks? What about my job at the Wild West show? I can't do that without both arms."

"No need of stewing over that which can't be changed. Now let me help you lie down."

The doctor lifted Nick's feet onto the bed then eased him back down. The irony of a man many years his senior helping Nick into bed wasn't lost on him. Too tired to protest, he surrendered to the soft bed as Doc O'Cullen pulled up a chair and sat.

"I'm sorry to tell you, lad, but Bill Cooper's Wild West Show left town. They've moved on to England."

"What?" Surprise knocked down the pain for a moment, numbing his limbs as his thoughts raced ahead. If he couldn't perform, he'd lose his job—a job he loved. And while this was a beautiful country, Nick had no intention of staying here. What else could he do? Maybe when he'd recovered, he and Storm could catch up to the show.

"How long will I be laid up?"

"Till you're well, me boy. I'm a doctor, not a fortuneteller. It all depends on the man."

Without his job, he'd need his money. . .the year's earnings he kept in his leather bag. "Where are my things?" he asked, his panicked gaze darting around the room.

"There now, don't trouble yourself. We've brought all your things to me house, even your fine horse. He's being tended in the stables. You just rest now and feel better." The doctor wadded up the old bandages.

"How long till I can get out of bed?"

Doc O'Cullen stopped and turned. "Like I said, it all depends on you." When Nick nodded, he continued. "You're a young lad. . .probably only a few days. But don't go stewin' if that's not the case. You took a grand knock on that noggin of yours. Concussions heal in their own time. You rest, and I'll send Keely back up with some broth for you."

A big fat juicy steak sounded better than some watery broth, but he wouldn't complain. Anything that made his stomach quit begging for food would satisfy him.

He grinned at the thought of Miss Keely O'Cullen having to come back into the room after the way she'd hightailed it out.

Though she denied it, he was sure he'd seen her in the arena just before he fell, and like it or not, he was going to get to the truth—and maybe enjoy the process.

Chapter 3

Keely slumped against her bedroom door. Oh, why had she lied? She knew in her heart that running into the arena when she did had caused Nick's horse to shy away and made Nick fall. She glanced heavenward. "Forgive me, Lord."

She hadn't meant to be deceitful, but when that *cowboy* accused her of causing his accident, her thoughts grew as mixed up as an Irish stew, and for the life of her, she couldn't get the truth out. She'd thought it safe to watch over Nick while he was asleep, but who could have known he'd wake up so quickly, much less remember seeing her before his fall? The best thing to do was turn the cowboy's care over to Alana. Aye, that was the answer.

As Keely reached for the handle, someone pounded on her door, startling her. When she opened it, her father stood, hand raised, ready to knock again.

" 'Twould seem our cowboy's awake," he announced, pleased as a leprechaun who'd found his pot of gold.

"He's not *my* cowboy, Da. He's *yours*." She crossed her arms over her chest.

Her father waved a hand in the air. "Matters not. He's doing better and needs some broth. Fetch some for him, please. . .and keep him company. With the knock he took, I'm not liking his being left alone this soon."

Her heart stumbled at his words. "Da, you can't ask me to do that. You know how I feel regardin' his kind."

"*Whessit!* 'Tis time you learned that all cowboys aren't like that Dusty King."

Keely braced herself against the doorjamb. "And how is it you can be so certain?"

Her father grinned down at her, melting her resistance. He smoothed one of the bushy gray eyebrows over his twinkling blue eyes. "I've lived a few days longer than you have, lass. You know good and well that you can't judge one man by what a similar man has done."

"God does. It says in the Good Book that the sins of the fathers are visited on their children."

"Forgive as you be forgiven. I'm thinking that's in there as well." He rested his large hand on her cheek. "Go now, and take that young man some of Alana's fine broth and soda bread."

She wanted to argue, but the past few days her father's spirits had ridden higher than they had in months. Rather than dampen things with her stubbornness, she relented for his sake. Better to handle Nick Dalton's presence any day than her father's melancholy. She sighed out an "aye."

" 'Twould be a good idea to read to the lad while you're sitting with him. I doubt he'll feel like entertaining himself till his head clears a bit. Read to him from God's Word. If he's not a believing man, 'twill do him some good."

Her references to God had annoyed Dusty. Perhaps the true Nick Dalton would make himself known if she did read the Bible to him. Still, it meant she had to face him again after the way she'd stormed out.

Groaning inwardly, Keely nodded to her father and shuffled toward the kitchen. Just what she needed, to spend even more time in Nick Dalton's company.

"And just what's gotten in to ye?" Alana asked, as Keely shuffled into the kitchen. The family cook lifted a large butcher knife and whacked it down on the cabbage she was chopping up for supper. "Ye're about to trip over yer chin."

Keely grabbed a bowl from the shelf and slunk over to the pot of Irish stew on the cast iron stove. "Da says I need to take food to that—that *cowboy*, and he wants me to read the Bible to him. Lotta good it will do."

Alana smiled and shook her head. "Keely, me lass, what am I going to do with ye? Will ye be goin' about for the rest of yer life fearing men in those big-brimmed hats and stackin' stones around that big heart of yours? Don't ye be judging the poor lad before ye know the truth."

Keely winced at Alana's last word. *Truth.* Sooner or later she'd have to tell Nick the truth about her part in his accident. Perhaps if she put it off a bit, he'd heal quickly and leave before she had to apologize.

Och! She'd hardly spoken half a basketful of words to the man, and he was already making her life miserable. Pushing herself into action, she took the lid off Alana's pot of stew. The fragrant scent of lamb, potatoes, and herbs made her mouth water as she spooned broth off the top and into the ceramic bowl. *If it works as good as it smells, I'll be rid of the fool in no time at all,* she fumed, slapping the wooden ladle down with so much force that Alana jumped. Keely felt like a naughty toddler under the cook's stern glare. She sent Alana a beguiling smile and placed a chunk of soda bread on a plate.

Hoping that her patient would be asleep, she carefully made her way back upstairs and tiptoed into Nick's room. With a sigh of relief at seeing that providence was with her, she prepared to set down the tray and make a hasty exit, but before she let go of it, Nick turned his head.

"Mmm. Something sure smells good," he said in a slow drawl.

Dusty's accent had been short and clipped, not at all like Nick's smooth, easy, toe-curling one. And her toes were dug into her slippers as though her life depended on it.

"I'm so hungry, I could eat an elephant."

Keely reined in the smile tempting her lips at the thought of him trying to manage such a feat. It was easier to maintain her distance if she wasn't on friendly terms with this man. She set the tray on a wooden teacart parked against the wall near the chimney and wheeled it over next to the bed.

Nick attempted to sit up, but she pressed him back down. "Da says you're not to get up for two days. So down you'll stay."

"He didn't mean I couldn't sit up." His dark gaze captured hers, making Keely want to dart for the door. "And beggin' your pardon, ma'am, but I can't eat lying down."

"You can if I feed you."

His lips tugged into a lopsided grin. "Well, now that's a right pleasant thought, but I assure you I can feed myself." He shifted his elbow under him and pushed up, grimacing as he rose.

Obstinate man! "You just be putting that head back on that pillow right now. I'll not take any arguing." She pressed against his good shoulder, rock solid beneath her hand. Faith, to make matters worse, she was touching his long-handle underwear. "Lie down," she ordered, half-strangled by embarrassment.

"No." His eyes locked with hers. Pain tilted his eyebrows,

but he didn't yield. His expression softened for a moment. "My momma taught me to fend for myself. I don't need no woman waitin' on me."

With one arm, he wrestled the sheet that held his legs captive. He tugged and yanked, despite the pain it obviously caused.

Nick Dalton was just as stubborn and senseless as Dusty. But then she could be kin to a mule when she put her mind to it. "Wait. I have a suggestion."

He ceased his struggles and looked at her. A damp sheen of moisture brightened the area between his eyebrows. "And what would that be?"

"If you'll halt that flailing about, I'll get some more pillows and prop you up a bit. Then you can eat your bread by yourself, and I'll help with the broth. Agreed?"

It almost looked like relief that passed over his face for a brief moment. Nodding, Nick fell back to the bed, as if he'd spent all his energy. A thread of sympathy wound around her heart to see this strapping man reduced to being spoon-fed soup in bed—even if he was a cowboy. But the sooner he ate, the sooner he'd regain his strength and leave, she reminded herself.

Half an hour later, after spooning more soup in Nick than on him, Keely sat back in a chair and opened the large family Bible that her aunt Ellen had brought her from England. All she had to do was read Nick some verses on forgiveness so that when she got up the nerve to confess how she and her dog had caused his accident, he'd be in a forgiving humor.

That Nick didn't protest at all to her offer to read him scripture was a pleasant surprise. Dusty had never liked it when she "got religious" on him. It shamed Keely to think how she'd put good looks and charm above godliness. And now, sneaking sly glances at Nick as she read, Keely wondered what it was that had attracted her to Dusty. He couldn't hold a penny candle to Nick's tall, dark, and handsome features, especially with two-days' growth of dark whiskers enhancing his ruggedness. And that slow accent that almost stroked a woman's heart with its velvet fingers. . . She brushed the observation aside, lest her heart pitter-pat from her chest into those capable hands of his.

After reading several passages in Psalms about forgiveness, Keely flipped and rattled the thin pages of the big family Bible, searching for another appropriate passage. Glancing up, she saw that Nick had settled back down, his eyes shut. Maybe now she could just slip out, and he wouldn't notice. But as she stood, her chair creaked.

Nick peeked out one eye. "Going somewhere?"

He grinned, sending her stomach into a somersault. *Heavenly Father, this won't do at all.* Pressing the Bible against her belly, she took a step back.

"I'd rather you stay, if you don't mind, ma'am. A fella can sleep anytime, but it ain't every day he gets to share the company of a pretty Irish colleen." He pointed toward her abandoned chair. "Sit down and tell me about yourself."

Keely straightened. She wasn't about to tell him anything. But she would obey her father and read to the wounded man. "You need to rest. So if you close your eyes and relax, I'll continue reading."

From the crease in his brow, Nick didn't like her response, but he didn't press her. He'd most likely never had the Bible read to him before. Resigned to the uneasy tradeoff, Keely sat down and opened her Bible to 1 Samuel 25:28. "I pray thee, *forgive* the trespass of thine handmaid," she read, "for the Lord will certainly make my lord a sure house; because my lord fighteth the battles of the Lord, and evil hath not been found in thee *all* thy days."

Well, maybe that wasn't the best one. She flipped the pages to I Kings 8:36, grateful that she'd had the foresight to look up the verses earlier, and read, "Then hear thou in heaven, and *forgive* the sin of thy servants, and of thy people Israel, that thou teach them the good way wherein they should walk, and give rain upon thy land, which thou hast given to thy people for an inheritance."

Oblivious to her stolen glances, Nick's scowl deepened. Perhaps she'd hit a nerve, and her subtle emphasis of the word *forgive* was doing its work. "Judge not, and ye shall not be judged: condemn not, and ye shall not be condemned: *forgive*, and ye shall be forgiven."

Shifting onto his side as though to get more comfortable, Nick turned his back to her.

"Had enough, have you?" she asked hopefully.

"Nope." But the clip of his response said otherwise.

Nibbling at her lip, she searched for another verse on forgiveness. By the time she was finished, there'd be no way Nick could avoid overlooking her transgression. In Matthew she found one that fit her motive just fine. "For if ye *forgive* men their trespasses, your heavenly Father will also forgive you: But if ye forgive not men their trespasses, neither will your Father forgive your trespasses."

Nick groaned. "On second thought, I think I *will* rest for a while. A man can only take so much harping on forgiveness."

Harping was it? Keely snapped shut her Bible and stood. "Suit yourself." Bending down, she pulled up the bedding that lay across Nick's hips and covered his shoulders.

"Thanks," he mumbled.

Pleased, she all but skipped out of the room, knowing that

God's hand of conviction was upon Nick Dalton. With God's Word, she'd paved the way for Nick to forgive her—if only she could find the nerve to confess.

Nick gazed across the room and stared out the window at the clear blue sky. White fluffy clouds drifted along like they had nothing else to do. The window's lacy curtains fluttered on the afternoon breeze. He caught a faint whiff of livestock nearby.

Nick smacked the bed with his fist. He hated inactivity. Give him good hard work, and he was happy. He'd sure worked hard enough back on his ranch in Texas.

The sharp stab of pain that came with each memory of his old home hurt worse than the ache in his head and shoulder. How could his father have betrayed him like that? To gamble away all they'd worked for. He closed his eyes against the burning in his gut. That ranch had been his dream. He'd worked alongside his dad most of his life to make it successful so that one day he could take over and be proud of all he'd done and raise his own family there. But now it was gone. Poof. All because of a stupid game of cards.

He rolled onto his back, hoping to relieve the pressure in his injured shoulder. Why had Keely sat there and read verse after verse about forgiveness? She had no way of knowing what he was struggling with.

Was God trying to get his attention? The picture of his sobbing father was burned into mind. His father had begged Nick to forgive him, but he'd ridden off without even saying good-bye. When he arrived in Houston and saw a poster advertising tryouts for Bill Cooper's Wild West Show, Nick hadn't wasted a second. He'd always been a great shot and a good rider, doing tricks to impress his friends as a teenager. Why not? He needed a job.

But now eight months later, that was over—at least for now.

Nick knew that he had to find it within himself to forgive his dad. But how? God's Word was clear; he needed to forgive his father if he himself wanted forgiveness from the Lord. But God didn't say how to overcome the anger and pain that festered inside. All he wanted to do was to go back home to the States and work his ranch, but the thought of facing Pete Dalton again brought bile to the back of Nick's throat.

Maybe he could buy another ranch. He'd earned a nice stack of greenbacks, but if he used that money to travel back to America and then to Texas, he wouldn't have enough left for a ranch—not even a small one.

There was no solution to his dilemma. He stared at the ceiling as if the answer might be there. "God, I don't have it within me to forgive Dad. I've tried, but I'm still angry that he lost the ranch. Make me willing to forgive like Your Word says. Please, God. Help me. Show me what to do.

Chapter 4

Nick had a new respect for soldiers who'd lost a limb during the Civil War. Simple things he'd taken for granted were now a struggle since his arm was still in a sling. At least he'd managed to shave without cutting his throat. One-handed, it had taken him nearly ten minutes just to get his pants buttoned up. He stood beside his bed trying to figure out a way to get his shirt on. He didn't want to leave the bedroom dressed only in his long-handles and pants, but he had to get up and move around. Nearly three days of bed rest was making him loco.

The murmur of voices drifted in the open window, drawing Nick to it. Below, Keely stood with her arms crossed, facing a tall, auburn-haired man who looked a few years older than she. He held the reins of a bay horse that Nick recognized as one of Ireland's Connemara ponies. The Wild West show had bought several of the gentle horses during their travels across the Emerald Isle.

"Not again, Declan McLochlin." Keely declared with a stomp of her dainty foot. The soft hands with which she'd soothed Nick's aches planted themselves on her hips. "This has to stop."

" 'Tis truly sorry I am."

"If ye'd built a stone fence like most the folks in all of Ireland, yer cattle wouldn't be comin' onto our land and frightenin' our sheep."

Nick chuckled, amused at the way Keely slipped away from her educated speech to a common brogue whenever she was flustered or angry.

As if stung by the fiery colleen's scolding, McLochlin struck a proud, stubborn pose. "I'll not be arguing with ye over livestock. I'll save that bit of business for yer father. I've come to ask ye to go to the Ballymara festival with me Saturday next."

Keely remained silent for a moment then mumbled a reply that Nick couldn't make out. Realizing that he was eavesdropping, Nick crossed the room to the other window. It didn't matter to him whether Keely went to a festival with that thick-necked Paddy or not.

Beyond the window were some of the greenest hills he'd ever seen, each rolling upward toward a bigger one in the distance until they reached the round-topped mountains. A man could make a home here if he was of a mind to, though it was a far cry from Texas. The only time it was this green in west Texas was in the spring, unless they had a year with lots of rain. The summer heat withered most everything except the hardiest of plants.

Nick wondered how his father was doing now. Had he found work? Or was he begging for handouts and wallowing around as the town drunk? Would Nick's staying have made any difference? All he had salvaged from his old home were his clothes and Storm Cloud, but with a horse and willing hands, maybe they could have started over. But then he wasn't willing.

Thank the Lord his mother hadn't lived long enough to see her husband gamble away their home. Course, the good

Christian that she was, she would have had a good cry and then said God had a plan even in this. She wouldn't have liked how Nick had run out on his dad.

The words about forgiveness that Keely had read to him out of the Bible played in his mind and, not for the first time in the last few days, made him chuckle. If God wanted to snag Nick's attention, He'd sure chosen a unique way of getting it.

"All right, Lord, I can take a hint," he said, rubbing his sore shoulder. "I'm sorry about the angry things I said and did. . .and for not forgiving Dad. Just show me how to make things right with him and show me what You'd have me do while I'm here."

The curtains fluttered against his arm as the cool morning breeze brushed him with a sense of well being. Like a tumble-weed in the wind, the anger and unforgiveness that knotted his chest rolled away, leaving peace in their place. Just as soon as he could use his injured arm, he'd write a letter of apology to his dad.

Turning back to the bed, Nick was ready to tackle the chore of getting his shirt on. He lifted the sling over his head and dropped it on the bed, wincing when his stiff shoulder moved.

"Here now. What's that ye're doing?"

Keely entered the room with his breakfast tray. Nick's heart surged as if he were caught committing a crime.

"Did me—" She caught herself. "Did my father say you could get up today?"

Nick shook his head. "No, but I'm sick of lying here. You're not gonna keep me hog-tied to this bed any longer. I'm stiff all over. I need to be moving around, missy."

"You're not to be using that arm yet," Keely warned, set-ting the tray on the teacart.

"I don't plan on usin' it. I just wanna get my shirt on, so's I won't go walkin' around in my long-handles."

Embarrassment painted her cheeks a becoming red at the mention of his underwear.

"No. I suppose not." Tearing her gaze from him, she lifted a wrinkled shirt out of his open leather bag that sat on the bed. "Could use a good ironin'."

"Never mind that. Just let me have it so I can get dressed."

Keely's gaze steeled for battle. Nick didn't know whether to run or stay and enjoy the fireworks. "I'll help you," she announced, as if it was the last thing she wanted to do.

She held up the dark blue shirt while Nick worked his way into the sleeves. He pulled it onto his shoulders, and she reached up to button it. Nick pulled back. "Whoa, partner. I can do that. I'm not a helpless baby."

"Fine then, do it yerself." She swirled around in a huff, her flaring skirts smacking his leg, and stormed out of the room.

Nick hadn't meant to upset her. He just wasn't used to having help getting dressed. It had nothing to do with the fact that she was the spunkiest, cutest filly he'd ever laid eyes on. Or that his heart was bucking like Storm Cloud the first time he'd been saddled.

After a couple days of Nick's proving that he could navigate around the house, Doc O'Cullen finally cleared him to go outside. First thing, Nick headed to the stables to check on Storm Cloud. The Appaloosa gelding that he'd raised from a colt had been a birthday gift from a Nez Percé Indian friend of his dad's named Osiah. Storm stuck his head over the stall gate and nickered a greeting.

"Hey there, buddy. Did ya miss me?"

The gray horse sniffed Nick's hand then nudged him in the chest. Nick opened the gate and stepped into the stall. Laying his good arm across Storm's back, he leaned against the horse and whispered a prayer of thanks to whoever had thought to send Storm with the O'Cullens when they'd brought him to their home.

"C'mon boy, let's take a walk." Nick strolled out of the stall with Storm Cloud following. Outside the stables, he got his first good look at Glencullen, the O'Cullen estate. The large, two-story home had a Georgian flair to it, with a columned overhang shading the main entrance. Large, evenly spaced windows stretched across the flat, white front, allowing in plenty of sunlight. Three chimneys rose from the steep roof, but only one had a plume of smoke drifting lazily gray against a blue sky.

With Storm at his heels, Nick followed a path that led up a round-topped hill. As he reached the pinnacle, he stopped so suddenly that Storm nudged him in the back, sending a sharp pain radiating through his shoulder. He rubbed at the ache and stared, horror mingling with dismay. Furry black-faced sheep dotted the rolling hills as far as he could see. "Why did they have to be sheep, Lord?"

As a cattleman himself, he despised sheep. There had been many wars in the States in the last few years between cattlemen and sheep owners. Cattlemen hate that sheep pull grass out by the roots as they eat, thus destroying any future fodder. Plus, sheep had to be the dumbest creatures on God's earth.

Suddenly, Keely's conversation with that McLochlin fellow made sense. Cattle and sheep. Why hadn't it soaked in before?

Storm let out a loud whinny, and the nearest ewes scattered in a frenzy, *baaing* in complaint. Nick couldn't hold back the chuckle that erupted as he continued down the trail he'd discovered. He knew, as he walked more, the tightness constricting his leg muscles would disappear and he'd be back to normal.

Then what?

Find the show and rejoin it? Even if he did, it would be weeks—maybe months—before he'd be able to do his normal performance routine. Most likely his shoulder injury would affect his shooting ability. He'd have to do a heap of practicing to get his dead aim back. And he just might give up that whole handstand routine.

The first thing he needed to do was write that letter to his dad. Tonight. He wouldn't put it off any longer. He needed to make peace. And maybe even return home.

To his surprise, Nick wasn't in as much of a hurry to get back to the States as he'd been a few days ago. Part of the reason was his beguiling nurse, although Keely never went out of her way to charm him. She was always putting barriers between them, as if he were some sort of threat to her. If only Keely would relax around him and not be so flustered all the time, she might actually find out that he wasn't so bad to be around. He remembered the zing that charged up his arm the first time he touched her as he helped her exit the stagecoach. No woman had ever affected him like that.

Her long, wavy black hair was beautiful. Normally, Keely wore it up in a little net thing, but he much preferred it when, in a morning rush, she left it hanging down her back, bound with a ribbon. And those Irish eyes of hers dealt out blue thunder and summer sky warmth at the whim of her mood. But what he really wanted to see was her smile. She'd come close on several occasions but hadn't quite given free rein to the sense of humor he'd seen dancing in her gaze.

From the top of another hill, Nick noticed several tiny cottages spread out over the flatter land. A stone fence or hedgerow divided each of the farmsteads, giving the landscape a patchwork-quilt look. These must be the tenant farmers he'd heard about from some of the Irish workers at the show. Several of the temporary laborers had been teen boys from such farms, making money to take back to their families.

As he approached the nearest house, the degree of poverty struck him, causing him to feel a deep sense of thanksgiving that he'd never had to live in such a ramshackle place. It was no bigger than a soddy he'd seen once on a cattle drive through the Oklahoma Territory. Some of the whitewashed plaster had fallen away in places, revealing the stone and mud wall that supported its thatched roof.

Three skinny young boys dressed in rags sat near the front of the house, digging holes in the dirt with sticks. As he approached, the urchin trio looked up in unison. Eyes widening at the sight of him and Storm Cloud, they jumped up and raced on bare feet into the house.

A moment later, a large man came out, carrying a shepherd's staff. Nick hoped the man didn't plan on using it on him. He'd done nothing to scare the children. Their reaction seemed strange to him, especially here in Ireland where most folks were more than friendly.

"Howdy." Nick smiled and offered his hand to the scowling farmer.

The man looked him up and down then glanced at Storm. "Top o' the morning to ye. What business do ye have here?"

Nick lowered his hand when the man didn't offer his. "No business. I'm a patient of Dr. O'Cullen. I finally got well enough to take a walk. I just ended up here."

"Ye're not the new overseer?" The farmer's eyes narrowed with deepening suspicion.

Nick shook his head. "No. I was a performer in the Wild West show that was in town a few days ago. Got hurt in a fall off my horse."

The farmer relaxed from his rigid stance and leaned against his staff. "Ah, well, me children saw yer horse and thought ye were an overseer. His likes is about the only kind we ever see here on horseback, and he don't take too kindly to the wee lads and lasses."

"Sorry if I scared them. Didn't mean to."

"Don't ye worry a whit about them. They'll be fine. Come in and join us." Finally the man smiled and held out his hand. "Me name's Patrick Connelly."

"Nick Dalton. It's a pleasure to meet you, Patrick."

After a bone-crunching handshake, Nick followed Patrick into the stone cottage, ducking to keep from hitting his head on the low doorframe. He knew Storm Cloud would be content for a while to nibble on the stubbly winter grass nearby. It took a moment for his eyes to adjust to the dimness inside the smoke-filled dwelling. Nostrils stinging, it was all Nick could do to get his breath without coughing.

"We've a guest, Lorna. Mr. Nick Dalton is here for a visit."

As his eyes adjusted to the dark, hazy room, Nick saw that Patrick was seated on a mat near a small fire located in the center of the room. No chimney, he noted with incredulity, just a smoldering fire. Along the back wall, the three young boys huddled quietly beside an older girl who held a baby. Four sets of eyes stared at him with a mixture of curiosity and apprehension. Nick brandished a smile to put them at ease. The girl glanced shyly away, but the three boys continued to stare, solemn as church elders.

" 'Tis a pleasure to meet you, Mr. Dalton." Lorna ducked a curtsy, before leaning over to stir a pot of something simmering over the fire.

"Call me Nick."

"These are our fine children, Nick. Jodie, our daughter, is the eldest, then there's Jamie, Dylan, Colin, and Molly, our wee baby girl." Patrick pointed out each child as he named them.

"You have a nice family, Patrick."

The farmer smiled, chest puffing with pride. "Aye. That I do."

Nick tried not to stare at the hovel the Connelly's called home. There was no furniture of any kind, save for the tiny table Lorna worked at, only straw or rush mats, evidently their chairs *and* bedding. A pile of dried peat in the corner served as fuel for the small fire, which was also the only source of heat. And he didn't want to think about how awful it smelled.

"This land part of Glencullen?" Nick asked, as he folded his legs and sat across the fire from Patrick.

"Aye. 'Tis that."

Nick clenched his jaw at the inequality of the situation. How could Taig O'Cullen and his feisty daughter enjoy such a life of prosperity and dwell in a mansion while these poor people lived in such poverty? As landowner, it was the man's duty to watch out for those living on his property. How could he accept rent money from people this poor?

"Would ye care for a bowl of boiled potatoes and some

bread, Nick?" Patrick poked the fire with a stick, sending flickers of fiery ashes dancing in the air. He smashed out a couple that landed on the straw mat.

Nick shook his head. He wouldn't take food away from this family. "No, thank you. I just had breakfast a short time ago."

"Ye'll be offending me fine wife if you don't let her feed ye. Ye wouldn't want to do that now, would ye?"

He had forgotten about the stiff Irish pride. He smiled. "Well, maybe a little bread. I really did just eat breakfast."

"Good then." Patrick waved his hand in the air, which set Lorna in motion. She quickly returned with a chipped bowl containing a large hunk of brown bread. She also handed him a mug of milk.

Nick suppressed an inner shudder. Even as a child he had never cared for milk. He tore off a piece of bread and shoved it into his mouth. "Mmm. Good." Lorna smiled a shy smile then busied herself in the corner with some sewing.

"We enjoyed ye're fine show." Patrick shoved a chunk of bread in his mouth.

"You saw it?"

"Aye, from the hill near the castle. 'Twas a fair distance away, but we were able to see most of what went on."

The poor man couldn't even afford the few shillings to see the Wild West show.

" 'Twas a fine job of shooting you did."

"Um. . .thanks." On seeing the three boys' eyes light up at his words, he added, "Maybe I could give your kids a ride on my horse today? He's really pretty gentle. Would that be all right?"

Patrick grinned. "Aye. Me boys would like that, I'm thinking." He looked over his shoulder at his kids. "Eh, what say ye? Do ye want to ride Nick Dalton's grand horse?"

Heads bobbing eagerly, the boys scooted up beside their father. Though she seemed less inclined to accept a stranger's offer, Jodie nodded as well. Judging by the lads' sizes, he would guess them to be between the ages of four and eight. The oldest boy—Jamie, he thought—sidled over next to him.

"Are ye a real cowboy, Mr. Nick?" The boy's dark red hair matched that of his father and brothers, while Jodie had her mother's dark brown mane.

"Yep, I am. I was born and raised in Texas."

"Texas?" Jamie whispered it almost reverently. "Where's that?"

"Leave the man be, Jamie." Patrick ruffled his son's head. "So, Nick, will ye tell us some stories about yer travels or yer life back in Texas?"

Nick smiled again. It would seem the father was just as curious as the son.

As he told the story of the first time he saddled Storm Cloud, the young boys moved around the small fire until they were practically sitting on his lap. He opened his mouth to tell about the time he'd nearly been bitten by a rattlesnake back home when a ruckus outside captured his attention.

"Patrick Connelly," a deep voice called. "Have ye taken to consorting with the enemy?"

"Or are ye now raising spotted horses?" The voice belonged to a different man.

"This fine horse has no markings and no owner. I think I'll be makin' him mine."

Chapter 5

Behind the house, Keely sat on the stone fence separating the sheep pasture from the garden and watched Ian, the shepherd, work Corky. The young dog was learning his shepherding skills, although the animal loved to frolic in the grass and would just as soon chase butterflies as wayward sheep. Fiona, her favorite black-faced ewe, *baaed* for attention. Keely wove her fingers through Fiona's coarse wool and smiled as she remembered the image of Nick walking out the front door earlier. Mr. I-can-do-it-myself had gone outside with only the front and right side of his shirt tucked in and no belt looped through his denim pants. 'Twould seem he couldn't dress himself as easily as he thought.

From her pocket, she pulled out her journal. Savoring a quick sniff of the fragrant leather cover, she opened the page with the ribbon marker in it and silently read the words she'd written just this morning:

> *I can no longer deny my attraction to Nick. His slow,*
> *soft drawl touches a restlessness inside me that makes me*
> *want to curl up at his feet like a fat cat and listen to him*
> *talk for hours. And those dark eyes are enough to lasso my*

*heart. He's not a heathen like I thought; he even has a
relationship with God, which was a stunning surprise.*

His knowledgeable discussion about the Bible had fueled a
few good arguments as they voiced their differing opinions on
what certain verses meant. Yesterday he'd made the comment,
almost under his breath, that clipped wings can fly again. She'd
thought it odd then, but as she stewed on the words, they'd
taken root and grown. He didn't literally mean wings, but he
meant that God could heal a person who'd been wounded, and
in her case, God could heal the heart that Dusty had stomped
on. She'd prayed last night that He would.

She looked at the first line of her entry again. *I can no
longer deny my attraction to Nick.*

Just because she was attracted to him didn't mean she had
to act on it. The fact was it irritated her that she had actually
grown to like the man. Maybe if he weren't leaving in a few
days—

"Hey there, beautiful."

Spinning around so fast that she spooked Fiona, Keely
dropped her journal and nearly lost her balance. She'd been so
deep in thought that she hadn't heard Nick's approach. And
here she'd done such a good job of avoiding him except, of
course, when she read the Bible and tended to him.

Nick reached out with his good arm to steady her. Tingles
charged up her shoulder in a way she'd never before experienced. Oh, this wasn't good. She didn't want to be feeling such
an attraction to this cowboy, even if he called her beautiful. But
then Dusty had said the same thing. Thoughts of Dusty were
like throwing a bucket of chilly water on her. She stood and
looked beside Nick, to see his horse with its big head hanging

over the fence, sniffing Fiona. The horse blew a muffled snort. Fiona lunged sideways to escape, *baaing* as she went.

Bully! Keely crossed her arms over her chest, hoping Nick wouldn't hang around too long. The last thing she needed was for him to discover her attraction to him.

He leaned down and picked up her journal from the ground. Her heart somersaulted when he raised it up as if to look inside, but instead, he blew off the dirt on the corner edge and wiped the leather cover against his pants before handing it back to her.

"Do you know Patrick Connelly?" Nick asked.

Giving herself a moment to collect her composure, she watched Fiona settle down and start grazing again before she looked back at Nick. She searched her mind for a moment, trying to put a face with the name, but came up blank. "Nay, should I?"

Nick caught her gaze and held it, as if looking for something. Did he doubt her? She hiked her chin and stared back, hoping to ignore the butterflies tickling her belly. For the first time, she noticed his eyes were closer to black than brown. Could it be he might have a little Indian blood in him?

After a moment, Nick looked up and stared at the field where the O'Cullen sheep grazed. Keely turned and looked out at the pasture, too. Corky must have noticed Nick because he ran toward them with his tongue flapping and a doggie grin on his face. Ian shouted for him to return to work, but the contrary pup had other things on his mind. Nick's horse raised his head and whinnied as if not sure he wanted to be near Corky again.

"I just thought you might know Patrick since he lives on your land." A muscle in Nick's jaw ticked. He bent down and patted Corky's head, receiving a slobbery kiss. At Ian's whistle, the dog turned and raced off.

"He's a tenant farmer?" Since she knew the names of all the house and stable workers, that was her best guess.

"Yeah." He looked at her again, squinting from the sun's glare. "I thought maybe you would have met him before. He's a nice man with a young wife and five small children."

She shook her head. "My mother never allowed Connor and me to socialize with the tenant farmers. Oh, sure, Connor would sneak off on an occasion and play with some of the boys, but I never did. Mother said they were dirty, uneducated folks, and that we might catch sickness from them."

Nick snorted. "And you believed her?"

Keely narrowed her eyes and faced him square on. "And just why should I not be believing me own mother?"

He softened under her glare. "I guess as a child you wouldn't have had any other choice. But she was wrong, you know." His eyes begged her to believe him.

Why was a single tenant farmer so important to Nick? More importantly, what reason would her mother have had to tell her a lie? Even though she'd been gone for several years, Keely remembered her well. Her mother had been distantly related to English royalty and insisted the family associate with others of good lineage. Could she have simply wanted to keep Keely and Connor away from the tenants because of their social status? She'd never considered her mother that petty, but looking at it from that angle gave Keely a whole new perspective.

She glanced at Nick. "Why are you wantin' to know if I'm acquainted with this Patrick fellow?"

Nick squatted on the heels of his boots and tugged loose a stem of grass. Keely looked down on his thick, dark brown hair.

With the white bandage still wrapped around his head, he reminded her of an Indian—minus his feather. She liked him without that big cowboy hat, which made him more intimidating. Thinking of the hat reminded her that she needed to see if Alana had been able to get it cleaned and straightened after Nick had landed on it in his fall.

"Who's Glencullen's overseer? Patrick mentioned him." He twirled the grass stem with his fingers. "Is it your father?"

"Nay, 'tis Declan McLochlin, our nearest neighbor. Da was too busy with his doctoring before he retired to tend to the tenants, so he hired Declan to watch over them, collect rent, and handle any disputes."

"So what kind of man is this Declan guy?"

"Why are you asking?"

Nick stood to his feet, put the hand free of his sling on his hip, and heaved a sigh. "I'm wondering if he's skimming off the top of the rents he's collecting."

"And just why would ye be asking such a thing?"

He turned to face her, a passion blazing in his eyes that made her take a step back. "You need to see how these people live, Keely. It's downright inhuman. They live in a tiny stone cottage smaller than any room I've seen in your whole house. They have no furniture and sleep on thin straw mats on the floor. Their kids wear tattered old clothes and go around barefoot. You're blessed with so much, and they have so little."

"You sound like ye're blaming me."

He plowed his hand through his hair, leaving stiff, spiky rows that Keely wanted to straighten in spite of her irritation. She had nothing to do with the tenant farmers.

He blew out another sigh. "I'm not blaming you, but you could do something to ease their struggles."

"What? What could I do?" How could he expect her to do anything when she knew nothing about the tenant farmers?

"I don't know. Talk your father into lowering their rent maybe?"

"Rents have already been made fair by the Land Acts and Plan of Campaign, which lowered rents for farmers all across Ireland. I learned about them in school. The peasants should be better off now than they've ever been." She tucked a strand of hair that insisted on tickling her cheeks behind her ear then crossed her arms over her chest again.

"Well, something's not right. If these folks were any poorer, they'd be dead. No one should have to live on boiled potatoes and bread. Those kids are entirely too skinny." He shook his head. Turning to look at her, a spark lit in Nick's eyes. "Let me take you for a visit, and you can see for yourself."

Apprehension washed over her like a flash flood. She had no desire to visit the tenant farmers, and yet, if children were going hungry, how could she not? Still, her mother's fierce warning overpowered her doubts. "Nay, 'tis not a wise idea."

Nick's lip curved to one side in a disgusted sway. He stared her in the eye, disappointment evident, then walked away. Amazingly his unbridled horse nickered and followed like a faithful dog, even though Nick hadn't signaled to it.

Keely watched Nick stride away until he crossed down the other side of a hill and out of view. Guilt weighted her down as if someone had tied her to the pledging stone and dumped her in a lake. Why did it bother her so much to think that she'd disappointed Nick? She kicked a small rock, and it skidded across the ground. Fiona dodged to her right, let out a *baa*, then dipped her head and started eating again.

Why was he so set on helping this one family in all of

Ireland? Dusty certainly wouldn't have bothered. She'd never bothered.

She didn't want to believe that this American stranger had more compassion for her fellow Irishmen than she did. Hugging her journal to her chest, she tried to squelch her mounting guilt. Guilt that maybe she'd overlooked the needy who practically lived under her own roof. Guilt that she'd allowed the seed of Dusty's betrayal to take root and grow into a gnarly, barren bush of unforgiveness. And guilt that she hadn't been honest with Nick about the cause of his accident.

She slumped down on the short rock fence that separated the sheep pasture from the garden. Verse after verse about un-forgiveness tracked across her mind. She'd meant those verses to soften up Nick, but now God was using them to reveal her own shortcomings.

Tears slipped down Keely's cheeks as she thought of children going hungry while her family always had a wealth of food left over after each meal. She lifted prayers heavenward for God to show her what she should do. Had her mother been wrong about the tenant farmers? Was Nick right?

How could she believe the man she'd only known a few days rather than her own mother? Maybe she'd just have to see for herself.

❧

Nick strode away. Disappointment at Keely's response surged through him like a bad case of influenza. His stomach churned at her lack of compassion for those who had less than she. Somehow he'd expected more of her.

But why should he? Because she read the Bible?

No, that wasn't the reason. He wanted her to care, because

he cared for her. Somehow, Keely O'Cullen had become important to him in the past few days. Listening to her lilting voice was like hearing a slow-moving creek as it rippled and splashed over rocks in its path. It was beautiful. And in spite of her aloofness, he'd grown fond of her.

That was more than he could say about Patrick's buddies. Where Patrick had been warm and friendly after their initial meeting, his friends had been cold and unwelcoming.

A smile tilted his lips at the memory of the three men Patrick had called Clancy, Michael, and Breck trying to control Storm Cloud. The faithful steed was a one-man horse. Nobody could ride him unless Nick was nearby. Clancy had found a piece of rope and attempted to construct a bridle of sorts to guide Storm. While Storm submitted to the device, a comedic dance occurred as the three men tried to mount his horse. Patrick's kids had laughed out loud at the bumbling group. Breck had barely missed getting kicked in the leg.

Nick chuckled. Maybe the Irish trio would have been friendlier if they hadn't been bested by a horse. They sure didn't have any friendly feelings for their overseer. They all held the same low opinion of Declan McLochlin that Patrick had. The overseer was hard-nosed, impatient, and charged rents above what he should. The tenants needed someone to champion their cause, and Nick believed he was that person. Maybe he'd see what he could find out about the Land Act that Keely mentioned.

He reached for his hat, realizing for about the hundredth time that it wasn't there. "Everything has its purpose. That's what the Good Book says, right, Lord?" Nick glanced skyward, squinting his eyes against the brilliant fingers of the sun. "Is that why I'm stuck here in Ireland? To help the farmers?"

Storm nickered and nudged Nick in the back, evidently thinking Nick was talking to him. Stopping, he turned and patted his horse on the neck. At least he had one friend in Ireland. He longed to jump on Storm's back and ride off with the wind blowing in his face, but that would have to wait a few more days until his shoulder was better.

Lifting prayers heavenward, he headed back to the O'Cullens' house. God would show him what he needed to do. If he had any other way of getting back to the States, he'd give Patrick his entire earnings from the show. Not that the man would take it. That stubborn Irish pride was hard to swallow at times. Keely was a prime example. Maybe a few more prayers could soften even a pretty colleen's pigheadedness.

Chapter 6

D a, you can't keep lowering the tenant farmers' rents."
Keely stood with both hands on the back of her chair at the dining room table as Nick walked in. She glanced up and met his gaze without smiling.

"I don't plan to lower them again, lass. But such talk is between Declan and me. Don't you be worrying yourself about it." Taig lifted his cup and sipped the steaming tea.

Keely pulled out her chair and plopped down. "I don't understand how the farmers can be having such a rough time when your rents are already fifteen percent lower than required by the Land Act."

"Keely, talk of business is not for women or my dinner table. Eat your food before it takes cold."

Nick cleared his throat, unsure if he should intrude on their conversation. Taig turned his head at the sound, and his face lit up with pleasure.

"Nick, me boy, come and join us for some lamb chops and colcannon."

He sat down, eager to dig into the creamy mashed potatoes with onions and chopped greens mixed in, not to mention the lamb. Who would have ever thought a rancher could develop a taste for it?

As he ate, he considered the information he'd overheard. If Patrick and his friends paid lower rents than they had to by law then why didn't they live better?

Keely watched him with those blue eyes of hers as he swallowed a mouthful of colcannon. When he caught her gaze with his own, a lovely blush reddened her cheeks, and she looked away.

Remorse that he'd soon have to leave threatened to disrupt his meal. At least he was thankful today wasn't that day.

"Corky! You come back here, ye daft dog."

The barking black and white blur of fur dashed over the green hilltop and out of Keely's sight. Struggling with the weight of her basket and the heavy skirts clinging to her legs, she hurried to catch up to the overgrown pup before he caused any mischief.

Her confrontation with Nick about the tenant farmers wouldn't leave her alone until she saw for herself their situation. She couldn't stomach children going without. And while she wouldn't admit it to his face, Nick's admonition had gotten through to her.

As she topped the hill a woman's frantic voice rang out. "Dylan, get ye back here. Right now! Jamie, run and get yer father."

A boy heeded her order and ran toward a tiny cottage in the distance, while Corky chased a goose into the waters of a small loch with a little boy hot on his trail. Her heart jolted. The dog and goose could swim, but like as not, the child couldn't.

"Dylan!" The mother waded out knee deep in the water, her skirt darkening as it absorbed the moisture. Suddenly, her gaze turned toward Keely. "Help, miss. Me boy can't swim."

Dropping her basket, Keely hiked her skirts, and rushed down the hill, not sure how she could help, since she didn't know how to swim either. The boy had ceased chasing Corky and thrashed about in his effort to stay above water. *Please, God. Send help.*

No sooner had her prayer left her heart than she heard the pounding of hooves behind her. Keely spun about. Nick, looking like a majestic knight from the days of old, raced forward on Storm Cloud.

"Nick!" the woman screamed in grateful recognition.

As he reached the water's edge, Nick yanked off his western hat—the one Keely had just returned this morning. His toss sent it spiraling toward dry ground. With a loud splash, horse and rider plowed into the water. Storm Cloud took several leaping hops before being forced to swim.

By this time, Corky had heard the lad's cries. Giving up his goose chase, the dog swam back toward the flailing child. Keely watched in disbelief as the child latched on to Corky's collar. Disbelief turned to sudden horror when she realized that, in his panic, Dylan's thrashing was taking the dog under.

"Lord save 'em," the mother prayed at Keely's side. Nick suddenly tossed the sling off his injured arm and grabbed the rope he kept lashed to his saddle. He spun a loop over his head as he'd done at the show.

Keely realized he was using his bad arm. Her heart caught in her throat. Nick's shoulder had barely healed. He could ruin it for rope tricks forever.

Ignoring the frigid cold of the loch, she joined the frantic mother in the knee-deep water. The rope sailed from Nick's hand and landed in a wide circle around the struggling dog and its panicked burden. In a few short seconds, Nick hauled the two over to Storm. He set the dog free to swim on its own. Rather than hauling the exhausted boy up behind him with his bad arm, Nick lashed him to the saddle horn so that Storm could drag him safely in at Nick's side.

Keely held her breath as the horse brought man and boy to the safety of the shallows. At the sound of loud splashing behind her, she turned to see a large man in ragged clothing plunge into the water and trudge past her toward Nick and Storm.

"Da," the boy cried, going eagerly into his father's arms as Nick released his hold on the rope.

"I'll never be able to thank ye for such as this," the man said to Nick.

"Nay, never," the woman added, pushing deeper into the cold water to join them.

Though pain grazed his face, Nick forced a smile. "Glad to help, pardner."

"Nick," Keely said, overcome with the myriad of emotions the rescue had wrung from her heart. "Let me help you."

The father moved his family away from the water's edge. Several other people, earlier drawn from their farms by the mother's screams, gathered around them. After leading the horse out of the loch, Keely held Storm's halter as Nick dismounted, grimacing as he hit the ground. Water welled over the rim of his boots from the impact.

"You risked your career for that boy," she said.

She knew her voice was filled with a mix of wonder and thanksgiving, but something else filled her mind and heart. Nick had managed to lasso them both with love. It was more than physical attraction. That she could disregard. But she couldn't ignore his noble character and godly spirit.

"Surely God will increase His healing on your shoulder after your kindness to the boy."

Nick chuckled through his obvious discomfort. "I just wish He'd hurry up—and you can let loose of Storm. He won't go anywhere."

At that moment, Corky bounded up to them, circling Keely's dripping, muddied skirts as though to get his share of attention.

"Off with you, troublemaker," she chided as she linked her arm in Nick's good one and led him to a downed log lying under the willow at the water's edge. Feeling useless, all Keely could think to do was to remove his boots and get rid of the water that must have collected inside them.

"I wouldn't be so hard on the pup," Nick said, as she bent over and grabbed one of his boots. "He did his best to save the boy."

"He's nothing but trouble," she said, tugging at the boot with all her might. Nick raised up his palm to stop her. But in that instant, the boot sailed off, the momentum of her pull taking Keely and the boot backward over the loch's edge.

She landed with a squeal and a full splash, boot clutched to her chest. Her neck craned in protest as the icy water engulfed all but her head.

"Are you all right?" Nick called from the bank. At her uncertain nod, he gave in to a loud laugh that drew the attention of the others from the half-drowned boy.

Embarrassment, backed by indignation, zinged through Keely, offsetting the chill of the water. How could he laugh at her when she was trying to help him? And she thought she loved the beast.

Keely struggled to stand in the shallow water. After dumping the liquid out of Nick's boot, she threw it at him. Still chuckling, he dodged the weapon, slowly rose to his feet, and held out his hand. She wanted to pretend she didn't see his proffered hand, but she couldn't ignore the heart-grabbing earnestness of his gaze.

As Nick helped her up the muddy bank, the others gathered round. "Are ye all right, mum?" the woman's husband asked. "We're very sorry that we've caused ye so much trouble."

Here she was meeting their tenant farmers for the first time, soaking wet and covered in mud. No, she wasn't fine. Her clothes and her pride were soggy, but Keely nodded, managing a smile.

"Thank ye, mum, fer trying to help me boy. He's a fey one, running about before thinking."

" 'Twas my own foolish dog, I'm thinking, is the culprit here. He rushed in and all but teased the child into following." Keely wadded up a section of hair that had escaped her chignon and squeezed out the water.

Both parents glanced at each other with surprised relief. Was she so intimidating?

"It'll take more than a little water to dampen this pretty lass's spirit," Nick said, slipping his arm about her waist.

"Patrick," Nick said to the husband. "This is Keely O'Cullen, the doc's daughter."

Keely watched both parents' faces pale. Did they think she might throw them off their farm over something so insignificant? Here was her chance to prove she meant well for them. She held out her wet hand. " 'Tis a pleasure to make your acquaintance."

The man seemed shocked. He glanced at Nick, whose eyes

were lit with something that looked like admiration. In spite of her wet clothing, warmth charged through her.

"Well, go on, Patrick. Shake the lady's hand." Nick's grin lit up his whole face.

"Aye, Patrick," the woman said, "shake the lady's hand."

Finally, Patrick reached out with a genuine smile. " 'Tis a pleasure, Miss O'Cullen. A true pleasure."

"I didn't think they'd accept the basket I brought," Keely said as she strolled through the sweet meadow grass toward the estate beside Nick. She had suggested they walk so their clothes would dry out, but Nick suspected she didn't want to ride on Storm with him.

"They probably wouldn't have if you hadn't said it was for the children. They're proud folk." Speaking of pride, Nick could burst with it over Keely's acting on his suggestion that she get to know the farmers. Not to mention her charging into the water to help without thought to her fine dress.

And her gaze, that smolder of admiration and concern, when she'd met him coming out of the water. It almost made his shoulder stop aching. He rubbed the sore spot but couldn't keep the smile from his face. "I'm proud of you for heeding my advice."

Her gaze darted to his. A shy grin tilted her lips before she looked away. "I noticed none of them had shoes, except the father. And those rags the children wore—" Keely's voice broke. She cleared her throat and continued. "You heard my conversation at dinner with Da. Why do you think they're so poor when my father charges them less rent than he has to?"

Nick sighed with relief. Finally she was realizing what was

happening in her own backyard. "I suspect it has to do with the middleman."

"Declan?" Keely stopped, turning. The heavy lashes that shadowed her cheeks flew up. "Why would you think that?"

Impatient, Storm Cloud nickered behind them as Nick replied, "Think about it. Your father is fair in the rents he charges. The farmers live in poverty, barely surviving, while McLochlin's cattle prosper to the point that they need to graze on your land."

Keely nibbled her lip. Nick wanted to reach out and smooth her brow. Even more, he longed to kiss her, kiss away all her worries.

"But Declan's family has money," she objected, oblivious to his thoughts. "It doesn't make sense that he'd cheat the farmers."

Licking his lips, Nick adjusted his hat instead of acting on his desire. Disappointed, he moved ahead, soggy socks squishing in squeaking boots. "Men will do just about anything for money, Keely." Thoughts of his father threatened to overturn his pot of forgiveness. But, no, he'd dealt with that. His father was forgiven, and his letter telling the man so had been mailed home.

Keely shivered when a gust blew past. Yellow gorse shrubs and multicolored wild flowers fluttered in the stiff breeze.

"Are you cold?" he asked. Even though the sun warmed him, the wind worked against it.

She nodded. "Aye. A wee bit."

Nick put his arm around her and pulled Keely against his side, surprised when she didn't sputter and fume or throw something at him. He liked how she fit tucked under his arm. His side warmed with her next to him.

"You know, although I grew up on a ranch in Texas, this sheep farm is growing on me."

Keely leaned against him. "Tell me all about it."

He told her about how hard he'd worked to build up the ranch and of the illness that had taken his mother last year. "It changed my father from a hard-working man into a gambler," he said, amazed that he could talk about it now and not feel anger. "Once Dad lost the ranch, I joined Bill Cooper's Wild West Show."

" 'Tis all so sad, Nick."

"No, not at all. I had a good, happy childhood and two parents that loved me. I learned ranching from Dad, and Mom taught me to read and to be a Christian, though I haven't always walked God's path."

"You're a good man, Nick Dalton." Keely's heart was in the gaze she raised to him. "Not at all like that Dusty King, and 'tis sorry I am that I misjudged you so."

Able to resist no longer, Nick lowered his head, drawing Keely around to claim her mouth, but she pressed her cold fingers to his lips, stopping him.

"What?"

"There's something I need to tell you." As she removed her hand, he sandwiched it between his, rubbing it, warming it with his breath. "I—that day—" She pulled her hand away and shoved it behind her. "I can't think when you're doing that."

"What if I do this?" He caressed her velvet cheek with the back of his hand. Then he fingered the damp wavy hair that hung to her waist, drying in the sun. "Keely. . ." The huskiness of his voice surprised him. He was in uncharted waters here, and his heart was stroking for all it was worth.

"Nick, don't. Let me finish." Keely stepped back, bumping into Storm Cloud. "I have to tell you about that day you were hurt. It's my—"

"Keely Noreen O'Cullen, where have you been?" Holding her skirts high, Alana hurried down the road toward them.

" 'Tis father?"

"Nay," she shouted. "Declan stopped by to say he'd pick ye up in an hour to take ye to the Brian Boru Festival. Make haste, or ye'll not be ready."

Chapter 7

Whom Declan looked for a place to park the buggy, Keely stared up the hill at the pale stone ramparts of Ballymara Castle. Perhaps next year, after the repairs to the walls and bailey were finished, the festival might be held there instead of downhill in the same spot where the Wild West show had been less than two weeks ago.

Had she really known Nick such a short while? Sure as time had taken down the castle walls, he had done the same to those barriers around her heart with his gentle spirit and noble desire to help others. Disappointed as she was that she'd come to the festival with Declan instead of Nick, this might be her best chance to find out if Declan was really cheating her father.

Once Declan secured the horse and buggy to a tree, he helped her down. Adjusting his brown corduroy cap, he offered his arm to lead her into the fairground.

It felt as though they had walked into an ancient Irish village in the days when Irish hero Brian Boru chased the Danes out of the Emerald Isle. Participants dressed in the clothing of the period demonstrated traditional crafts such as weaving and woodworking. Dancers kicked up their feet in a merry jig to fiddle and banjo, while farther along, a harpist strummed a tune for another audience.

It was simply glorious. If only she could be here with Nick instead of Declan. But she was on a mission. "So, Declan, tell me how things are going with the tenants."

He gave her a sideways glance. "Why would ye be interested in their likes, a lady such as yerself?"

She shrugged. "I guess I'm feeling the need to learn more about the estate. One day Glencullen will be mine, unless, of course, Connor returns."

"Well, there's no need for ye to worry about that. Once we're married, I'll handle the business side of the estate, and you can run the home."

Keely stopped aghast. "Just what gives you the idea that we'll be married?"

"I've known it to be so, ever since we were young. Ye worried me a bit when that Dusty King was about, but he didn't stay long. Besides, who else would have such a fiery, stubborn lass as yerself?"

"Och! If that's yer notion of flattery, ye best save it for another." Keely strode over to a booth displaying Irish jewelry. Picking up a silver Claddagh ring, she slipped it on her finger. Its heart design represented love and the clasped hands, friendship. A crown for loyalty made her think of Nick. He now held her heart like the hands on the ring. What would he do if he knew? Would he stay in Ireland?

"Maybe I'll see about getting for us something to drink," Declan offered upon catching up with her. "Would ye like that?" The dolt hadn't a clue that he'd belittled her, much less that she wanted nothing to do with him.

Nodding, Keely replaced the ring and picked up one with

small crosses etched in the shiny silver band. The old woman on the other side of the table watched her with expectant eyes.

After a few moments, Keely moved down to study the necklaces. Her attention was caught by a gold chain with a shamrock inlaid with some kind of dark green gem. She lifted up the dainty chain and allowed the shamrock to dangle freely. The afternoon sunlight sparkled against the shiny gold, making her blink.

The shamrock reminded her of the pledging stone. Would she ever stand there with Nick, the man she envisioned sharing her life with? He was all that Declan was not.

"Such a pretty Irish colleen ought to be wearing that lovely piece of jewelry."

Clutching the necklace to her chest, she looked up at the sound of Nick's voice. He leaned casually against the trunk of a huge oak that reached its long arms over the old woman's tent. Her heart raced in tempo with the lively music playing nearby. "What are you doing here?"

Nick seemed taken back by her question. "I came with the doc."

"Da's here?" Keely searched the crowd for her father's familiar face.

"Yeah, he wanted to come, so I brought him in the wagon. He's over there." Nick jerked his thumb toward some men arm wrestling.

"Nick." Keely moved toward him then laid her hand on his chest. "You have to stay away from me tonight. You'll ruin everything."

His dark brows knitted. "And just what would I ruin? Your little romance with that swindling neighbor of yours?"

"Och! You're almost as daft as he is." Keely laid the necklace on the table and moved to the side of the tent for more privacy. "There is no romance with Declan. I'm trying to find out if he's cheating the tenants."

"Keely," Nick circled her waist with a protective arm. "I told you I'd look into the situation. I went back and visited the farmers after I cleaned up this afternoon. I may have some evidence to prove Declan's been charging more rent than your father knows about and siphoning money into his own pocket."

"Men!" Keely stepped away, arms crossed. "Why is it ye all think a woman has no mind for business?"

"That's not what I think."

"I'll be spending this evening with Declan to find out what he's been up to," she declared, adding with a glower, "without your help."

"Here now, what's this? Is the American giving ye trouble, lass?" Declan walked around Nick, scowling and holding two glasses of lemonade.

"No, he was just leaving. Nick came with Da so he could keep an eye out for him." Keely lifted a brow, daring Nick to disagree.

For a moment, she thought he'd take her up on it. Cheeks puffed with a sigh, he tipped his hat and headed toward the wrestling match.

Forcing aside pangs of guilt over her impatience, Keely accepted the glass Declan held out to her and sipped the tangy beverage. She'd have to patch things up with Nick later. For now, she had a job to do.

"How much longer is he going to be at yer home? Looks pretty healed up to me." Declan watched Nick's retreat. "Ye'd think a lass would learn a lesson after being jilted by one cowboy."

Keely swallowed back the reprimand she wanted to give Declan. "I'm not as slow-witted as ye'd think, sir. He'll be leavin' soon enough. And one cowboy's about the same as another. They matter not to me." Keely hoped she was convincing, that her heart would not betray her.

"Well, I for one will be glad when he's gone." Declan swigged down his lemonade in one big gulp. "Shall we be seein' the sights then?"

As Declan offered her his arm, Keely caught a glimpse of Nick waiting a short distance away for a wagon to pass. Hoping he hadn't overheard her remark, she reluctantly placed her hand on the rough fabric of Declan's sleeve. It was going to be a long evening.

As the orange ball of the sun began to set, Keely and Declan followed the rest of the crowd up the lane toward Pledging Stone Chapel. The Brian Boru Festival always ended with a local priest or minister saying a blessing over the town and the townsfolk. Looking for Nick and her father, her gaze scanned the crowd. Old men helped their elderly wives up the cobblestone path. Children skipped along, playing and laughing, while young couples cuddled or held hands. It was too blithe a time for such a troubled heart as her own.

All afternoon, Declan refused to talk about tenant affairs, insisting that it was men's business. For all her efforts, Keely could have spent the evening with Nick and have had a glorious time instead of having to stall Declan's unwelcome advances.

The crowd gathered around the stone chapel, some in front on the grass and others standing behind them. The minister silenced the crowd with a wave of his hand and offered a long prayer. After a shout of "Amen," he raised his hand over the crowd in blessing. "May your neighbors respect you, your enemies neglect you, the angels protect you, and heaven accept you."

He waited until the townsfolk's cheer quieted then continued, "And may your blessings outnumber the shamrocks that grow, and may troubles avoid you wherever you go."

The ceremony over, some of the people took a moment to speak to the holy man before following the others back to their homes. As Keely started to join the downhill progression, Declan stopped her.

"I need to be talking with some folks. You wait for me by the chapel." He stalked off before Keely could stop him.

Tired and melancholy from her lack of success, she made her way to the pledging stone, built into the entrance of the country chapel. The cold rock chilled her fingers as she ran them along its smooth surface.

"As sure as the shamrock is green, as sure as Three are in One. . ."

Keely spun about at the sound of Nick reading the inscription on the stone from behind her. She pressed her fingers to his mouth. "Don't. 'Tis a vow to be made to God in the presence of the one you love and want to spend your life with. 'Tis not to be taken lightly."

Torches on nearby stands illuminated Nick's soul-filled gaze. Could it be that he felt for her the same way she did about him? Confusion swirled in her mind. If she confessed her love for Nick would he stay in Ireland? And if not, could she go with him and leave her father alone?

The truth drained her of any hopefulness. She couldn't leave her father. She wouldn't.

Pushing past Nick, she walked around to the side of the

chapel and stared at the stained-glass window with a shepherd on it. As a child, she had loved sitting inside the church on a sunny day and watching the brilliant rays of sun illumine the colorful window.

From the outside at night, the windows lost their vividness, just as her heart had. Keely brushed away an unbidden tear from her cheek.

At least she'd lost her hatred for cowboys and Americans. *That's something, isn't it, God?*

"Keely. . ." Nick placed a warm hand on her shoulder. "Look at me, darlin'."

Keely turned in obedience, but she couldn't look up. He would see her tears and know her feelings. But when Nick tucked his finger under her chin and lifted it, there was no hiding the pain that blurred his handsome face.

"Don't cry, honey. Don't you know—"

"Here now! What's that yer doin'. Unhand me girl."

Keely and Nick turned in unison to see Declan and his friend Shane O'Toole standing a stone's throw away. "You'll not be stealin' Keely from me. I mean to marry her."

"Declan—" Nick's tightened grasp on Keely's arm halted her words.

"Ye told me yerself that them low-down American cowboys are all the same and that ye want nothing to do with 'em," Declan said. "I heard the words from out of yer mouth just tonight. Come here, woman, and stand by yer future husband."

She had never fainted before, but she just might now. Nick's wounded expression at Declan's comment punctured any hope she had left that she and Nick might share their love. He let her go, hand dropping from her arm.

"I've got something to ask you, McLochlin." Nick challenged, his voice ringing across the shaded glen overlooking the river below.

Keely noticed her father shuffling up the hill behind Declan. Nor was he alone. A remnant of townsfolk gathered round to witness the confrontation, for from the stubborn jut of Nick's chin, that was what was building. Among the crowd were Patrick and his family as well as some of their neighbors.

Panic that the news of Declan's announcement of their betrothal would soon be all over town was exceeded only by fear of a physical clash between Nick and the overseer. Declan was a brawler in the first degree, and Nick's shoulder gave the oaf the advantage.

Looking heavenward, Keely sought God. *Please, Father, forgive me for my stubbornness and for telling Nick that lie. I never meant to. I've been a coward, and I'm sorry for that. But, God, please don't let anything happen to him.*

"Why don't you tell the O'Cullens how you've been cheating their tenant farmers for the past year and pocketing the proceeds?" Nick challenged.

Declan straightened, tucked his thumbs in his jacket lapels, and held on tightly. "I don't know what ye're talking about. And I'll not have a foreigner slandering me good name."

"I have proof." Nick reached into his pocket.

"Nay!" Eyes wide with rage, Declan pulled a pistol from his pocket and pointed it toward Nick.

Keely turned her head just in time to see Nick diving at her. The full weight of his body crashed into her, knocking her to the ground at the same time the gun shattered the night calm in a flash of light and thunder. Behind them, glass exploded.

Her pulse pounded in her ears as the weight of Nick's body

pressed her into the chilly grass. The crowd roared its disapproval. "Grab McLochlin," someone cried out. A scuffle ensued. Nick jumped to his feet and pulled her up with his good arm. Dizzy, she swayed against him, holding tight to his arm until the faintness passed.

"I told ye that ye'd get caught one of these days, didn't I?" Shane O'Toole shouted to Declan.

Wrestling against the men who held him, Declan scowled at his old friend. "Ye didn't seem to mind when I bought yer drinks at the pub!"

The magistrate plowed through the crowd. "Here now, what's all this about?"

"Are you all right?" Nick's breath warmed her ear.

Keely dusted her hands, trying to ignore her aching body. "Aye. I'm fine." Looking past him, she stared in horror at the remnant of the shattered stained-glass window.

"You there," the magistrate shouted at Nick. "Seems ye're part of this. Come to me office so we can get this mess straightened out."

"He's got a gun," Declan yelled.

Hand resting on his pistol, the magistrate lifted his bushy eyebrows at Nick.

"No. Honestly, sir, I don't have a weapon. I was reaching inside my pocket to get this accounting of how much rent each of Taig O'Cullen's tenants have been paying." He held the paper out toward the officer. "I think you'll see a discrepancy between this list and the one Declan McLochlin kept. It seems McLochlin's been skimming some of the rent."

"Go on, Nick, and talk with the magistrate. I'll see Father home." Keely avoided his gaze. What was there to say? She loved him but wouldn't leave Ireland with him. It couldn't work, no matter which way she looked at it.

"You're sure you can spare me?"

With a twitch of a sad smile at his attempted humor, Keely nodded, moving to where her father made his way toward them. Tears held at bay, she longed for the privacy of her bedroom. A deceiver like her didn't deserve a man as honorable as Nick. Somehow she had to put Nick Dalton out of her heart and mind forever.

Chapter 8

Nick felt like a yellow-bellied coward who'd been kicked in the gut. He checked his bag to be certain he'd packed everything. He'd never slunk away from a fight before. But then this wasn't really a fight. It was an opinion. That it belonged to the woman he loved hurt all the more.

Last night at the festival, he'd overheard Keely's snide comment about cowboys, only to be reminded of it by Declan repeating it to the whole town. Somehow, Nick had thought Keely's feelings for him had softened. How could he have been so wrong?

After the magistrate had hauled Declan off to jail, Nick had ridden back to the O'Cullen estate. Keely had already gone to bed. There was no putting off what he had to do. It was time to hit the road.

In his pocket rested the envelope that contained the note that he'd written to Keely, explaining why he was leaving and wishing her well. Also in the missive was a little token to remember him by. *If* she wanted to remember him.

He would never forget the fire in Keely's blue eyes or her feisty spirit. At least, he'd been successful in opening her eyes to the needy living on her own estate. His heart had swelled with pride when he learned that she was working to make things better for Patrick's family and the other tenant farmers.

Picking up his leather bag and boots, he slipped downstairs, hoping not to awaken anyone. In the dining room, he set Keely's letter on her breakfast plate, which Alana had already set out, and then laid a letter down for Taig, which contained some money for his doctoring services and a thank you.

"So ye're leaving, are ye?"

Nick spun around at the sound of Alana's voice.

"It's best I move on now that I'm better."

"Best for who? You? Or Keely?"

"You know how she feels about cowboys. And that's all I'm ever going to be." He pulled on his boots then grabbed his bag and reached for the door handle.

"I'm thinking she just needs the right cowboy." Alana lifted her chin a notch.

"Maybe. But I'm not the one for her. She made that clear enough. Thanks for your great cooking. I even learned to like lamb. Good-bye, Alana."

"May the Lord keep you in His right hand and never close His fist too tight, lad." Alana held the back door open for him, a broad, motherly smile on her face. "Never be afraid to trust an unknown future to a known God, Nick."

Half an hour later, Nick reined Storm Cloud to a stop in front of Pledging Stone Chapel. Rain dripped from his Stetson onto his shoulders and down his arm in a frigid stream. The morning's gray mist mirrored his attitude.

He tied the horse to a nearby fence and moseyed up the cobblestone path that led to the chapel's entrance where the pledging stone gave silent testimony to centuries of vows. How many young couples had pledged their love here? Hundreds? Thousands?

If only he had more to give Keely, he'd pledge his love faster than a bronco could bust out of a gate. But he was a man of small means, not unlike the farmers that tilled her land. He couldn't give her the wealth she was used to.

The landscape blurred before him as he leaned against the cold stone of the chapel. The black pain raging in his heart was worse than all his father had caused him, but Nick couldn't simply will Keely to return his love any more than he could bear to be near her without it.

Not even the peek of the morning sun trying to bully its way through the clouds could brighten his mood. Heaving a despondent sigh, Nick turned away from the chapel. He'd been gone long enough. It was time he headed back home to America.

Keely threw back the thick drapes covering her window. It was a glorious day, even though a gray mist dampened the earth. Last night she'd wrestled with God. He'd made His will clear to her, and today she'd tell Nick of her love for him.

Not even her remorse for lying about how he'd gotten his injury could wilt her joy. The good Lord had forgiven her for her wrongdoings and apathetic heart, and she was certain Nick would, too. God would see to the details.

Keely slid into her slippers and hurried down the stairs. Father and Nick were probably already eating breakfast. As she reached the bottom step, she wiped the smile from her face. She didn't want an audience when she told Nick. If only she could get through breakfast without her love spilling from her eyes.

Rounding the corner into the dining room, she saw her father standing near his chair, shoulders sagging. An opened letter hung from one hand, and an envelope dangled from the other. Her heart plummeted from its pinnacle. He looked as stricken as the day Connor had left.

"Da?" she said, her heart seizing in her chest.

Alana entered from the kitchen, holding a covered serving dish, her face mirroring the same gloom as the doctor's.

Keely searched the room with a frantic gaze. "Where's Nick?"

Her father turned toward her and held out the envelope. " 'Tis for you. I'm afraid 'tis sad news, lass. You'd best have a seat."

Keely took the envelope and clasped it to her chest. Limp as a piece of wilted lettuce, she collapsed into the chair her father pulled out for her.

No. This couldn't be happening to her again. Dusty had left a letter and slunk off, coward that he was. She never expected Nick to do the same thing.

Hands trembling, she ripped open the envelope. Something fell into her lap. A gasp escaped her lips as she recognized the shamrock necklace she'd admired yesterday at the festival. So that's what became of it. Prodded by second thought, she'd gone back later to buy it, but the necklace had already been sold.

Clutching the cherished pendant to her heart, she read Nick's letter:

Beloved Keely,
    It's killing me to walk away without telling you good-bye in person, but I think it's for the best. Like you said on

several occasions, I'm nothing but a low-down cowpoke. I've worked hard all my life, and I'm not ashamed of that, but even with hard work, I can't give you all the things you're accustomed to. I wish I could. I wish my love was enough. But now you've seen how the tenant farmers live, and while I've never known the poverty they have, I couldn't keep you in the style you're used to. You deserve so much more.

Please keep an eye on Patrick's clan for me, and tell him I said good-bye.

Remember, there's nowhere you can go that God isn't with you, helping and comforting you. Enjoy the shamrock necklace. I'll never forget how your eyes lit up like blue diamonds when you first saw it. Hope it reminds you of the promise you'll make at the pledging stone some day. I'm just sorry that I'm not the man you'll be saying it to.

Live well, Keely O'Cullen. And remember the cowboy who loved you, if only for a season.

All my love,
Nick Dalton

"Oh, Da, what have I done?" Keely hugged the letter to her chest. The necklace warmed in her hand, but nothing could warm her heart. She wailed in anguish loud enough to put a banshee to shame. "I've chased him away, just when I realized how much he means to me."

Her father drew her against him, patting her head. "There now, I loved him, too."

The catch in her father's throat made her sob even harder. God had given her a jewel, and she'd thrown it to swine out of pride, determined that she didn't need Nick's help to prove Declan a liar and thief. How could she live, knowing she'd run off the man who loved her?

And he truly did love her. He said so in his note.

Alana set the covered glass dish down so hard the clank gave Keely a start. "Are ye just gonna sit there and let the man get away? He's a good man, Keely. And he loves you. I seen it in his eyes and in them kind words he's always had, even though you weren't so kind to him. Go after the man and bring him back to us. You aren't the only one who loves Nick Dalton."

"Aye!" Her father smacked the table with his fist. " 'Tis a grand idea." The letter he'd been holding spiraled to the ground, along with several American dollars. Her father was already headed for the front door.

Hope surging, Keely leapt to her feet, wiping the tears from her eyes. "But how will we find him? How long has he been gone? He may have left last night for all we know."

"Nay. 'Twas but half an hour ago, if that."

Keely stared at Alana in shock. "You knew he left, but you didn't tell me?"

" 'Twasn't my place to meddle. 'Sides, I knew sure as the mornin' sun that ye'd be down for yer breakfast any moment." An ornery twinkle lighted in the cook's eyes. "I did happen to leave me cookin' long enough to follow that fine lad to the road and see that he headed for Ballymara."

Keely couldn't hold back her grin as she hugged her friend. "Oh, thank ye, Alana. Keep the food warm. When we return, we'll have reason to celebrate."

"Make 'em go faster, Da."

"The ponies are doing the best they can, lass. We're almost to the river."

115

Clutching the side of the wagon as it bounced and shook down the rocky road, Keely counted the seconds until they rounded the bend and could see the stone bridge crossing the Killibadh River.

Please, Lord, let us find Nick before he leaves town. Don't let it end this way. Please.

Her heart sank as the ancient bridge came into sight. No cowboy on horseback could be seen, only a lone man crossing the stone bridge on foot.

Keely shaded her eyes with her hand. The sun had evaporated the earlier rain clouds and now burst forth with fingers of light and warmth. A sudden river of hope flooded through her as she realized the man striding toward her was quite tall and wore a hat—with a brim. Her heart leapt in recognition. Nick!

"Stop, Da!"

"What?" His bushy eyebrows lifted. "Go faster. Hurry. Now stop. Make up your mind, lass."

"It's Nick, Da."

He looked down the road from under the brim of his cap. "Glory be! 'Tis himself. . .an' he's coming our way."

Keely leaped to her feet, prepared to jump off the moving wagon if necessary. "Nick!" She waved her hand above her head.

Looking their way, Nick slowed then burst into a dead run that matched the excited beat of her heart. As her father stopped the wagon, Keely jumped free in a billow of skirts and ran to meet her love.

Colliding in an embrace, Nick spun her around in his arms, devouring her with his gaze. Embarrassed, she lifted a hand to smooth down her rebellious tresses, curling in the humid air.

"Allow me." Nick ran his hands over her hair as though touching something more precious than gold. Keely swayed against him, reveling in his touch. "I never thought I'd see you again, and it was killing me," he said, moving her at arm's length and staring as if to be certain that she was real.

"Me, too." Keely blinked away her tears. "I came downstairs this morning all ready to confess my love, only to find you gone. Do you know what that does to a woman's heart?"

Nick's brow shot up. "You love me. . .a low-life cowboy?"

"Aye. I do love you, but you're not a low-life. And I'm sorry for saying such. You're a kind, noble man. And if you'd not been in such a big hurry to run away, you'd have known it before now."

Nick lowered his gaze. "Sorry. I didn't think there was a chance for us."

"Now who's being the doubter?" Raising his chin with the curl of her hand, Keely gave him a no-nonsense stare.

Nick fingered the shamrock necklace around her neck. "Do you like it?"

"Aye," she whispered. "You know I do. And it will always be special because you gave it to me."

Nick tipped his hat back. "I tried to leave. I visited the pledging stone then got on Storm, but the loco horse wouldn't budge. I kicked and clicked my tongue. It was the strangest thing."

Keely grinned. "A bit like Balaam's donkey in the Bible, I'm thinkin'."

"You know, you just might be right." Wonder filled Nick's face. "God must have had a hand in it."

"No maybes about it." Keely pulled what she hoped was a beguiling pout. "Are ye going to stand there till St. Paddy's Day, or are you going to kiss me, Nick Dalton?"

The twinkle in Nick's dark eyes sent the leprechauns leaping in Keely's stomach. With a mischievous grin tugging at his lips, he lowered his mouth to hers.

Nick's kiss was all she'd dreamed of and more. His soft, warm lips stirred her, conveying an unspoken promise of more to come. Keely could hardly wait.

All too soon, he pulled away, cold rushing in to fill the gap between them and dashing Keely with reality. They'd admitted their love, but Keely had yet another admission to make. "Nick, I've something to say."

"Go on," he encouraged, with a lopsided grin on his handsome face.

"I—" She swallowed, gathering courage. " 'Twas me that caused yer accident."

Nick's brow quirked. "What do you mean?"

Keely licked her lips. "Corky ran into the arena. I ran in to get him, but 'twas me that spooked yer horse." She looked down at her feet and whispered, " 'Twas my fault ye got hurt."

Nick's snort brought her head up again. "Why didn't you say something sooner, girl? I've known what happened from the beginning. Your dad told me the day I woke up."

Keely stared, dumbfounded. He'd known all along and still wanted her?

"Keely Noreen O'Cullen, it'd take more than a banged-up shoulder to come between me and the woman I love."

With that, Nick set about proving it, taking her in his arms and kissing away all her doubts.

Epilogue

Two months later, Keely stood at the pledging stone, looking at her handsome groom. Nick wore the western suit that his father had brought from America when he came to attend the wedding. A gentle warmth filled her being that father and son had made peace. Even better, the wayward father had found God and was making a turnaround.

A letter from Connor stated he was doing well, though he had parted ways from Dusty. And it would seem that before long Keely would have an American sister-in-law as well as an American husband.

The chapel window that Declan broke had been replaced by one to honor Nick. From now on, people would look at the stained-glass window of the shepherd holding a lasso and remember the cowboy who made peace at Glencullen with his gentle persistence and noble example. She'd learned from Nick that the tenants had been so upset about the rents that they were considering a boycott, and there had even been talk of burning down her home. Nick's intervention had brought Declan to justice, and her father had reimbursed the tenants' money that Declan had taken. Keely had even made friends with Patrick's family and several others.

Nick squeezed her hand, drawing her attention back to him. How could she be so blessed to marry such a kind, honorable man?

"You ready?" His bright smile radiated heartrending tenderness and love.

She nodded and took hold of his other hand. Their voices melded in a forever promise.

"As sure as the shamrock is green, as sure as Three are in One, our love shall be redeemed by the Father, Spirit, and Son."

VICKIE MCDONOUGH

Vickie's first novella was included in the historical romance anthology *A Stitch in Time*. Her writing has been recognized with awards in a number of prestigious contests. She has written over 300 book reviews, which have appeared on various websites, ezines, and in her book review columns in several newspapers. She is the mother of four boys and makes her home in Oklahoma with her husband of almost thirty years. When she's not writing, Vickie enjoys reading, gardening, watching movies, and traveling.

Vickie loves hearing from her readers at vickie@vickiemcdonough.com.

A Legend of Love

Part 2

by Linda Windsor

Chapter 5

*D*ia duit ar maidin, Mrs. O'Cullen, Moyra Rose," Father Mackenna announced at the back door of the publick house the following morning.

"Mornin', Father," Moyra mumbled over her cup of tea. Somehow, she failed to see the good of it.

"If ye call it a good morning, Father," Gran echoed Moyra's thought. She stepped back so that the priest might enter the kitchen. "Me granddaughter's marryin' an alien, and me own spinster granddaughter is the laughin' stock of the town."

Moyra winced from the round table where the family gathered, hit and miss, most mornings. Polly O'Cullen never minced words, priest or nay.

"Will ye have some tea and rolls?" Gran offered.

"No time today," the priest replied, astonishing Moyra. Gran's butter rolls were known all over Ballymara. "I just came to see what Moyra Rose thought of her great-great-grandmother's story.

"A cowboy in Ireland," Gran exclaimed, "and all the while I never knew." Like Moyra, she'd been fascinated by the account of how Keely O'Cullen came to marry Nick Dalton.

" 'Blessed are the peacemakers,' " Mackenna quoted, " 'for

they shall be called the children of God.'"

"Many's the time I've seen that rope in the shepherd's hand just above my bench, but never did I guess he was a cowboy," Gran twittered on.

"And what are your thoughts, Moyra Rose?" Father Mackenna asked.

"I'm thinking of a good use for that rope," Moyra muttered over her cup of hot tea. The reply clever, it did not reflect the whole of her heart. At the moment she saw herself in her ancestor's place, saddled with an American. But this American was hardly Nick Dalton. He had no redeeming qualities.

"I'm thinking of you as Nick Dalton, Moyra Rose. You're the one who must win the skeptical heart with your goodness. . . make the peace, so to speak."

Moyra jerked in rebellion. "Has your mind gone fishin', Father?" Yet even as she challenged the priest, she knew in her heart that was the only hope for Ballymara. "It's not my nature," she declared, aware of Gran's study.

"Doing the right thing is often not in our nature," Father Mackenna answered, "but with God's help, we can do the right thing."

He was right, Moyra realized, but it wasn't what she wanted to do.

Peg poked her head around the doorjamb. "Has anyone seen Buttons?"

"Aye," Gran replied. "I let the poor cat out this mornin', so heavy her belly's draggin' on the dew."

"But, Gran, you know she's due to drop the kittens any day."

"And she'll do it inside, where she's always chosen," Gran assured the young woman. "In the furnace room where it's warm and comfy."

"Well then, I'd best be off," the priest announced, his mission complete.

"Jack has finished his breakfast, Moyra Rose. He's ready to 'hit the road,' " Peg quoted with a giggle. "These Americans."

"Remember, Moyra Rose O'Cullen," Mackenna said from the door. "What we feel like doing and God's will are oft at odds." He gave her a little wink. "And the Father always knows best."

"That scrawny little man loves sayin' that," Gran muttered as she closed the door behind the priest. "As if t'were himself." She gave Moyra a silent appraisal. "So how much money do ye think a man such as Jack Andrews makes in a year's time?"

Moyra's gaze sharpened. "Not nearly enough for what you're thinking." She got up and gave Gran a kiss on the cheek. "Don't go there, Gran. I may be a spinster in your eye, but I'm not desperate."

As she walked out of the room, Gran called after her. "Put on your sweet face, dear. No need in frightenin' the gent away right off."

Jack nearly toppled the coffee mug he set down on the checkered tablecloth as Moyra swept into the Mugger's Loft like a breath of spring, making straight for his booth. And those eyes—Jack braked his mental wandering. They were an incandescent battleground reflecting the struggle he'd put there.

"Top of the morning, Moyra Rose," he said as she slid onto the bench opposite him, a cover girl for a day of sport in autumn tweed slacks and a russet sweater. "Do we do the castle today?"

" 'Tis Saturday, Mr. Andrews. You've mixed up your days. I believe you have a practice with Killbog this afternoon."

"That's Jack." Gradually her answer set in, forcing him to

look at his watch. "Aw man, I'm so befuddled I'm not sure if I'm coming or going." Probably due more to her company than the time change. "And what's a Killbog?"

"It's the neighboring village team. The game's for practice this week, but next, it's for real." She hesitated, searching his face. "What did you think of our own Irish cowboy story?"

"Fascinating, actually." While Jack didn't lie, he was more interested in hearing about the game. It had been years since he'd played soccer.

"I knew the Wild West shows toured Europe but never thought beyond that. And a cattleman settling the disputes of the sheep farmers—that's a first and last, as far as I know."

"Because he followed God's calling and not that of his purse."

Jack winced inwardly as her words struck dead on target. He supposed he deserved it. His career was his money, and that was the driving force behind exposing the pledging stone. But trusting his career to God, well, that was just talk. "But scripture points out that God helps those who help themselves."

Moyra frowned, the arch of her auburn brows riveting Jack's attention. "I don't think that's in scripture, Jack. Isn't that some kind of proverb?"

"Is there a book of Proverbs?" he kidded with a dismissive chuckle. He dug out the money for the check and left it on the table. "Shall we?" he asked, catching Moyra pulling the humor at his play on words from her lips.

"I'll be over to the park in a bit," Moyra told him. "Besides, you'll need to get your kickabout and change into something more suitable for having the stuffings knocked out of you."

Something told Jack that she'd like that as he followed the fiery colleen out of the loft.

Chapter 6

The early morning mist lingered over the day, but it took more than dampness to keep the fans of the Ballymara Rams inside. The bleachers were filled on the home side and not far from it on the visitors' side. While the team was an amalgamation of pensioners and pups hardly old enough to shave, the town enthusiasm for them made up for their lack of physical prowess and skill. Moyra joined the cheer as they walked onto the field. Among them, clad in sweats, Jack Andrews joked with Tim Ryan, the curly blond who'd talked him into playing for a member out with a sprained knee.

For a writer, the American looked fit, Moyra admitted reluctantly. She watched the way the breeze tossed the feathered wings of his sandy brown hair, wishing that Keely O'Cullen's story had spoken to him as much as it had to her. If she was willing to suspend animosity, the least he could do was suspend his skepticism.

"I've got the coffee," Peg announced, setting a large Thermos and bag of pastry boxes on the reserved bench beside Moyra. Since Gran's Publick House provided the team refreshment, the family had the equivalent of box seats. As the Killbog players trotted onto the field to the roar of their supporters, Peg pulled a Styrofoam cup from the plastic sleeve. "Want one?"

The chill made hot coffee sound delish. Best to get it now before they were surrounded by the football players. By the time Moyra cut the coffee's bite with some milk, the team swept in like a pack of locusts, consuming everything Peg had brought.

"So are you ready to play?" she asked Jack as he crumpled his cup and tossed it into a nearby garbage can.

"Ready as I'll ever be." He nodded toward the field. "The field's a bit larger, and the goal looks like a cross between soccer and our gridiron football, but the fundamentals are the same. . .I hope."

His grin was positively beguiling. If only he weren't who he was, Moyra thought—the man who would end her new career and rob the mouths of Ballymara.

The loud clearing of a throat drew her attention to where Peg stood, holding her backpack. Upon snagging Moyra's attention, she withdrew a little bell.

"To cheer the team?" Moyra teased.

"It's a wedding bell," her niece informed her in light-hearted indignation. "All the guests will get one to ring as we pass."

"The chapel bell isn't good enough?"

Stars twinkled in Peg's eyes. "I read that it's an old tradition. . .to ring away discord between Ned and me. The guests ring them in the church as we pass by."

"Discord?" Moyra snorted. "You've been so close, one dose of salts would work the two of you."

"And then there's this," Peg said, ignoring Moyra and pulling out a little hanky. "They call it a Magic Hanky. I carry it on my wedding day, and when we have our first child, with a few stitches, it's a christening bonnet."

Moyra fought the pang of envy over Peg's happiness. But

Moyra was a modern woman in a modern time. Maybe marriage wasn't for her.

The shriek of a whistle drew her attention to the game about to begin.

A flurry of kicking and grunting ensued as Killbog and Ballymara scrambled for control of the ball. Jack played a halfback, defensive for the most part. Well-matched in age, paunch, and athletic skill, the teams ran neck and neck through the first half.

"Get shod of it, Jack!" someone shouted when three Killbogs zeroed in to take the ball from the American.

Jack was good at maneuvering the ball with his feet, but surrounded, it was impossible.

"The hands, Jack, the hands," another shouted. But it was too late. . .again. The ball was Killbog's, and a goal scored.

"What's the matter with our Jack?" Peg exclaimed in exasperation. "Does he think the ball's dirty?"

Moyra crinkled her eyes in the sunlight that eked its way through the cloud cover. "I'm thinking maybe American soccer players don't touch the ball."

A few minutes later during the halftime break, Jack confirmed Moyra's suspicion. "I can't get used to being able to hold the ball."

"Only for four steps," Moyra reminded him with more sympathy than she intended. The flush of his cheeks made his mercurial gaze bluer today.

"Think of it this way, Jack. If you hadn't hopped in for Billy Kelloug, there'd be no game," Peg consoled him.

Jack arched a playful brow at her. "So half a player's better than none, eh?"

"Precisely," she replied, as bright as the glitter on her eyelids.

"In full sun, she could send signals with those," Jack mumbled under his breath as Peg ran off to meet the love of her life, who'd just got off work from the farm. "Cute kid."

"And so in love, it's almost annoying." Moyra caught herself. "And only a week before the big day. . .and the game." Turning, she found herself the object of Jack's scrutiny. Great, now he'd want to know why she'd said what she'd said and find that beneath her Miss Independence attitude lay, at least partly, an envious heart.

"What does *give it a skelp* mean?"

The man was clueless on more than one count, thankfully. "It means to try."

"Aha! That makes sense now," he declared. "I thought *give it a skelp with the hands* meant skin the ball."

Moyra laughed outright. "I don't think that would go over well, seein's the town has a limited budget for recreational equipment."

"Yeah, and I'd hate to have to outrun thirty angry men."

Her smile lingered as Jack rejoined the team for the second half. With soon-to-be newlyweds all but canoodling next to her, she focused on the game and one particular player. Jack broke himself of the habit of avoiding hand contact with the ball, but he still rid himself of it as if it were a hot potato. His improvement evoked huzzahs from the home benches. After he'd sent the ball back to his team more times than the Killbog forwards thought prudent, the gloves came off for the American rookie. Shouts of "Killbog" took on the emphasis of *kill*.

"Knock Killbog's knickers off," Moyra shouted back with the same bloodlust when Jack finally got into the collision-tolerance of the play and defended himself against a burly forward.

"Look, Aunt Moyra," Peg said in delight, drawing Moyra's attention from the end game play. "The Klingon daggers came in for the table setting."

How on earth she and Peg could have come from the same genetic soup was beyond her, Moyra thought, staring at the black and gray plastic wedding favors.

At that moment, a collective gasp from the Ballymara bleachers drew her gaze back to the field. In the short span of inattention, Jack had gotten knocked end over tea biscuits upon the field. The gasp turned into a cheer as Ballymara's forwards took over the ball and tore off to the other end of the field. Coach Burns rushed to Jack's side, but Jack shook off the help, climbing to his feet on his own. Beyond, Ballymara scored a winning goal.

"Game!" the Ballymarans cheered, spilling off the bleachers and onto the field like supercharged lava.

"He's got bottle, your American," one of them said to Moyra in passing.

"Hear that, Moyra Rose, *your* American, he says," Ned said, as if he wanted to infect everyone he knew with his giddy-headed happiness.

"He's not mine, nor would I have him," Moyra snapped. . . a little too quick to her liking.

"Ned's mam says *'tis a lonesome wash without a man's shirt in it*," Peg quoted dreamily.

The words drenched Moyra's urge to rush to Jack's side with congratulations like a bucket of ice water. "Aye, no doubt," she shot back. " 'Tis one less shirt his dear mam'll have to launder."

Chapter 7

Jack flinched as Moyra gently placed a bag of ice over his swollen eye.

"You should have let me tend it when I offered," she said, as though he deserved every hammer of pain in the affected area.

At the time, he'd been anesthetized by the adrenalin of the *shebeen*—what the guys called the celebration. But as the night wore on and the hungry players finished off their meals, his eye and temple began to feel as bad as the expression on Moyra's face when she'd first seen it. Prim and stiff as a broomstick, she straightened on the edge of his bed. "At least you'll have Sunday to recover, though I doubt you'll want to be in any of the castle pictures come Monday." Humor tugged at her lips.

"I didn't think it was Christian to take delight in another's agony."

Her eyes flashed. "Now don't be making a pepperpot of things, just when I'm starting to think you have some thread of decency."

"I think I like seeing you in a pepperpot. Puts fire in your eyes."

Her lips parted, as though uncertain whether to lash out or

caress. Jack hoped for the latter.

"You, Jack Andrews, have been knocked off your trolley." As she rose, Jack caught her hand before she bolted for the open bedroom door. "What is your story, Moyra Rose? Do you have a boyfriend?"

Frozen to the spot, she shook her head. "I've no time for one, Jack. Much like yourself, I'd imagine."

"Oh, yes, my ex-fiancée." He coaxed her back with his hand and the anticipation of an explanation. "But she wanted a man on demand. My job wouldn't allow it. What's your story?"

She started to draw away again, but Jack held fast. "Now, now, no fair. I told mine."

"In case you hadn't noticed, I have a fierce pride and temper," she said, gaze fixed on one of the hand-hooked rugs scattered about the cozy room. "Not exactly the makings of a good wife. . .or so Gran says."

"A little spirit never hurt anybody." Jack meant it. It enchanted him. The impish quirk of her brow as she shifted her focus to him sent a frisson of awareness through him.

"Bear in mind, Jack Andrews," she warned softly, "a little is all you've seen, thanks to the good Lord's intervention. And come tomorrow—"

The ice bag slipped off his eye. As Moyra leaned forward to catch it, Jack caught the edgy colleen in his arms and sought her lips with his own. Startled, she tensed and drew away, but the firm, yet gentle, circle of his embrace held. He watched a wary tolerance claim her face. Moyra Rose was no more to be carried away in one fell swoop than her ancestor Keely O'Cullen Dalton had been.

He loosened the fold of his arms, taking pleasure in the fact that she didn't bolt like a wild horse into the hall beyond.

Instead she returned to her schoolmarm posture, straight as the ladder-back chair by the hearth nearby. Clasping her freed hand in the other, she rose.

"Well then, Jack. I'm glad we—" She scowled. "You, I mean, got that out of your system. And seeing as how you're so improved, I'll be leaving you to your rest."

Jack watched her back toward the door opening as if she half-expected him to lunge after her. It wasn't beyond the realm of his imagination either.

"Best you get some rest, or you'll be knackered in—" Leaping high as a step dancer, Moyra shrieked in concert with the potbellied cat that had scampered out from under the chair in time for her heel to catch its tail. "Buttons, you'll be my death!" Hand still clutched to her chest, she turned. "I'll call you for church in the morning."

"I'm not really into church—" Jack broke off as she locked gazes with him.

It was only a split second of time, but Jack felt as though he'd seen a kindred spirit.

"Suit yourself." She closed the door behind her as though she'd seen the same thing and was as unnerved as he. From the other side she called back, "Monday then. . .and Ballymara Castle."

Chapter 8

What had he been thinking, Jack wondered as Moyra drove him up the winding road toward the conical tower of a castle just visible above the tree line on the mountain ahead. Kissing the woman whose career he was about to ruin was the last thing he needed. It was far easier to devastate her from a distance, but maintaining detachment from her and her quaint little town was growing harder.

Even with the news that he was out to discredit the pledging stone and possibly ruin their livelihoods, the citizens of Ballymara had drawn him into their lives as one of their own, just as they had Nick Dalton. Jack had a new understanding of the assimilation of the island's conquerors into their society. The invaders couldn't resist Erin's charm. . .and her colleens.

"So did you enjoy the service yesterday?" Moyra asked, slowing to a stop as a herd of sheep crossed the paved road, unhurried.

And he'd gone to church for the first time since youth-group age. "It wasn't bad at all. I want Padrac to try to capture the glow inside the chapel from the stained-glass windows. Hollywood tries to capture that ethereal quality with special lighting, but I tell you, they don't come close. It knocked my socks off."

A smile lighted on his companion's lips. " 'Tis the Holy Spirit. Like as not, that quality doesn't come on Hollywood's demand. . .or any man's. Just when two or more are gathered in His name. . ."

Jack cut her off. "Yeah, I know. There is love."

"There is God, who is love," Moyra corrected, "surrounding them with His lighting. Name me anyone who can match any sunrise or sunset." She shook her head. "Granted they capture it on film, but even so, it isn't as magnificent as the real thing."

Jack didn't answer because he had none. In his heart, he knew that she was right. He also knew that he'd never felt so at home, surrounded by the light in that small chapel.

The Irish life was infectious; awakening a part of him that the concrete and diesel fumes of the city had hardened.

Halfway up the hill to the castle, Moyra pointed out the two-story manor house that had belonged to her ancestor, Keely O'Cullen. Today Corbin Sheehan, the Donald Trump of Ballymara, lived there.

"He owns the hardware, the market, and the radio station. Mrs. Sheehan is giving a bridal shower for Peg, Ned being her nephew," Moyra informed him. "If you wanted to come early to get some pictures, I'm sure she'd not mind. Not nearly as stuffy as himself."

Her little sniff of disapproval was a cross-twitch between Jack's childhood loves of *Bewitched* and *I Dream of Jeannie*, although he'd never considered himself a nose man until now. Moyra would never be a whiner or a clinging vine, that was certain. It was a shame they were at cross-purposes.

"Maybe Padrac can take a picture or two for the article after they leave the castle."

As they approached Ballymara Castle, Moyra told him about the round tower, which, like the many surviving in Ireland, had once stood alone as a refuge from the Vikings. Later, when the Norman-Saxons from Britain occupied the Pale, of which Ballymara was a part, they incorporated this particular tower into a greater castle.

"Pierce and Mary Brennan bought it at a bankruptcy sale and are renovating it a section at a time," Moyra said.

"I imagine the cost of modernization is staggering," Jack remarked, studying the tower against the blue gray morning sky.

"More than staggering," Moyra agreed. "It's been used commercially since the nineteenth century as a public gathering place for fairs, exhibits, and such."

The walled-in compound conjured the image of an ancient convention center.

As Moyra parked the SUV next to Padrac's beat-up white compact car, the photographer climbed out. "Perfect timing," he said as they climbed out of the Land Rover. He gave Moyra a toothy grin. "Moyra Rose, *conas tá tú?*"

Moyra's gaze fell on the *Ballymara Tribune* rolled in his hand. She obviously didn't know what was the lead story, but suspicion lit in her eyes. "I'm fine, Padrac. . .at least until I see what you've got there."

Padrac handed over the paper, which Jack had already seen that morning. Now he knew why the feisty colleen hadn't chewed him up for breakfast. He watched Moyra's eyes snap. The Irish television station hadn't picked up the video footage, but the challenge made the *Tribune* headlines.

"Any feelings of love yet, Moyra?" the photographer taunted.

Jack fisted his hand at his side. Padrac was becoming a barracuda for a story. It was like looking into a mirror to see who was the most ugly of them all.

Moyra looked up from reading the caption beneath the picture of her and Jack at the chapel. "I told you I needed to put on some makeup. I look like great-grannie's ghost." She handed back the paper. "And you call yourself a photographer."

As he followed Moyra to the heavy double oak doors, Jack smiled at the dumbstruck Padrac, who evidently had expected her to turn into a gnashing tigress. Gracious, but sharp enough to draw blood, Jack thought, surprised yet caught in admiration.

Chapter 9

At the first knock, Pierce Brennan opened the door, clad in a fourteenth-century costume. "Good day, Milady O'Cullen." Of height and build enough to carry the robes and what looked to Jack to be tights, he extended his hand upon seeing Jack. "And you must be Sir Jack Andrews. Welcome to Ballymara Castle."

Jack accepted the handshake, more struck by the genuineness in Brennan's intelligent gaze than the absurdity of an outfit best saved for the tourists. Of course Brennan had cause to make a good impression, but an inner sense told Jack that this was the real deal, whether the article in the paper rolled under the man's arm brought business to the place or not.

"Mary's made hot cinnamon rolls and scones in the kitchen. . .and coffee," he added, with a solicitous glance at Jack. Self-conscious, he brushed at his velvet overcoat. "The costume was her idea. She thought it would give you the flavor that we are trying to achieve."

Jack patted his full stomach. "Perhaps later," he said. "I'm still stuffed with ham, eggs, and Gran's butter rolls. But the outfit is apropos."

"Ah, then I imagine you'll have room later then. It takes

awhile to go through the archives."

"But the coffee will help me stave off sleep," Jack said. "I'm still adjusting."

"Consider it done."

After crossing a courtyard, Brennan led them into the hall. *Great Robin Hood*, Jack mused, taking in the long room with high ceilings. It was perfect for grand parties or receptions. Beyond the two rows of columns supporting the vaulted ceiling was space aplenty for tables.

"My wife and I thought you'd like to do your research like a king on the dais." Brennan pointed to a floor lamp that looked out of place on the raised section at the head of the hall. "Although we made for some modern allowances, lest you find yourself blinded by the chandelier light."

Actually there was plenty of light inside the hall, something that surprised Jack. Long, narrow windows on either side of the room allowed shafts of it into the room, despite the overcast sky outdoors. Again, he was struck that an island with a reputation for its mists was so bright and colorful.

Padrac glanced at his watch. "What say we shoot the pictures you want first, so I can be off? John wants me to head north to get a shot of the beached whale carcass."

Jack snickered. "Big news, eh?"

"Least for the whale," Padrac quipped.

"Then I'll start the tour," Brennan offered. "Will you be coming along Moyra, or would you rather chat with Mary?"

Jack watched Moyra weigh the decision, not daring to linger on her gaze too long for fear of getting lost there. What was it about this town and its people that made him *want* to be Irish?

Moyra shook her head. "No, I'd like the grand tour. I'm new at this," she reminded them. "Perhaps Mary might join us, if she can. It's always good to get the woman's insight as well. And if she's in costume, she'd be a lovely addition to Padrac's photos."

Padrac shot a full roll and a half by the time the tour was over. Jack would have to decide which ones to use for the article, but it was the story behind the castle that intrigued him. It was primarily written as seen through the eyes of the fourteenth-century Anglo-Norman Lady Breanda of Ballymara, whom Mary Brennan played on the tour to her husband's Ardghal of the O'Cullen clan.

"I hope you don't mind Pierce and me using you as guinea pigs for our tour idea," she said to Jack. "Especially you. Since this is your specialty, I'd hoped you might let us know if it's too off the wall or not."

"No, it's very interesting," Jack answered. And he was definitely using the picture of the replica amulet that belonged to Ardghal, displayed in the museum off the hall. The real amulet, exquisitely crafted of silver with a ruby center, was in a Dublin museum.

"I had no idea that the O'Cullens were associated with the castle," Moyra marveled. "I mean, it was Anglo-Norman construction and the round tower had been built during the Viking era by priests."

"When we researched the castle in Dublin, we found more history from that period than any other," Pierce Brennan explained. "You know O'Cullen is a modernization of *O'Cuilinn*. . . from *cuileann*, which means holly tree."

"Heard that. . .but it fits," Jack said, drawing Moyra's attention. "Pretty and prickly."

"Ah, go away," she said, waving her hand in dismissal.

But the berry blush that tinged Moyra's cheeks caused Jack

to dig into the soles of his shoes with his toes.

"Lady Breanda was a letter writer and keeper," Mary Brennan went on, "so we know more of her story. She and Ardghal were orphaned by the plague and taken in by his predecessor, Lord Garland. So grateful were the two that they built an orphanage."

"So it was probably destroyed?" Moyra asked.

Mary shook her head. "No, it's the old almshouse by the church."

"The Sunday school building?" Surprise claimed Moyra's face. "We had refreshments there after church," she told Jack.

"The very one."

"Hey, that'd make a good local interest column," said Padrac, who'd been taking notes as fast and furious as Jack, now that the photos were taken.

"The beatitude over the door of the almshouse is *Blessed are the merciful: for they shall obtain mercy*. That's because both Breanda and Ardghal were plague orphans, lost without loved ones, and taken in with mercy. They wanted that legacy to go on," Mary told them.

"From an orphanage to an almshouse and now it still serves the church," Moyra wondered aloud. "God doesn't waste a stone."

"Or a heart," Mary put in.

"The scripture is in the church, too," Jack observed. "Think there's a connection?" A warmth rolled over him as he caught Moyra's taken-aback glance. Obviously, she now deemed him not quite as heathen as first thought. Fact was, he'd never been completely lost to his faith, just estranged, as he'd been with love.

Mary shrugged. "It could be. Maybe there's a story for each

of the four beatitudes used in the church. There's Conn's verse for bringing the light of Christ to the people, and Ardghal's beatitude for mercy. . . ."

"And Nick Dalton's peace beatitude," Moyra said. "He's the shepherd with the rope—a nineteenth-century cowboy who settled a dispute between the landowners and the tenants," she added at Mary's puzzled look.

Pierce laughed. "Now you've told me something that I didn't know. But we can tell our guests to be sure to look for the shepherd with the lariat at the chapel."

"If we get any guests," Mary lamented. Upon realizing what she'd said, she cast a hasty look at Jack that confirmed she'd read how he was out to debunk the legend of the pledging stone. "Not that I'm trying to change your mind, Mr. Andrews," she added hastily, "but for what it's worth, you'll read in the letters that Lady Breanda and Ardghal pledged their love at the stone as children and that, against the odds of treachery, not to mention a marriage law prohibiting Irish to marry Anglo, their love and faith were redeemed."

"Aye, sir," Pierce chimed in. "Do what you must do, but a favorable write-up can make or break Ballymara Castle. 'Tis our livelihood at stake."

"And mine," Moyra spoke up. "But let God be your guide."

Jack steeled himself against the tug at his heart. That's why discrediting the pledging stone was so important to him. It was his livelihood at stake, too. And with opposite goals, the chances of the stone working for Moyra and him were as good as a snowball surviving in the desert.

"My mind is still open," he assured them, slipping his arm around Moyra's trim waist. "We've another few days for something to happen."

"I'll fetch the rolls and coffee," Mary offered hastily as if grabbing at the chance to escape the cloud of tension that enveloped them.

"But with God all things are possible," Moyra said to no one in particular, although Jack felt the brightness she intoned was as much to convince herself as the others.

Meanwhile, Jack felt the utter cad. Unlike the castle's Lord Garland or Ardghal and Breanda, he couldn't afford mercy.

A Legend of Mercy

by Pamela Griffin

Dedication

Special thanks to my critique partners in this project, especially to those grand lasses who share the collection with me. Linda, your help was above and beyond, your patience as pure as gold, your friendship highly treasured. Ditto, Tamela and Vickie—I couldn't have done it without either of you. To my friend Robin Bush, a big thank-you for fulfilling my dream of going to Scarborough Faire and discovering the medieval world. And to my sons, Brandon and Joshua, whose enthusiasm to hear Ardghal's story spurred me on—I cherish you, two of my most encouraging and loving supporters.

Dedicated to my Lord and Savior, whose mercy is as far-reaching as the widest rainbow, as refreshing as the mist that waters the land, as timeless as the green hills of Erin. To You, my Lord, I give my all.

Blessed are the merciful: for they shall obtain mercy.
MATTHEW 5:7

Prologue

Ballymara, Ireland, 1359

A cold shiver of air whispered down from the distant Wicklow Mountains. It stirred the treetops as though to tell of ancient secrets and chilled the three who trekked near the forest edging the castle on the highest hill. Eight-year-old Breanda grew even colder when she caught sight of a boy lying on the snow-covered ground.

"Is he alive, m'lord?" she asked in shock.

Before the earl could answer, Breanda slipped her hand out of his soft one and ran toward the boy, who lay huddled against a huge rock.

"Breanda—wait, lass!" Lord Garland called. "He could be dangerous."

More troubled about the boy's health than with obedience at the moment, she dropped to her knees beside him to see his face better. He appeared not to be breathing. Fearful, she brushed a damp chunk of his black hair away. He was so pale. No pink colored his cheeks, and his lips were blue. She frowned. She had seen that look before on the face of a poor tenant who'd caught his death from winter's cold.

All at once, the lad grasped her wrist hard, and his eyes shot open. Breanda drew back in surprise. His eyes shone a deep, dark blue and held an uncertain look that captured her young heart.

"Wh–who are you?" His voice shook. "What d' ye want?"

"I'm Breanda. Be ye ill?" Strangely, she was not afraid that he held her captive, though his skin felt like ice. The coarse fur wrap he wore made it clear that he must be one of Ballymara's tenants. She'd thought him younger, huddled up as he was, but when he released his hold and awkwardly tried to stand upon Lord Garland's approach, she saw that his limbs were longer than hers and he must be older.

The boy fell back against the rock. "C-cold," he whispered, his voice hoarse. "I no longer f-feel me legs."

"Who are you?" The earl moved closer. "Why have you come to the castle grounds?"

"I–I am Ardghal. I seek Lord Garland."

The earl's bushy brows lifted higher. "I am he."

Ardghal sighed in relief. He reached inside his tunic and pulled out a silver amulet hanging from a thick chain around his neck. A red stone glimmered from its center as if lit with a hidden flame. "I was told to give ye this."

At sight of the medallion, the earl's ruddy skin lost color above his pointed brown beard. He crouched low to study what the boy held. "Who gave this to you? Speak, child."

"Me *máthair*." Tears glistened in Ardghal's eyes, but he brushed them away with a grimy fist. "Afore she died this week past, she told me to c–come here. I journeyed two days from the mountains."

"In the cold?" Breanda thought of the wind and rare snow that had chilled the area.

"Aye."

"Have you no father?" Lord Garland's voice was quiet.

"Me *athair* died of the Black Death. Years ago."

"There is no one else?"

The boy studied the earth below him. "No one, m'lord."

The strange bond that Breanda felt ever since Ardghal opened his eyes and looked at her strengthened. She, too, had lost her parents to sickness. Not four moons after she'd come to live with Lord and Lady Garland as their ward, when she was seven, her own mother and father died. She looked toward her guardian. "May we take him to the castle?"

Lord Garland peered closely at Ardghal. "What is your age, lad?"

"I've lived on the earth one and ten winters, m'lord."

The earl shut his eyes.

"Father?"

Both Breanda and Lord Garland turned to look at ten-year-old Cormac. Upon spotting Ardghal, Breanda had forgotten all about Lord Garland's only son, who often straggled behind like a shadow. From his place on the path where they'd been walking, the skinny boy with flaxen hair curiously stared at Ardghal, Breanda, and Lord Garland in turn. "Should we not return to the castle? The light wanes, and Mother will wonder what keeps us."

"Aye." With a determined look, Lord Garland lifted the shivering Ardghal into his arms. "We shall see you fed and warm, lad. You shall have a home at my castle."

Ardghal's expression filled with relief. "The amulet, m'lord," he reminded, offering it to him.

Lord Garland gave the silver disk a fleeting glance. "Keep it. Perhaps one day it will bring you good fortune."

Breanda fell into step beside Lord Garland, every so often

casting a shy glance at Ardghal, who watched her. It pleased her when he returned her smile with a faint one of his own. Quickly, they made their way up the snow-crusted hill toward the stone castle, which now shone ghostlike against a darkening sky.

Chapter 1

eight years later

Ardghal stood on a grassy knoll, his unbound hair whipping about his face. He watched the beautiful maiden in the churchyard below him. Unaware of his presence and with no one else in sight, she continued her graceful dance beside the narrow round tower. With eyes closed, she lifted the skirts of her blue cotehardie and twirled about the area. Even from this distance, he could see her smile. Brown silken locks flowed past her hips, unencumbered by braids or coils. A flower garland adorned her hair, which captured the sun's fire, dazzling the curly strands into ruby and dark gold brilliance.

Ardghal smiled and stooped to pluck a shamrock from the ground. Descending the hill, he had almost come upon her, when she opened her lovely green eyes.

"Oh!" Her face was flushed from her exertions. "Ardghal. I did not expect to see you this morn. I supposed that you would lie in repose before the tournament."

"Disappointed?" He raised his brow, his smile never faltering.

"Nay, merely startled. I came to speak with Father Stephen."

"And is this what has you so joyful, my lady?"

Breanda bridged the short distance between them. " 'Tis much more. After what was said between us last night, I thought you would know—" Sudden shyness cloaked her, and she glanced away, though they'd been friends for years and shared many secrets.

"Aye." He lifted her chin with a curled finger. "And I meant every word."

Since they were children, Ardghal had loved Breanda, but only last night had he dared act upon that knowledge and told her so. Today was the sixteenth anniversary of her birth, and he fully intended to query Lord Garland on a most important matter.

"Fair Breanda," he murmured, "how long have I loved you? Forever, perhaps?"

Her luminous eyes answered in kind as she lifted her smooth palm to his cheek. He grasped her wrist and kissed the palm, his heart aching with the love he felt for her. "Come," he said, relaxing his hold and slipping his fingers through hers. "I've something of import to say, and only one place is worthy enough in which to speak it."

He led her to the stone arch fronting the church. Generations ago, 'twas said that his ancestor Conn, the holy man who brought Christianity to Ballymara, and his wife, Sorcha, first pledged their love at that same stone, now part of the entryway. Damaged during battle years ago, one of five stained-glass windows depicting shepherds had been replaced by Lord Garland and dedicated to Conn.

Once beneath the arch, Ardghal lifted her hand. With care he wrapped the shamrock he'd earlier plucked from the hillside around her finger. The stem was too short to tie, so he held it in place, looking beyond the splendor of her eyes to the sweetness of her soul.

"Breanda. . .As sure as the shamrock is green, as sure as Three are in One, our love shall be redeemed by the Father, Spirit, and Son."

His voice was soft, yet fierce with sincerity. Once, when they were very young, he'd recited those same words to her, though neither of them understood the full significance at the time. Now he spoke the words with all his heart. The ancient pledge etched beneath Conn's window was sacred, not one to be given in haste, and a vow a man would only give to the woman with whom he wished to share his life.

Breanda's eyes widened. "You. . .I. . ." She shook her head, dazed. "You are certain?"

"Aye. With all that I am I wish to make you my wife."

Joy blossomed upon her face, rivaling the beauty of any flower. "You'll ask Lord Garland? Today?"

"After the tournament ends, two days hence, I shall speak with him. I only hope he considers the match between us a worthy one."

"He will agree, Ardghal; he must. He holds you in high regard. You're one of his most trustworthy knights." A faint crease marred her smooth brow.

"Something ails you?" His hand tightened around hers.

" 'Tis nothing." She gave a slight shake of her head as if to dislodge a thought. "A foolish premonition clouded my joy for a moment, but it will soon pass."

"An omen?"

"Ardghal, I'm not one to put my faith in such things. You know this. Perchance, I simply cannot trust this abundance of joy that is now mine, a joy I've so long coveted. I fear 'tis only a dream, and when I awaken, it shall all be stolen from me."

He smiled wide in an effort to recapture her happiness.

"Ah, Breanda. What can steal such joy away? Nothing on the earth, if you will it, nor in the heavens above. 'Tis yours to keep, and I'll wield my sword against any fiend who dares attempt t' take it from you."

Twirling the shamrock near her lips, she giggled as he waved an imaginary sword. Then, swinging her up into his arms as if to rescue her from a foe, much in the manner in which they'd played as children, he dashed with her toward the trees and the glimpse of the river beyond. Yet children they were no longer. And Ardghal again became conscious of the manifest difference between present and past, her soft, womanly form no longer the girl's he remembered. The lighthearted mood drifted beyond him as surely as dew fades from the grass.

Gently he set her upon her feet. "Forgive me. I should not have—"

"Ardghal." She laid her palm against his linen surcoat where his heart now fiercely pounded. "We've no need for such words between us. I've always loved you; I always shall."

Their eyes met. . .and held. Like a prisoner long denied refreshment, he drank in the nectar of her words.

"Wilt thou favor me with a kiss, my lady fair?" His own words were husky as he gave voice to the question never before asked in all their childhood play.

"Aye," she whispered, lashes fluttering downward as she slowly lifted her face to his.

His lips were but a breath from hers when a thick shadow blanketed them. At the sudden absence of light and a shrill horse's whinny, Ardghal turned to look skyward. An ominous cloud had swallowed up the sun, casting the countryside in darkness.

" 'Tis Cormac," Breanda murmured.

Indeed, Lord Garland's son sat on his mount atop the hill, watching them—always lurking in the background like some oppressive phantom. He remained that way awhile longer, motionless, then pulled his steed's head around and disappeared from sight.

Breanda stiffened beside Ardghal. The shamrock flew from her fingers, swept away by a sudden strong gust of wind. If he didn't know better, Ardghal would believe Cormac to be a sorcerer, such dread came over his beloved's face.

"Breanda?"

"You must ask Lord Garland with all haste. Do not delay. Promise me."

Her urgency infected him. "As soon as the opportunity presents itself, I will."

She looked at him a moment longer before delivering a fleeting kiss to his jaw. Then, as swift as the wind that tore through the trees, she picked up her skirts and ran up the hillock to the milk-white mare tied beside his black stallion. Mounting her horse with the aid of a rock for a stepping stone, she turned the mare toward the path edging the forest and galloped toward the castle on the highest hill.

Ardghal watched her retreat. Was he unwise to elevate her hopes in view of the prince's recent edict? Yet most assuredly he could sway the earl to resist the intolerant decree. Both in battle and in peace, Ardghal had proven his merit, also demonstrating good stewardship. All of Ballymara respected him. Surely the earl would deem him capable of managing the land left to Breanda by her father; or he might instead issue him a small tract of land for his services, on which to live with a wife and raise a family. 'Twas the earl, himself, who'd knighted Ardghal, once he served his apprenticeship as a squire to Sir Rolf. The earl had even gifted him with plate armor and a fine warhorse.

This time, too, Ardghal was sure to win his favor.

Within the large stretch of land known as the Pale, the sole part of Ireland under English rule, and at a meeting point between the two noblemen's castles, Lord Garland's knights battled against the knights of Lord Roscoe. The reason for the tournament was twofold: to celebrate Breanda's birthday and to entertain an emissary of Prince Lionel, Earl of Ulster, whom King Edward III appointed as viceroy years ago.

Breanda fanned herself with her stiff imported silk and looked toward the tromped field of grass. At a distance, two knights on powerful steeds faced each other within the list, the low fenced area used for the joust. In their coats of armor, glinting silver in the hazy afternoon light, the knights were barely distinguishable from one another. Only by their coat of arms on their shields and surcoats and by the colorful cloth trappers their horses wore could Breanda tell which contender was Ardghal. That, and by her blue veil with which she'd favored him before the heralds had lauded their knights and the trumpets' blasts had announced the start of the joust. Ardghal wore her veil fastened around his arm.

Heart brimming with love, she studied her valiant champion. He had bested each of Lord Roscoe's knights who earlier competed with him in the events of wrestling, axe throwing, and sword fighting. Accomplished at the joust, he would likely prove himself in the next competition as well.

Breanda thought back to this morning. She had been disappointed when the fulfillment of their first kiss was waylaid. Often of late, she wondered how it might feel to have

Ardghal's lips touch hers and hoped the chance would soon revisit itself. Her face warmed at the prospect, and she fanned it more violently, bringing the fan closer and accidentally striking her nose. She sneezed.

"Have ye caught a chill, m'lady?" her lady's maid, Elaine, asked.

"Nay, I am well."

Rubbing the bridge of her stinging nose, Breanda determined to rein in her thoughts before she did herself true bodily harm. Along with other onlookers seated on the elevated stand built for ladies and important guests, she watched from beneath a fluttering crimson canopy that made a *thwupping* noise as the wind tried to tear it from its stakes. A flag bearer stood to one side of the list. He lifted a flag high then let it down with a mighty sweep.

Both horses charged toward one another as the knights held their lances ready. More than the length of a man, the narrow weapons were fashioned of hollow wood and blunt steel at one end; still, Breanda knew they could inflict damage. Pressing her hand to her bodice, she held her breath as the knights came abreast of one another. A dull *clang* of metal on armor made Breanda gasp then exhale in relief when she saw Ardghal was unharmed. His contender remained seated on his horse but was unsteady. The knights turned about to face off for a second charge.

Out of the corner of her eye, Breanda glimpsed Cormac riding toward her. He stopped near where she sat with her lady's maid on the third row. Seated on his horse as he was, they were almost eye-to-eye. He leaned over his mare's neck, closer to her.

"Breanda, have I told you how lovely you look?" His words

were low, meant for her ears alone. "Your face shines as brightly as the noonday sun."

Thinking the flattery odd, since a thick cloud had recently swallowed that great orb of light, which rarely made its presence known anyway, Breanda kept her focus on Ardghal. She paid little heed to Cormac but perceived his continued stare. Of late, his attentions toward her had been a source of discomfort, and she was still angry with him about his conduct this morning.

On the tourney field, Ardghal and his opponent again raced toward one another. This time Ardghal's lance knocked the other knight off his horse. From the stand above, Lord Garland cheered, loudly proclaiming Ardghal's prowess to Lord Lumpston, the viceroy's visiting emissary.

"He makes a fine warrior," Breanda murmured to Elaine. "Does he not?"

"Indeed he does, m'lady."

"I know what you must be thinking," Cormac said testily, his voice low. "But you realize a union between the two of you will not be permitted?"

Breanda's focus snapped his way. He had removed his helmet, and his tawny locks blew over his armor. Ruddiness washed his cheeks, a sure sign of his anger.

"If you'll excuse me, m'lord," she said, not really caring if he excused her or not. "Come, Elaine."

'Twas best that she seek temporary respite in the thicket, so as not to shame her guardian by a display of temper toward Cormac. With her tongue seized between her teeth lest it yield to temptation, Breanda drew her cloak about her and left the stands. As she moved toward the privacy of a copse of trees, she lifted her eyes to the rounded, smooth peaks of the distant mountains, praying for calm.

Cormac's gray steed cut her off before she could reach her destination.

"You cannot escape the truth, Breanda. Since the Statutes of Kilkenny have been enacted, we're forbidden to continue with Gaelic customs, dress or otherwise, as well you know. Why suppose you that the tourney today is focused on the matches exercised in England? To appease the emissary, who's been sent as a spy to see that all the king's subjects uphold the new law, of course."

She blew out a short breath. "Your reasoning?"

" 'Tis simple. Your father was a baron and a subject of the king, as is my father. You and I both possess Anglo blood, while Ardghal's blood runs as Gaelic as the Wicklow Mountains, with nary a drop of Anglo to it."

Ire rising, Breanda addressed Elaine. "Leave us. I will return anon."

Once her lady's maid retraced her steps, Breanda turned on Cormac. "I have yet to understand why you deem yourself an authority to interfere in my affairs. Aye, we've shared friendship these past years, Cormac. But that does not give you license to tell me what I may or may not do, or with whom I may do it. Your father is my guardian, and to him only will I answer. Ardghal may have been born to clan members, but Lord Garland reared him. He looks upon him with favor, as well you know. In truth, Ardghal may possess the wild Gaelic in his veins, but he's become one of us."

" 'Tis of little matter." Cormac's thick brows beetled together. "First and foremost, my father is a subject of the king. He'll not risk being demoted and having his lands stripped away—all to appease the whims of a foolish young lass who acts with her heart and not her head. The statute decrees that any alliance with the Gaelic-Irish by marriage shall be punishable as high treason."

She was aware a statute had recently been decreed, though she knew little about it. She'd only been instructed by the earl to dispense with any Gaelic form of dress or music. Nor was she to speak the language.

The uncertainty Breanda experienced at the church revisited her, but she tried to mask it. "Why do you speak thus, Cormac? Why do you seek to wound me with your words?"

His blue green eyes gentled a fraction, and he dismounted to stand before her. "From the day you came to the castle, Breanda, when you were but seven, it has been understood that you and I would wed once you came of age."

"I knew of no such arrangement."

"Nevertheless, 'twas understood."

She studied his face. He was a handsome man, and once she considered him a friend and as close as a brother. But the lust for power had changed him, and sometimes his brash actions caused her to regard him as a stranger. His cruelty toward the serving wench at table this morning when she spilled his wine and the heated altercation Breanda and Cormac shared afterward were two reasons she had avoided him all day.

"You speak in truth when you say I act with my heart," she admitted quietly. "I've loved Ardghal for many years. And if what you say is true and I cannot have him for my husband, then I should prefer to remain cloistered the rest of my days."

"He's not worthy of your undying affections, Breanda," Cormac growled, taking a step closer until little space separated them. "I'm as great a warrior as he! What traits does he possess that I lack? Why have you always favored him over me? Indeed, I can give you so much more—anything you desire— since all that my father has will one day be mine." He grabbed hold of her hand and kissed it.

His emphatic declaration reminded her of something he might have said in their youth; indeed, he was acting childish. Did he think her so shallow that the promise of greater wealth or lands would sway her to accept his offer? Did he suppose it was merely Ardghal's strength and courage in battle that drew her to him?

"It grieves me to learn that you think so little of me, Cormac." She pulled her hand free of his tight grasp. "I seek no excess of earthly riches, and I cannot marry you. Indeed, a similar vow I've already given. This morning, I pledged myself to Ardghal." Too late, she realized she should not have uttered the last until Ardghal had spoken with Lord Garland.

"He's taken you from me!"

"Cormac, no. What nonsense do you speak? I was never yours for the taking." She gentled her demeanor, knowing she'd unintentionally hurt him. "I hold affection for you in my heart as I would toward my brother if he were alive. To be sure, you and Lord Garland are all the family I have left aside from a distant cousin."

"I want you for my wife, not my sister, Breanda."

"In good faith, Cormac, I cannot give you what you ask."

A nerve pulsed near his jaw. His eyes glinted with danger- ous fire. "We shall see—as we shall see who is the better man."

"What do you mean?"

He stormed away from her and mounted his horse.

"Cormac!"

He wrenched his horse's head in the direction of the joust

and galloped toward the others.

Fear clutching her heart, Breanda lifted the skirts of her cotehardie and ran after him. Breathless upon reaching the stands, she saw an intermission was underway. Across the field, Cormac rode to where Ardghal had dismounted. Ardghal's helmet was absent, his raven black curls glistening with sweat from his recent victory.

"Ardghal!" Cormac shouted, his hand going to the hilt of his sword. "Before all gathered here today, I challenge you. Let us see if the hand of a cur can successfully wield his blade against mine."

Dear Father in heaven, no! Breanda's blood froze in her veins. The crowd of onlookers quieted then began to murmur. A challenge issued in such a manner meant one thing.

The fight would be to the death.

Chapter 2

Ardghal peered into eyes filled with hate. His friendship with Cormac had disintegrated since they'd grown into men. Glancing toward Lord Garland, he caught sight of Breanda beside the stands. Her face was tense, white. She clutched the scaffold as if it were her only support. Any simpkin could see that Cormac now knew they had pledged their troth. And Ardghal was no fool. Still, he sensed the challenge was over more than Breanda, though jealousy must have spurred it. Ardghal had discerned the younger man's affection for their lady friend, though he doubted it could compare with the love he himself felt for her.

"Cormac, my son." The earl stood and pressed his fingertips together near his waist then spread his hands wide in a gesture solely his. Ardghal had seen him use it often when addressing a difficult issue brought before him by his tenants. "Today is a day for merriment, not for blood to be spilt. Whatever slight you deem Ardghal has inflicted, whatever ill will has sprung between you, let the matter be settled in a match—a joust—but let it be *à la plaisance*."

À la plaisance. Of peace.

Cormac's stare hurled daggers through Ardghal. Tense

seconds elapsed, but he finally called out, "Yea, Father. It shall be as you will it. But let the victor claim the prize of the loser's battle horse."

"So let it be done," the earl approved.

Relieved that he would not be forced into a situation that could result in his taking the life of his benefactor's son, Ardghal inclined his head toward Cormac. "I accept your challenge, my lord."

Cormac opened his mouth to respond then shut it and jabbed his heels into his destrier's sides. Ardghal turned to the young squire who helped him suit up.

"Padrac, my armor."

"Aye, Sir Ardghal."

Within a short time, Padrac again laced the protective armor of greaves to Ardghal's legs, placed the gauntlets to his hands, and outfitted him with the coat of plates for his torso. Ardghal pulled on his helmet, impairing his vision to what could be seen through the two slits. He swung atop his battle horse, its head and chest also protected with armor, and resumed his position at one end of the list. Padrac handed his shield and lance up to him. With his steel glove, Ardghal held the weapon horizontally under one arm.

His armor of chain mail and steel plate were the weight of a robust lad. Moreover, after contending in three matches and taking a hard blow during the last, Ardghal was weary. Nonetheless, Cormac was not as adept at the joust as he was at swordplay; a fact Ardghal ascribed to his own favor.

Ash-dark clouds rolled across the gray firmament. Rainfall would impair his vision all the more, but there was little to be done if it did rain. Sitting tall in his high-backed saddle, he impatiently waited for the flag to drop. To be done with this match was his sole desire.

At the signal, he urged his destrier to charge. Horse hooves pounded, jarred him, as Ardghal worked to keep his lance steady, aiming for Cormac's breastplate. As they drew alongside each other, their lances made contact. The agonizing force of a blow to his chest knocked the breath from Ardghal, and he barely kept his seat. 'Twas the second time today he'd been hit in that spot. While the crowd cheered, he and Cormac turned their horses about for a second charge. This time, only Ardghal's lance made contact, the wood shattering upon impact. Cormac almost fell from the blow.

Padrac handed up a fresh lance to Ardghal just as the clouds opened and drops blew at a vicious slant toward him. He grimaced. A third charge was made, and he struggled to see past the blur of rain. Cormac's lance struck his helmet. Lights flashed inside Ardghal's head. Thrust backward from the blow, he lost his grip on the reins, crashing to the earth.

The next thing Ardghal became aware of was the roar of the crowd in his ears and Padrac kneeling beside him. "Are ye injured, sir?" the boy asked as he helped to pull off Ardghal's helmet.

Pain mixed with heaviness made it difficult to move. Trying to rid himself of the wooziness, Ardghal shook his head. "No blood is apparent. I'm able to bend my limbs." He sat up stiffly. With the way his right shoulder throbbed, he must have landed on it first.

Suddenly Breanda knelt in the mud beside him, her cloak's hood fallen back from her hair. Her face was flushed, wet from the rain. Her eyes shimmered with anxiety. "Are you hurt?"

"Nay. Merely winded." Unease filtered through him that she should see him in a weakened position, one he rarely suffered.

"You should not be here. You'll ruin your new gown."

"I care not for the gown. I care only for you." She looked at Padrac. "Is he hurt?" she asked, as though not believing Ardghal's assurances.

With the aid of the boy, Ardghal stood to his feet, keeping his gauntlet on Padrac's shoulder until the dizziness abated. Breanda stood as he did.

"Behold." Ardghal kept his voice light. "I am unscathed, my lady. You must return to the stands. We will talk later, at the banquet."

"Aye." Her eyes told him what her lips couldn't say since they shared the company of others. Indeed, he felt her love so strongly it was difficult to refrain from taking her in his arms.

As he watched her hurried retreat, Ardghal reveled in the knowledge that he possessed the love of a virtuous woman, the favor of the earl, and a promising future. To be sure, the man he once considered a friend seemed bent on making life wretched.

However, Cormac had just bested him and won Ardghal's powerful destrier. At least Ardghal owned another, swifter horse, one he used outside battle and had gained during a prior tournament with a contending knight. He harbored little doubt he would win additional horses in future tourneys. Yet for the present, let Cormac reign as conqueror. Perhaps he would be satisfied with his small triumph, and this would be the end of the discord between them.

From beneath the hood of her velvet cloak, Breanda stared at the mist that fell from a twilight sky. 'Twas fine weather for ducks, but little else. Thrice, this day, the dismal clouds had wept over Erin's sod. Earlier, Breanda had escaped the gala at the castle, secretly hoping Ardghal would seek her out and they could talk, but now she retraced her solitary steps.

To her left, the narrow river wound like a silver veil billowing in a gentle breeze. Beyond Ballymara Castle, the timeworn Wicklow Mountains sloped toward the heavens as if presiding over the area, ancient lords to the grounds beneath them. Thin bands of receding sunlight escaped their imprisoning gray clouds and caught myriad droplets that misted the air, transforming them into iridescent jewels that bedazzled the eye.

Breanda stared at the many-colored rainbow shimmering a stone's throw away. She thought of the first rainbow, given along with the Almighty God's promise that He would not flood the earth again to destroy it.

Lord, wilt Thou allow my heart to be flooded with this pain it now carries? For surely it shall be Thy servant's destruction. Wilt Thou guide me and reveal to me a fitting solution? Is there one?

Again, Cormac's bitter words resounded in her mind, and she cast her gaze upon the path before her feet. To him she'd shown a measure of bravado, implying she would prevail. To herself, she knew she could not act in a manner that would reflect badly upon Lord Garland. As was often the case with noblemen's children, she'd been sent to live with a family of higher nobility when she was very young. During her past nine years at Ballymara Castle, she'd developed affection for the earl. She would do whatever he asked. She would make her requests known to him, yea, and if he refused her, she would appeal to be sent to a nunnery.

"Why do you tread the grounds and with such downcast countenance? Surely this is a day for rejoicing?"

Startled, Breanda looked up into the dear craggy face of

her guardian. Since his wife had died two years past, a stoop had claimed his broad shoulders, and he exhibited greater tolerance toward her than when she was a child. Though he'd always been kind.

"My lord." She sought for appropriate words. "Might I speak with you about a matter that concerns me?"

"Let us converse as we return to the castle." He held out his hand. "The mist falls more heavily, and I would not wish you to catch a chill."

Breanda left the path she had traversed along the river's edge and looped her fingers around his. Glistening blades of lush grass swept against the hem of her cloak and dampened her thick hose. Thorny shrubs of yellow-flowered gorse grew in abandon over the emerald green hills that were speckled with all manner of wildflowers.

"Do you recall when we walked in such a manner when you were but a child?" Lord Garland's fond words stirred Breanda's memory. "You with your little hand in mine?"

"Aye. And 'twas during such a walk that we found Ardghal."

"Ah, yes. Ardghal." He chuckled. "You were his champion, rushing to his side even then—much as you did today, when he was knocked from his horse. The speed with which you reached him amazed even Lord Lumpston. I've never seen a lady leap over a fence so gracefully, and in full skirts as well."

Heat singed her face; the cooling mist did little to help. She slipped her hand from his. "My lord, if I displeased you with my behavior, I ask pardon. Verily, I gave little thought to what I was doing—"

He raised his ringed hand to stop her apology. "Breanda, I'm not angered. You've had lads as companions and no mother or other woman to instruct you in a lady's ways when

170

you came of the age to be taught. Any fault is mine, not yours, to bear. I should have looked to your future after my wife died and found you a suitable mentor. Perhaps I should have sent you to your cousin's for a season. But alas, those things that should have been cannot be recaptured."

She could not bear to look at him. "Then I *have* displeased you."

"Nay. I admire your spirit and strength. Those twin traits will serve you well in the future. However, a word of counsel. You've come of the age to marry, but you must curb your willfulness, at least before the wedding takes place. A man likes to think he'll receive a wife who's submissive and meek, not one who'll clash with him at every turn."

At his light words, a second wave of heat rushed over her face. Had he seen her confrontation with Cormac during the joust or heard their heated words that morning? Was he referring to his son when he spoke thus?

"As to the matter of marriage, it is on this subject I wish to speak," she said quickly before she lost all nerve. "I've chosen the man I wish for my husband."

"Indeed? *You* have chosen?"

"Aye." She swallowed over a dry throat. "It is Ardghal."

"And why does such a revelation not surprise me?"

She twisted her head his way, gratified to see him smiling.

"Even before this, had I not seen the brightness in your eyes when he walks into a room, your behavior at the tournament made it clear, and not only to me."

She looked away toward the square castle of pale stone with its crenellated curtain wall and round towers abutting it. "Cormac."

"Aye, Cormac. And every other guest in attendance today."

She closed her eyes in a brief moment of contrition.

"Be not dismayed, child. I'll admit, when you first came to Ballymara I had thought that when you reached the age to marry, Cormac would make a fitting choice. Yet I deem Ardghal just as worthy."

"Truly? But Cormac said—" She cut off her flow of words. She could not betray her friend to his father by revealing those things he spoke in what she assumed to be confidence. True, he had angered her, but she was loath to slight Cormac by revealing to another his profession of feelings toward her. Feelings of which his father must be unaware, contrary to what Cormac had implied, since her guardian had just stated that he approved of a match between her and Ardghal.

Lord Garland's brows almost met. "What exactly did Cormac say?"

Breanda nipped in her bottom lip, thinking of what to disclose. "He told me that, because of the prince's new statute, a match between Ardghal and me would not be permitted since he is Gaelic and I am Anglo. He said that for me to wed Ardghal would cause you to lose favor with the king. That it would be considered high treason."

The earl ceased walking though they'd reached the barbican. Two guards stood at attention on each side of the keep's entrance. Lord Garland grew silent, his focus going beyond them and to the inner courtyard, where Breanda could see people milling about. Most were servants tending to their duties. Others were guests and visiting knights, the ribald actions of the latter displaying their continued merriment.

Breanda returned her gaze to the earl. His face was ashen.

"My lord?" Concerned, she gripped his arm to support him. "Are you ill?"

'Twas a moment before he spoke. "Tonight, after the banquet, I wish to speak with you and Ardghal privately. I fear the time has at last come upon me. . . ." His final words trailed away, as elusive as the mist. He speared her with a sober gaze. "You will tell Ardghal? I must see to Lord Lumpston before he takes offense."

"I will tell him." Breanda's anxious thoughts took free rein as she trod quietly beside him and into the castle yard.

Chapter 3

After the feasting ended and many had slipped away to bed for the night, Ardghal proceeded to the earl's private chamber in the solar. Earlier, Breanda had whispered that Lord Garland wished to speak to both of them after the banquet. Before Ardghal could inquire further, a lady guest requested Breanda's audience, and Ardghal's curiosity as to the reason for the meeting went unquenched.

Nearing the entrance, he glimpsed Breanda standing in the light of several candles that lit the wide corridor. The muted glow from the thick beeswax pillars could not hide the apprehension on her face.

"Breanda?"

"Lord Garland ordered me to wait. He seemed upset."

As though he heard them, the earl cleared his throat from within the chamber whose door stood ajar. "Breanda, Ardghal. Come."

They exchanged glances before Ardghal led the way inside. Lord Garland stood with his back toward them, staring out a glazed window that overlooked the river. Hands clasped behind him, his stance appeared resigned, his shoulders slumped.

" 'Twas there, near the forest, I met your mother," he said

as if to himself. He turned to Ardghal, his gaze solemn. "The time has come for you to know. . .I am your father."

Ardghal felt as if he'd been struck by another lance's blow. "My lord?"

"I met your mother while I was out riding. My father was then overlord, and a fine thing, too. I was young, imprudent, as yet unmarried." He shook his head in self-rebuke. "Your mother was gathering herbs when I crossed her path. She'd wandered far, and a storm was brewing. She accepted my offer of a ride home but would not give her name. Before we could reach her dwelling, she urged me to stop, dismounted, and ran from my sight. After that, I saw her thrice more before the fair, always alone, in the forest. She'd become a mystery to me, an intrigue. I was besotted."

He looked away, as if caught in the past. Ardghal could only wait for the earl's next words. His own voice seemed to have abandoned him.

"At the fair, my father at last persuaded the clan O'Cullen to sign a treaty of peace. For years, they had remained obstinate, refusing to serve as tenants though the king gave my father authority over them and the lands on which they lived. They agreed to wage no further war and to pay taxes in return for promises made by my father, and a pact was made. I knew little of this at the time. My sole desire was to indulge myself, and I did. Freely." He winced.

"I found her—your mother—and together we partook of the festivities. I learned her name—Maggie—but knew little else about her. Her mystique allured me, and I was enamored. The rich wine and music intoxicated me but no more than her beauty. I had to have her. She did not protest."

Ardghal focused on the waving treetops. He clenched his

jaw, tamping down fierce emotion.

"More than a moon elapsed before I encountered her again," the earl continued after a moment. "She seemed removed, anxious—though she'd set out to find me—and she told me she carried my child. I was stunned but assured her I would care for her and the babe in whatever way I could. My oath did little to appease her. She broke from my embrace and said I must never see her again if peace was to remain in Ballymara. 'Twas then she told me that she was a daughter of the O'Cullen chieftain. I made her vow that if ever she was in trouble to send me her amulet—the one you now wear—and I would come for her. With tears in her eyes, she kissed me one last time and fled into the forest. I desired to go after her, to pledge that we would find a way to be together. But we both knew that my father would never allow me, a nobleman, to wed a woman from a clan who'd been a thorn in his side for years. Nor would her father allow it."

The earl heaved a deep sigh. "Later, when I thought I might die from her absence, I attempted to seek her out. In the village, I learned that the clan had been torn asunder due to a disagreement. Half the tribe moved beyond the Pale into Wicklow Mountains. Your mother had married and left with them—but you are the child that resulted from our union. You are *my* son."

Ardghal managed a curt nod. His mother had borne only one babe. The man he'd thought was his father had hurled cross words at her, calling her cursed because she could only give him one son. Had he suspected Ardghal was not his son? Was that why he often exhibited violence toward them before the sickness took his life?

"I blame you not for despising me, Ardghal. When I made

peace with God, I realized the wages of my sin, my selfishness, and how it had wounded both your mother and me. But I never stopped loving her. And though I endeavored to show affection toward my wife, a piece of my heart always remained with my Maggie." The earl seemed to come to himself and shook his head. "But you have no need to hear all of what went on before. I took you into my castle so that I might atone for my grievous wrong. I've come to regard you as my firstborn, and I wish to give you all that is within my power to give."

He looked at Breanda. "I recognize that you have deep affection for my ward, who's become as a daughter to me. Due to the statute issued by the viceroy, Breanda feared a match between you would be considered unlawful. 'Tis for this reason I've chosen to divulge the truth. Your blood is as Anglo as mine, Ardghal. No opposition will come from those loyal to the crown. If you wish to wed Breanda, you have my blessing."

"Thank you, my lord." Ardghal could not look at him, could not give explanation for the sudden distance and anger he felt toward the man. "I do wish it."

"So let it be done. I shall announce your betrothal and post the bans once the emissary leaves and upon Breanda's return from visiting her cousin next week. I will host a feast then."

Ardghal watched as the earl embraced Breanda.

"Thank you, my lord." She pulled away, clasping his hands. "You've given me great joy."

Lord Garland approached. Casting his gaze to the floor, Ardghal still felt unable to meet his eyes. An uncomfortable silence ensued before the earl stepped back to the window.

"You may go."

As he turned, Ardghal glimpsed a shadow slip away from the flagstones near the chamber exit. He hastened to the area, but no one was in sight. Looking to where the corridor angled off in another direction, he strode that way. Did a spy lurk in their midst?

Breanda's light footsteps hurried up behind him. She put a hand to the sleeve of his tunic. "Ardghal, I see that you're troubled. Will you not talk to me?"

He turned and, sensing her distress, took a steadying breath. "In truth, I know not what to speak or think or feel. Once I can make sense of this matter, then I may seek your company." He touched his fingers to her silken cheek "You've always been an encouragement, Breanda. And I shall count myself blessed to have you for my wife." Feathering his fingers down to her jaw in caress, he dropped his hand away, preparing to go.

"Before you retire," she hastened to whisper, "I—I believe you owe me a kiss. Or perhaps 'tis I who owe you one?"

"A kiss?" He lifted his brow at her swift change of topic.

"Aye." She quietly cleared her throat. "Earlier, this morn, we. . .we were interrupted. I should like that kiss now, if you would be so inclined to give it. As a token of your affection."

Ardghal grinned, all former stiffness vanishing. "Indeed. I can think of nothing that would please me more."

He lifted his hands to cradle her blushing cheeks. In the candlelight, her eyes shone like jewels, and he gazed a moment longer into their jade green depths before lowering his mouth to hers. Brushing his lips lightly, slowly over hers, he thrilled in their softness, their sweetness. Her breath was fragrant and warm as it mingled with his. Her hands, so soft and gentle, touched his upper arms, then slid up to clasp his shoulders and move to his back, as she leaned into him and freely returned his affection. Her response ignited a blaze within, so fierce, he wanted nothing more than to crush her to him and deepen their kiss. Never stop kissing her, never stop holding her. . . .

Heart pounding so loudly he could hear it, Ardghal pulled back. Her eyes were luminous, marveling, questioning. He laid a forefinger against her lips when she opened her mouth to speak.

"There shall be opportunity for us to fully share our devotion, Breanda. Once we are wed." His words were husky. "Until that day, let us exercise caution. The hour is late. We should retire to our chambers."

Disappointment tinged her eyes, but she nodded. "You are wise, Ardghal. If you count yourself blessed to have my love, I count myself doubly blessed to have yours. May the Lord smile upon you and give you a sleep that is sweet," she added, as she'd said to him each night for eight years, since the evening he'd first come to the castle.

"And may it be returned to you a hundredfold, dear Breanda."

She offered a parting smile. He watched until she disappeared from sight.

A sudden scraping—what sounded like a shoe against flagstone—broke Ardghal from his tender thoughts, reminding him of his suspicion that he wasn't alone. He hastened in the direction of the sound. Yet when he reached the bend of the corridor and looked its length, again he saw no one there.

A sennight had passed since Lord Garland divulged the truth of Ardghal's parentage. In those seven days, Ardghal was distant, though he assured Breanda that he, too, was overjoyed that the earl gave his blessing. Why, in all these years, had she never guessed at the relationship between the men? Both possessed eyes of the same dark blue, and both carried themselves in a similar noble manner, though Ardghal's stance seemed prouder, stronger.

Breanda fidgeted against the bench of the closed, horse-drawn chariot that transported her to her cousin's and the wedding of her only relation to be held on the morrow. Yet again, she relived the kiss she and Ardghal had shared and felt the blush rise to her face. Never had she dreamt a kiss could be so tender, so poignant, so powerful. . . .

Faith, was she wicked to dwell on that kiss? With no one to ask, Breanda decided it best to steer her thoughts onto safer ground, befitting a maiden, and returned her attention to the landscape. Beyond the square window opening, forested hills in every hue of green occupied her sight. As the carriage jounced and rolled within the heather- and gorse-covered granite mountains around her, Breanda observed that fewer sheep dotted the grasses of the valley here than in Ballymara. On occasion, she spotted a Celtic high cross through lush foliage.

Another jolt shook her as the wheels rolled over an obstacle. Her body ached from the bruises she was certain she'd acquired due to the constant bouncing as they traveled over rough terrain. She missed the company of her lady's maid, who'd taken to her pallet with fever. A good thing she'd not had to endure this vexing ride, which lasted the greater part of the day.

Breanda didn't often venture from Ballymara and hoped she wouldn't appear plain to her elegant cousin. Taking inventory of her simple gown in deepest blue, she noticed dirt sullied its lap. Frowning, she brushed it away. The scoop-necked bodice hugged her to the waist, as all her cotehardies did, and ended in full skirts that hid her pointed-toe slippers. At least *they* were embroidered. No embellishment adorned the gown, but she did wear an ornamented girdle slung above her hips and, concealed within it, a small, jeweled dining dagger. Bandits were known to attack travelers, and though she had an escort of four worthy knights, Ardghal among them, she was grateful for the weapon which would serve a dual purpose, if need be.

In the distance, a round tower loomed near a thick copse of trees, snagging her attention. Ballymara's own belfry had been hit by lightning five years past, and the earl had used stones from its damaged side to build onto the village church. She preferred that church to the stuffy castle chapel, especially since the lovely and peaceful church site included the pledging stone arch. And near it the round tower. Such remains, once used as hideouts for priests during Viking raids centuries ago, were now used only for storage if they were used at all.

Father Stephen's tales of how priests would gather their gold and enter the tower from the outside high window—higher than the church itself—spawned hours of adventurous play for Breanda, Ardghal, and Cormac as children. Pretending they, too, were under attack from Vikings, they gathered stones as treasure to take with them while they ascended the rope ladder, afterward drawing up the ropes to protect their cache—until the day they were caught during one such escape. A wistful smile curled Breanda's lips at the memory of how Ardghal had championed her, taking the brunt of the blame. Nevertheless, Father Stephen had scolded them all soundly and sent them running home to Ballymara Castle.

The sudden clamor of approaching horses startled Breanda. Twisting toward the noise, she peered out the window. Eight mounted men galloped from the cover of trees.

Stunned, Breanda watched as one man aimed a crossbow behind the chariot. Its arrow whizzed past. A strangled cry came from one of the knights, followed by the sound of a body thudding to the earth.

Shouts rent the air. Ardghal sped into her line of vision on horseback, brandishing his sword as he charged toward the bandits. The alarming *clang* of steel striking steel rang within her ears. A second mounted knight appeared, his gleaming blade raised high as he targeted one of the fiends. Terrified, Breanda watched yet another bandit race up behind the knight, his weapon held ready for attack.

Save us, heavenly Father!

Everything was happening so quickly she could scarcely think. *Escape!* her mind screamed. But no—she'd been forewarned to stay inside the chariot in the event of danger.

The chariot's driver plummeted to the ground, a crossbow's arrow protruding from his back. A bandit jumped atop the chariot, causing it to shudder. Dropping her hand to her dagger hilt, Breanda threw open the door. Stay or flee—she would not be taken without a fight!

Before she could jump down, the horses pulling the chariot took off with a jolting start. She braced her hands to the sides where the door had been fastened. It swung wildly, banging against the outside of the hurtling chariot. Breanda nearly flew headlong into a massive tree. Struggling for balance, she dared to peer past the jamb and spied Ardghal fighting off a bandit. Another raced up behind him.

"Ardghal!" she yelled as loudly as she could in warning.

He turned, and in that instant, a bandit's sword plunged into him. He toppled from his horse.

"No!" Breanda screamed.

182

The wheel hit something hard. Legs buckling, she fell, striking her head on the bench. Darkness blotted out the sun as her world went black.

Chapter 4

Breanda awoke with a start. Her head throbbed. Carefully, she touched the back of it, discovering a lump. A canopy of dirty canvas stretched above her. Pushing herself up to sit, she noticed the sides of her world were round and similar in color. She lay in a tent on a sour-smelling bed of rushes.

Memory flooded her mind, increasing the pain.

Ardghal!

Quickly she rose. Dizziness swept over her, a merciless bird of prey. She grabbed the center stake that held the tent upright. Somehow, she must find him, tend his wound, do what she could to help. He *must* be alive.

Her vision clearing, she spotted the tent's opening. She felt for her dagger, surprised to find it. Her abductors must not have searched her. Grateful for that small miracle, she wrapped her fingers around the dagger hilt, unsheathing the weapon. Hiding it in her skirts, she moved toward the flap and pulled the canvas aside.

A bearded giant blocked her way. With a beefy hand thickly sprinkled in black hairs, he motioned her to return to her prison. Beyond him, men gathered around a fire in a clearing surrounded by a dense thicket. Her sentry roughly grabbed her arm when she did not budge.

"Unhand me, knave, or live to regret it." She raised the double-sided weapon chest high, pointing it toward him. The emeralds embedded in the silver hilt gleamed in the murky light, but no more so than the wicked point of her blade.

"Threaten me not, woman." His reply came in swift Gaelic. His eyes closed to slits, and his grip on her tightened.

She slashed the blade's point along his knuckles.

Yanking his hand from her arm, he cursed and wiped a thin line of blood onto his tunic against the red shield emblazoned there. 'Twas then that she noticed the O'Cullen crest. The guard took a menacing step closer. Again, she pointed the dagger toward him.

He ceased his advance and swore again. "Get back in there afore we both live to regret it."

"Who are you, and why have I been taken? What plans have you for me?"

" 'Tis not for me to say."

She tried once more. "Where are my escorts? What have you done with them?"

"All dead. Enough! Test not me patience."

Catching her unawares, he covered the scant distance and grabbed her wrist, wresting the dagger loose from her fingers. With a harsh thump of his massive palm against her shoulder, he forced her back into her prison. Her feet flew from under her, and she landed hard on the ground. He leered then wrenched the tent flap closed.

Alone again, Breanda pushed herself up on one elbow but could scarcely think. Dead? They were *dead*? Baldric. Gaston. Leonard. . .Ardghal. It could not be. It must not be. The ache of her bruised body paled in comparison with the anguish that ripped through her heart.

The dank smell of wet earth and the twittering of birds aroused his senses, and Ardghal opened his eyes. He lay stomach-down on the ground. Sharp pebbles dug into his cheek. When he forced himself to move, his left side burned as though impaled with a flaming torch. He clenched his teeth to keep from crying out. The pain brought with it the memory, and he examined the wound in his shoulder.

Fortunately the cut wasn't near his heart. The lesion had stopped bleeding but appeared deep. Apparently, the thick patch of black mud in which he'd fallen had acted as a poultice and quenched the blood's flow. His left arm useless, he relied on the aid of his right arm to help him stand.

The sight of his three friends and fellow soldiers lying in the grass, along with four lifeless bandits and the chariot driver, sickened him. But the absence of the chariot and horses had him falling to his knees. *Breanda...*

"Dear God, help me to find her."

Stunned to see the O'Cullen crest on the brigands' tunics, he tried to make sense of the matter. His mother's clan had attacked. Why? For what purpose would it serve to break a treaty of peace?

Ardghal's heart weighed heavy as he lumbered to each of Ballymara's knights in turn and found all of them dead. He paused a moment in prayerful silence over each man. Then, swiping at the moisture that rimmed his eyes, he collected his sword from the ground and blew out a shrill whistle that caused the birdcalls to fade then increase in intensity.

From a distance, the pounding of hooves struck the earth. Ardghal sheathed his blade and turned. A fine black steed burst through the trees, coming to a stop beside him. With a muffled snort in greeting, the animal tossed its raven black mane.

Ardghal reached up to stroke his stallion's glossy neck. "Faithful Destroyer. Always you are near when I have need of you." Using his one good arm, he mounted the powerful beast and took the reins, guiding his horse to the twin trails the chariot's wheels had made.

Paramount to all else, he must find Breanda. And quickly. There was no time to return to Ballymara and enlist the aid of fresh troops. He assumed Padrac, who was fleet of foot, had escaped the bandits and returned with news of the ambush, heeding an instruction Ardghal had earlier given. Urging Destroyer into a gallop, he winced, pressing his left arm to his side.

The sun had dropped a notch in the heavens before he approached a stream. Besieged with lightheadedness and pain, he dismounted, knowing he must rest. He stretched out on his stomach beside the stream to drink his fill then dunked his head beneath the icy water. It chilled his teeth and bones, but he hoped it would keep the dizziness at bay. Groping to a kneeling position, he shook his head like a dog, sending drops of spray everywhere.

Something scraped on the rocks behind him. A plunking of pebbles hit the earth.

Ardghal hastened to his feet as fast as he was able, grabbing the hilt of his sword as he spun around. Atop a low rock cliff, three bearded men circled, brandishing weapons. Their tunics bore the same crest as those who'd killed his friends and had taken Breanda. The shorter of them, obviously the leader, wore a sapphire blue cape.

Ardghal held his sword aloft, waiting, assessing. His fighting arm was not the one stabbed; yet that shoulder still ached from the fall he'd taken at the tourney.

Letting loose a fearsome shout, the wiry man in the cape leapt down from the rock shelf and rushed forward. Ardghal met the assault with all he had in him. The clash of steel rang in his ears, seeming to echo in his mind.

Vision swimming, he broke away and gasped for breath. A second man drew close through the blur. As if sensing Ardghal's strength abandoning him, the first brigand advanced, slicing his blade downward. Almost caught unawares, Ardghal swivelled, managing to parry the blow. The second man cried out in Gaelic.

"Fearghus, look. The amulet!"

Sword positioned, the first attacker stared at Ardghal's surcoat over its chain mail. Blades at the ready, the others crowded close, gathering in for the kill.

Ardghal wielded his sword in defense, but it grew heavy in his hand. A dense blackness descended like a shroud of death over his eyes. Stumbling to his knees, he lost his hold on the weapon and crumpled to the earth.

Nightfall swept its mantle of darkness over the land, as if to hide men's evil deeds. The only sounds to disrupt the silence were those of a crackling fire and men murmuring outside the tent. On occasion, the buzz of an insect or the rustle of a nocturnal animal could be heard outside the cloth wall. A tear in the canvas roof revealed a sharp slice of moon piercing the sky. Few stars shone. Breanda hoped there would be enough light to track her whereabouts, for she was certain someone must come.

After her altercation with the ogre guard, a lad with ruddy curls had brought her a hunk of bread and some pottage. He remained mute to her demanding questions, however, and had regarded her fearfully, as though he thought she might actually bite him. Good. With her dining dagger gone, little damage to his person could be achieved, but 'twas best these ruffians know she wasn't a woman to be trifled with. She could almost hear Ardghal chuckle as he had in their youth when he called her wild and unbroken—"worse than a mare with a thorn under her saddle." At the time she had growled in indignation to be compared to a horse and, waving an upraised fist, chased him over the hill abloom with wild orchids while he eluded her, laughing.

Breanda bit into the stale bread, surprised to find it salty, then realized it was her tears that seasoned it. She swiped them from her cheeks and raised her chin. 'Twould not do to show any sign of weakness to these ruffians.

Ardghal could not be dead. Surely the Lord would not allow it, as often as she'd prayed for his safety. Yet Breanda knew that the Almighty did allow tragedies to enter one's life. Her own parents had died shortly after she'd gone to live at the earl's castle. The sickness had stolen their lives, and her brother had died in battle. She would never visit her family or again see them on this earth. Father Stephen once tried to console her, attributing such circumstances to God's omnipotence, but Breanda barely listened at the time. In truth, she barely sat still long enough to pray, except when to do so involved something she desired.

A wisp of guilt unfurled within her, but she smothered it.

Were her prayers even heard? Or were they wasted on the heavens above that could hear nothing? The winds blew, the clouds produced rain, the sun and moon and stars gave off light. Yet they did not speak to her or reassure her. They were nothing. Acts of nature that had no voice. . .

Angered shouts broke the stillness, startling Breanda from her bitter ruminations. The murderous *clangs* of steel upon steel rang through the air. Eyes going wide, she hurried to the flap to see.

Chapter 5

Ardghal opened his eyes. He lay inside a wattle and daub hut on a mat of straw. The sky he discerned through the cracks of the thatched roof was black as pitch, but a fire nearby crackled close enough to produce a harsh yellow glow, also drowning him in heat. Sweat streamed off his face, into his ears, and over his scalp. He dragged his hand to his chest and found it bare. All his armor and the quilted garments he wore underneath had been removed. A rough fur blanket covered him to the waist. Something bulky and weighty wrapped his throbbing arm and shoulder. A poultice of some sort, if the stench coming from the cloth was anything to go by.

A figure came into his line of vision. By the outline against the fire, he assumed his visitor to be a woman.

"So, ye be awake," a feminine voice said. He placed it at no less than forty years. "The devil will not have ye, then."

"Where am I?" Ardghal asked, astonished at the raspy sound in his own throat.

"Ye be with the clan O'Cullen. And a fine thing it is that the amulet you were wearing."

The amulet! He slapped a hand to his neck but found no chain there. His swift action brought a ripping pain to his shoulder, as if ground glass had been smashed into his wound, and he groaned.

"Have a care, man. Are ye daft? Lie still. The fever is not gone from you, and the cut may flow a second time, though 'twas necessary to cauterize it."

Ardghal shut his eyes, remembering the searing pain, though he had trouble recalling how he'd gotten there.

"Aye. Sleep while ye may. The chieftain will soon be wantin' a word with you."

"Chieftain?"

She drew herself up proudly. "Niall O'Cullen. Me brother."

Ardghal stiffened in recognition. Niall O'Cullen. The man about whom his mother had warned him with her last breath.

While she lay on her deathbed, she made Ardghal vow that after her demise he would leave their clan and seek out Lord Garland. She stressed that he shouldn't remain in the camp. Anxious to calm her, Ardghal had agreed. Had the chieftain suspected that Ardghal was the son of an Anglo and not sired by a member of their clan, as had always been believed? Otherwise, why would his mother have feared him so?

The hulking, dark shape of a man entered the hut and came to stand beside the woman.

"Niall," she murmured. "If it is well with you, I'll take me leave."

"It is well." The newcomer's voice was gruff.

Ardghal steeled himself not to look away, though he could see little of the chieftain's face. The chieftain, this man. . .his grandfather.

Breanda's heart pounded fierce and without mercy as she stood with the tent flap parted and watched the battle. Along with several other knights, a flaxen-haired man wielded his sword against her abductors and guards. As he turned toward the firelight, his visage became clear.

Cormac! He had come to rescue her. . .yet there was a strangeness about the manner in which the rogues fought. Those who'd taken her didn't fight as fiercely as they had during the ambush. Was it the lateness of the hour that made them weary, the unexpectedness of the attack that made them sluggish, or her own weariness that prompted what was only her imaginings? Whatever the reason, Breanda was relieved when Cormac reached her prison of canvas and grasped her above the elbow. His eyes darted around the area, his sword held aloft to fight any who would try to stop them. The ogre guard seemed to have disappeared.

"Are you hurt?" he asked.

"Nay."

"Then let us be away from this place."

Cormac need not have spoken. Breanda was already running beside him toward a patch of murky white near the trees that proved to be Cormac's stallion. He mounted, swung her up behind him, and prodded the horse into a hard gallop, leaving the other knights to continue the battle. Behind, Breanda heard shouts; yet after a lengthy span of hard riding, it was evident no one followed.

Cormac soon brought his mount to a slow trot as they approached a deep glen. One of the cliffs descended at a slant, providing an overhang. Cascades of water shimmered over rocks nearby, emptying into a dark lake.

"We shall await the morning here," Cormac said. "The night is too dangerous for travel."

Breanda loosed her arms from about his waist and wearily dismounted. "Is it wise?" She watched him slide off after her. "Will they not pursue us?"

"I appear to have convinced them such a course would be folly."

"I fear for Ardghal." Despite what the ogre guard had told her, her heart refused to believe her beloved was dead.

Even in the scant moonlight, she noticed Cormac's scowl. "Must you always think of him? 'Twas I who saved you from those brigands!"

"Aye, and you have my gratitude. Yet Ardghal attempted the same and was wounded for his loyalty." The sudden desire for truth made Breanda clutch his sleeve. "Tell me. He is alive? For surely you must have come upon the place of ambush to learn I was in peril. Did he tell you?"

Cormac's lips thinned as he twisted his arm from her hold. His visage haughty, he lifted his head. "Your faith is misplaced, Breanda. You speak of loyalty, but a cur such as Ardghal knows no such word or deed." He moved to the lake and knelt to drink.

Resentment simmered within her as she followed. "How dare you speak ill of one who was willing to sacrifice his life for me!"

"Sacrifice his life?" Cormac let out a sneering laugh as he shook the water from his hand and stood to face her. "My dear, misguided Breanda. 'Twas a message delivered to the castle that informed us of your peril. I knew of no ambush."

"A message?"

"Aye. Signed by Ardghal, himself. He conspired with the lot of his worthless clan to kidnap you for ransom. Two hundred pieces of gold was the price for his loyalty."

Chapter 6

In the heavy gray light before daybreak, Cormac and Breanda resumed their journey homeward along with the other knights who'd earlier caught up to them. She found it curious that Cormac wasn't as hurried as he'd been last night. Did he not fear that the bandits might try to recapture her now that morning had dawned?

Twice during their sojourn, Cormac spoke of Ardghal, inferring that his knowledge of his illegitimacy and subsequent anger regarding the earl's duplicity must have sparked his rebellion. Breanda was astonished he knew the truth. To her knowledge the earl hadn't disclosed it to anyone, save her and Ardghal. When Cormac made his disparaging remarks, she turned a deaf ear to him, as she'd done last night when he first laid the blame on Ardghal. Each time, she didn't miss Cormac's reddened face or the infuriated sigh he heaved.

Let him be irate and think her a fool. She wouldn't believe evil of Ardghal. She had seen him wounded in his efforts to protect her. That he instigated her abduction or had taken part in it was folderol. The supposed letter of ransom had to be forged; surely the earl must know this.

The sky glowed a fiery red gold by the time Ballymara

Castle came into view. Seeing its high, curtained wall and round towers, Breanda relaxed. Tears sprang to her eyes, and she wiped them away. Oh, to be home again. Safe. She would speak to Lord Garland, and all this nonsense would be swept away like the rubbish it was. Ardghal would be found, and life, as she'd known it, would resume.

Once they dismounted in the lower bailey's courtyard, Breanda spied her maid hurrying toward her.

"Oh, mistress." Tears washed Elaine's cheeks as she flung her arms around Breanda's shoulders. " 'Tis glad I am ye be safe! Curse the sickness that kept me from your side. Would that I'd been with ye, where I belong, this mightn't have happened."

Breanda drew away, attempting a smile. "And what do you think you, a mere maid, could have done that four armed knights could not?" She sobered at the reminder of the lost noble soldiers. "I'm glad to see you recovered but relieved you were absent from me. I might have lost you to a brigand's sword as well."

Breanda turned to find herself encased in velvet as Lord Garland embraced her. "Breanda, child, you're home."

" 'Tis thankful I am to be home, my lord." She pulled from his embrace, alarmed at how lined his features appeared. Overnight, he'd aged into an old man. "If I may confer with you, I wish to speak of Ardghal."

Pain misted his eyes, and his jaw trembled. "Later. You must rest after your ordeal."

Breanda was weary from a full day of riding, but a sense of urgency prompted her to converse on the matter that had beset her ever since Cormac touted his lies. She parted her lips to speak, but caught Cormac's slight shake of the head. Tempted to ignore him, she gave the issue further thought. Perhaps it would be in her best interest to air her concerns when she and Lord Garland could speak privately.

She led the way to the inner bailey and the solar, where the family quarters were located, and ascended the spiral stairway to her chamber. Elaine followed and drew the heavy curtains back from the wooden frame bed.

Gladly, Breanda lay on the cool bedding. She shook her head when Elaine approached to help remove her soiled gown. Even to wash the dirt from her face and hands and neck seemed too much of a task. She inhaled the sweet scent of tansy, earlier sprinkled on her feather mattress to keep the fleas away and on the stone floor to freshen the air when crushed underfoot. . .so much nicer than her prison tent. She closed her eyes, her last thought drifting to Ardghal and his avowal of love at the pledging stone. A tear slid down her cheek.

When Breanda awoke from her slumber, a patch of inky darkness tinted the window. How much time had elapsed? Had the earl retired for the night? Without waking Elaine, who slept on a straw pallet nearby, Breanda quickly freshened herself, attempting to smooth the frizz that had come loose from her plaited hair. She dared not take the precious time to comb it out. The urgency to speak with Lord Garland about Ardghal prompted her to hasten toward the earl's chamber. Muted voices emptied out into the candlelit corridor. Breanda halted, surprised.

"I fear you are right, Cormac." Lord Garland's sorrowed words were low. "And it grieves me to air the edict that will most surely seal Ardghal's fate. Nonetheless, justice shall be met, and you'll be rewarded for your bravery."

"I ask only one reward, Father. Give to me Breanda. In marriage."

Breanda clapped her hand over her mouth to muffle a gasp. She leaned close to the chamber entrance, not wanting to miss the earl's reply. When it came, it chilled her very soul.

"Aye," he said quietly. "So let it be done."

When next he woke, Ardghal felt lucid. His wound didn't ache as much, and he struggled to a sitting position. The air held a chill that made him shiver. Through the hut's opening a pale sun shone beneath a white strip of cloud. Daylight. But how many days had passed? He recalled little of the conversation with his grandfather or how long ago it had taken place. The fever stole his consciousness during that first meeting, but he did remember the words Niall O'Cullen spoke before the world faded: "So, ye've come back."

Come back? His presence in their camp wasn't by his will. He'd been captured, though no fetters bound his hands or feet and no one seemed to be guarding him. Ardghal studied the area outside the hut. People moved about, but none took notice of him, save for some children who stood whispering in a group, a stone's throw away.

He frowned when he saw a child with hair the color of Breanda's. Had she been brought to this place as well? He must find her.

Awkwardly he pushed himself to his feet, holding the fur coverlet against him. He staggered and waited until a wave of dizziness passed.

A lass of approximately six years separated from the children and moved toward the hut. Her big inquisitive eyes, a hue of blue lighter than his own, studied him. He clutched the fur cover more securely about his waist, feeling like a turtle stripped of its shell.

She smiled, giggled, and ran off, shouting in Gaelic for her mother. Ardghal tensed. What malady would the child now bring upon his head?

The girl returned, followed by a plump woman with red braids and wearing a green gown of fine cloth. Ardghal was grateful that she carried his clothing and armor, evidently cleaned, but his sword and dagger were absent. She handed over his things, seeming embarrassed and amused at the same time.

"I'm Alma, the chieftain's daughter. Ye must dress, and I will bring food. Me *athair* will then speak with ye."

"How long have I remained here?"

"Five days."

Five days? What had become of Breanda?

The child continued to stare at Ardghal after her mother left the hut. The woman looked over her shoulder. "Isabel, come!"

"Aye, *Máthair*." The girl hurried to obey but not before giving Ardghal another big, close-lipped smile. He watched her scamper off before he turned to the task of dressing, favoring his injured shoulder as he did. So Isabel was his cousin. A fair and fetching lass, and at such a tender age. And Alma was his aunt. He had failed to recognize her, but then he'd only been a lad when last he'd seen her.

Once Ardghal wolfed down a bowl of vegetable pottage and tore his teeth into a hunk of wild boar—the first food he'd eaten in days—a short, wiry man entered the hut, announcing he was to take Ardghal to the chieftain. The man's tunic bore a red shield with a white chevron, three hands raised in pledge, two black shamrocks, and a shaft of wheat. The O'Cullen shield. Upon second glance and noticing the mole on his cheek above a sparse brown beard, Ardghal realized that this was the swordsman with whom he'd fought near the stream after the ambush.

Wary, Ardghal walked with his guard past other huts scattered within the confines of the rath. A sense of familiarity struck as he recognized areas of the wooden fortress.

"I've heard it said ye be Ardghal," his guard muttered.

"Aye."

"I am Fearghus. You and I hunted together as lads."

"Fearghus. . ." Ardghal recalled his boyhood friend, a snaggle-toothed lad who possessed a comic mischief. A chuckle escaped. "And do you still sling rocks at the crows that perch along the rath's outer wall?" He motioned to the sharp, pointed tips of the tall wooden wall that enclosed the compound, noticing a few of the black birds there now. For the first time, he wondered why the chieftain had built a rath of wood, as in ancient days, instead of a sturdier fortress of stone.

Fearghus's jaw clenched. "Why did ye side with the enemy?"

"I heeded a deathbed promise, asked me by my mother. But Lord Garland is no enemy, Fearghus. He took me into his castle and cared for me when I might have died." He spoke the words, though bitterly. What would Fearghus say if he knew Ardghal was the earl's son?

"Ye speak as the Anglo nobles do," Fearghus shot back as though he'd heard nothing said. "Ye dress like an Anglo, as well. Ye've become one of them. 'Tis surprised, I am, that ye be keepin' yer *máthair's* amulet."

"Where is it? And my sword and dagger?"

"I gave 'em to yer *seanathair*." Fearghus stressed the word for grandfather, spearing him with an accusatory glare, as if again to remind him of his supposed betrayal.

They approached the inner bailey, which housed the chieftain's quarters. Ardghal grabbed hold of Fearghus's upper arm before they went farther. "With all that I am, I vow to you that I mean no harm, Fearghus. To you nor any of the clan."

"Why then were ye on our land, if not sent as a spy?"

Ardghal chose not to remind Fearghus of the verity they both knew, that the English Crown ruled much of eastern Ireland. But he did speak of Breanda. "Is she here?"

"Think ye that we abducted the earl's ward?"

"Men bearing the O'Cullen colors ambushed our party."

" 'Tis a lie! Niall would not break a treaty of peace. Our number is few compared to the earl's army—of which ye appear t' belong. Would be to our destruction to raise his ire against us."

His words made sense. Ardghal continued to walk with Fearghus and caught sight of some children nearby. Their clothes were ragged, their eyes soulful, as if begging him for something, though they spoke not a word. "Who are these children?"

"Pitiful waifs, are they not? They scavenge what food they can find and keep to themselves. They have no parents. We lost both men and women during a clan war with the Byrnes two years past."

"Women?"

"Aye, they fought as well. Anyone who could raise a sword did so in defense."

Pity surged through Ardghal for the orphans. He wished he had the means to give them what they needed.

In a dim corridor, Fearghus halted in front of a chamber. Before they could enter in, Ardghal spoke. "You've become a fierce warrior, Fearghus, one I do not wish to clash swords with again. Let us not be enemies, when once we were friends."

"Ye made your choice eight years past. To be enemies is all

that's left to us now." Fearghus turned on his heel and left Ardghal to weather the storm alone.

Who is in the whirlwind or the storm? Who is in the fire? In the midst of one's distress, does a lone voice cry out to be heard? If so, from whence does it come? No, a thousand times no. There is no voice of comfort, no relief from one's distress. There is only the whirlwind, only the storm, only the fire. . . .

Breanda laid down her quill next to the vial of ink and studied what she had written. Lady Garland, when she was alive, had kept records of her daily activities. Since the day she'd reached the age of six and ten, Breanda had chosen to do the same on scrolls of parchment she kept safely hidden in a trunk in the wardrobe. Yet this day, the words that came to the shaved nib of her quill troubled her soul.

She turned her head in the direction of the window to stare out at the pearl gray sky. A peregrine falcon sailed past her line of vision. Drawn to the stirring sight, she rose from her bench at the small writing table and moved closer, placing her palm against the rock wall. Filmy white clouds brushed the horizon. In the distance, gently sloped hills of emerald green rose beyond Ballymara's forest.

I am not in the storm, nor in the fire, nor in the whirlwind, daughter. Hearken unto Me, for I am the still, small voice inside your spirit.

The gentle thought flitted through her mind, taking roost in her heart. It reminded her of a lesson Father Stephen once taught about the prophet Elijah, when God hid him in the cleft of the rock until the storms passed him by. And at last she began to comprehend.

Despite the whirlwind of Cormac's accusations. . .despite the storm resulting from the earl's belief in what surely must be lies. . .despite the agonizing fire that scorched Breanda at the very thought of becoming Cormac's bride—she recognized truth. God was in none of those things. He was the still, small voice that whispered to her heart. The voice that assured her of Ardghal's innocence.

She bowed her forehead to the cold stone. "Almighty Father, I seek forgiveness. I've been neglectful in my prayers and in seeking Thy face. I've yet to understand why this happened, but Thou perceive and understand all things. Protect Ardghal. Keep him safe. I beg Thee, let not Cormac's plan for vengeance come to fruition. Hide Ardghal in the cleft of the rock till the storms pass him by."

She shuddered at the thought of his possible capture. Four days now, the earl's soldiers had been searching for Ardghal, with Cormac leading the men. The earl commanded that he be brought back alive, but at the memory of Cormac's murderous eyes at the tournament, Breanda feared for Ardghal's life.

Her gaze lifted to the heavens and a flock of birds in the distance. "Where is he, Lord? Why has he not sent word to me by messenger? I believe he's alive. For surely, if he were not living, I would feel it within my heart."

Watching the birds, she thought of the pigeons the earl used to deliver urgent messages to remote districts. The birds flew to their original nest, in this case what used to be her parents' manor, and from there, another pigeon was sent to carry the message to another castle. . .

Elaine stepped into her chamber. "Pardon, m'lady, but Padrac, Sir Ardghal's squire, wishes to speak with ye."

"The lad?" She furrowed her brow. "Very well. I shall meet

him in the courtyard."

"He asked the meeting be private."

"Near the dovecote then. No one should be there this time of day." She assumed the reason she named the location was because she'd been thinking of the birds.

Within a short time, Breanda joined Padrac. Loud cooing could be heard from beyond the round timbered walls of the structure where hundreds of birds were kept. The squire, who was four and ten, raked a nervous hand through his dirty brown hair. His eyes darted about the area, as though fearful someone might see them.

"You wish to speak with me?" Breanda prodded.

"Aye, m'lady. On the day of the ambush, I ran with news to the castle as Sir Ardghal told me to do. But in the forest I came upon the men who'd attacked us. I hid close enough to hear them. Another man was there. He asked if the deed was done, and they said yea, that they'd left only my master, Ardghal, wounded, so he could not give chase. But that he was alive. The man said 'well done' and handed over a coin pouch."

Excitement tingled through Breanda to hear testimony that her beloved was indeed alive. "This man—can you describe him?"

"He stood taller than the others and was slight of build. Dressed in fine linens. But there's more."

"Go on."

"The bottom half of his ear was missing as though it had been shredded by a wild animal."

"Have you told the earl this?"

"Oh no, m'lady. His lordship mightn't give heed to a simple squire like me. But I knew you would listen. Sir Ardghal spoke well of you often."

"You've done a good service for your master, Padrac. I shall see that you are rewarded."

"I speak not for the reward, Lady Breanda, but for Sir Ardghal, himself." He looked down as though ashamed. "I delayed coming forward because I feared Lord Cormac, but I speak now. I would do anything to help my master."

Breanda smiled. "As would I. Now, go, fetch the keeper of the dovecote. Your words have given me a plan." She lifted her gaze beyond him, to the round building.

The boy scurried off, and Breanda mentally formed the message she would send. Surely, 'twas not coincidence that she'd been thinking of the pigeons and told Padrac to meet her here. Peace enveloped her, and she sensed God's guidance for the first time since the day of the ambush.

At last, she could do something to help Ardghal.

Chapter 7

Ardghal faced down his grandfather, who stared at him with the disgust one would show vermin. Graying brown hair hung to the shoulders of his crimson cloak trimmed in squirrel. His visage was lined with age, but his form appeared sinewy and muscular, and he stood tall, taller than Ardghal.

"Why are ye here?" Niall O'Cullen asked, pressing his palms to the long table that stood between them. "What curse has come upon me that ye bring the wrath of the Anglos upon our head?"

"The choice is not mine to be here. I seek Lady Breanda. She was abducted by men bearing the O'Cullen colors."

"No clansman of mine did such a deed."

"Someone did. We were ambushed."

Niall narrowed his eyes. "And so the lofty Lord Garland exacts vengeance upon us, even laying the blame at his own whelp's feet."

"*What?*"

"Your father seeks your capture and ours." Ardghal blinked, stunned, as the man continued, "Aye, I ken the devil who sired you. Me daughter was foolish in thinking she could hide it. She made haste in taking for herself a husband and clansman whom afore she could not abide. She should have drowned ye at birth, and I might have done the deed meself had I known the trouble you'd cause."

Ardghal fought the fierce emotion that threatened, both at the knowledge that the earl had declared him an adversary and that his grandfather knew his parentage. He struggled to keep his voice level. "If the earl has sent soldiers, they are strong in number. 'Twould mean war against your clan. You cannot survive such an attack."

"A conclusion I'd already reached."

Ardghal thought quickly; only one solution seemed apparent. "Niall O'Cullen, whatever our differences, we must put them aside and aid one another. Give me your word that you had no hand in this matter, and I shall do all within my power to return you to the earl's good graces. Give me Fearghus and other strong fighting men to accompany me, and we will find those responsible."

Niall scoffed. "Ye think me a fool that I would send me warriors with you and leave the rath at the mercy of the earl's soldiers?"

"Then give me Fearghus only. I give you my word; I mean no harm. I loved my *máthair* and would not hurt her people. Keep in mind the risk is also my own. Lady Breanda is pledged to me. My future hangs in the balance until I can find her *and* prove my innocence."

As though no longer concerned, the chieftain sank to his high-backed chair and plucked up a roasted leg of mutton from his wooden trencher. He took a bite, chewing as if his meal was of greater importance, though Ardghal sensed his tension. Niall peered at him with half-closed lids. "Me messenger gave word the girl's been found. By your half brother on the day of her capture."

Cormac? Ardghal digested the news. *How could he have found her so quickly?*

"I also heard the earl intends to give your betrothed to him in marriage. The announcement's to be made at a feast nigh unto a week."

The news struck Ardghal a mighty blow. *Breanda to marry Cormac? No! Does she, too, doubt my loyalty?* Working to keep his expression blank, Ardghal returned the chieftain's calculating stare with a steadfast gaze.

As if coming to a decision, the man grunted. "Take Fearghus. Find those responsible. Me word I've given, and we're none of us to blame. But heed this warning, Ardghal. If ye do anything to bring harm to our clan, I'll see you dead." He pulled a silver disc from his robe and tossed it across the table. It hit the wood with a clunk and shimmered in the firelight. The amulet.

"Fearghus will return your sword and steed. Go."

Ardghal retrieved the amulet and wasted no time in doing just that.

Having supped, Breanda prepared to leave the spacious great hall.

"A word with you before you retire to your chamber," Lord Garland said.

Tensing at his somber tone, she waited. Except for a few servants removing the remnants of dinner from the low trestle tables, they were alone. The knights had quit the building and headed for their sleeping quarters.

"I understand you made a visit to the dovecote today."

Breanda stiffened. The keeper must have revealed her plan. He hadn't been keen on her idea, without first gaining permission. Her duties as lady of the castle, a title gained upon her fourteenth year after Lady Garland's death, included overseeing the servants of Ballymara. Not issuing urgent messages to outlying regions.

"Aye, m'lord."

He released a heavy sigh and drained what was left in his chalice. "Ardghal's treachery is hard to accept—how well I know! Had I not seen the message or learned of the ambush, I would believe his innocence. The revelation that I'm his father was difficult for him to bear. 'Tis time for you to release fruitless hopes grounded in wishful fantasies."

"I cannot, my lord." A mist of tears veiled her eyes, but she lifted her chin in defiance to them. "His squire witnessed a meeting between those rogues in the forest, as I've told you."

Her guardian scoffed. "A lad given to wild tales."

"I believe him."

"Aye. But you've a gentle heart, often perceiving good that's truly absent. Ardghal wasn't among the dead, and he's not made contact with me. What else am I to surmise but that he's rebelled? Padrac reveres the ground upon which Ardghal walks. Is it so astonishing that the boy would concoct such a story to help his master?"

Breanda shot to her feet, but other than stiffening her shoulders and staring down into his shocked countenance, she did not move. "Perhaps not. Yet what I do find astonishing is how swift you are to accuse Ardghal, the man whom you've treated as a son for eight years. The man who *is* your son. And in that time, he's shown you nothing but selfless service and undying loyalty."

Working to rein in her anger, she gentled her voice. "Forgive me for speaking harshly, my lord, and I beseech you to grant me this petition. Delay the announcement of my betrothal to Cormac until a thorough search has been made for the evil men about whom Padrac spoke. Send soldiers to hunt them down." She inhaled a steadying breath. "And if they've not been found four weeks hence, I shall do as you say and marry Cormac."

His jaw tensed. "Matters of war are not for a maiden's shoulders to bear."

"But surely you do not wish to start a battle that should not be!"

"Breanda! Curb your tongue." Rare anger swept across his face as he upbraided her, startling her into silence. "You *must* accept the truth. Ardghal's heart has turned from us. He has sided with the O'Cullens, who've broken the treaty of peace. Cormac rescued you from those who would harm you, and it is to him I owe my good faith." He rose from the table, his expression grave, resolute. "The announcement will be given on the morrow, and the bans made. The wedding will take place *one* week hence when the nobles assemble here for talk of warfare. What I have decreed shall be so."

Helplessness gnawed at Breanda. Sinking to her chair, she watched him leave the great hall. Alone, she buried her face in her crossed arms and silently wept.

Ardghal, my beloved, I know you're not what he says, what any of them say. Prove them all wrong, and return to me. I've done all I know to do.

Ardghal and Fearghus rode past a thundering waterfall and

211

along a narrow path that led out of the copse of thick trees. They approached Glendalough's monastery. Beyond the nearest wooded hill, the glowing orb of the moon rose, and Ardghal's thoughts flew to his beloved. *My dearest Breanda, what must you be thinking. If only you knew how my heart yearns for you, how I long to hold you in my arms and kiss away your every fear. . . .*

"Someone comes," Fearghus said, breaking into Ardghal's reverie.

A monk in a cowl shuffled from the lit doorway of one of the stone buildings, cupping a candle with his hand.

"My sons. All is well?" he asked.

Ardghal reined in his mount. "We seek a place to rest for the night."

"Come, come. Have you eaten?" The man motioned to a small building near the church. "Stable your horses and share me table."

Within a short span, Ardghal and Fearghus sat across from their host, who introduced himself as Brother Cleary. His age-spotted hands were stained with red and blue ink at the finger-tips, doubtless from the illuminated manuscripts such monks were noted for composing, detailed paintings accompanying scripture verses. His tonsured hair was almost white. A spider web of lines stretched across his round face, but his blue eyes were merry. Chin to his chest, hands folded in prayer, he said a litany of grace over the meal. Fearghus squirmed, restless, but Ardghal put in his own quiet petition.

After spooning a thick brown pottage into his mouth, Brother Cleary looked up. "Have we met? I sense a familiarity about your face."

"I am Ardghal of Ballymara, but, no, we've not met."

"Ballymara?" The monk straightened in surprise. Peering

more closely at Ardghal, his gaze fell to the amulet. "I've seen that before."

Ardghal fingered the ruby in its center. "My mother gave it to me the night she died."

The monk sank back in his chair as if struck with a revelation. "Her name was Maggie, was it not?"

Ardghal's eyes widened. "You knew her?"

"Only twice did I look upon her face, when she sought my counsel." He grew thoughtful. "Such a comely lass but so weighted with sorrow. The Lord has blessed me with a keen mind, and she was not easy to forget."

Ardghal tore a hunk off the bread, stuffing it into his mouth. He didn't want to hear again how the earl had wounded his mother.

"I see you've not forgiven him."

"Who?" Ardghal looked up.

"Your father."

The bread went down with difficulty. "You know?"

"Aye. 'Twas for that reason your mother sought me. She could not conceive after she bore you and judged that she was being punished for her past sin. She made confession and sought the Lord's forgiveness the second time she visited." He thought a moment. "Nigh unto ten years past."

Ardghal blinked in surprise. "I never knew. 'Twas shortly thereafter she took sick and died."

"I'd heard of her death." The monk leaned forward, his expression compassionate. "My son, you must release this anger you hold toward your father."

"I've tried but cannot. And now he seeks my life."

Ardghal sensed Fearghus's body jerk as the man swung a look his way.

"Pride is a terrible thing," the brother commiserated. " 'Tis the root of a man's destruction. Your father's sins are his own; they're not yours to bear, nor must you regard them as grounds for punishing him. Make not the mistake of confusing sinful pride for righteous anger. 'Twill do you naught but harm. Rather, show those who've wronged you mercy, as our heavenly Father has shown you mercy by sending His Son to absolve your sins."

Astounded by the monk's perception, Ardghal choked down the emotion that rose to his throat with the last morsel of bread. "I fear my destruction is already upon me if I cannot find those responsible for laying the blame at my feet. Even Breanda, the woman dearest to my heart, doubts my fealty and love. Why else would she agree to marry my half brother, when she'd given her pledge to me?"

"Lady Breanda of Ballymara." The monk actually smiled. "Of course. Please, wait here."

Bewildered, Ardghal watched the elderly man shuffle from the room.

"So the earl be your *athair*?" Rancor seethed from Fearghus's tone.

Ardghal released a weary breath. "Be assured, the knowledge brings me little pleasure."

"Yet ye swore ye would help us try to prevent a war. Why?"

Ardghal seethed in incredulous anger. "D'ye think me so heartless I would not help me own clan? I'm an O'Cullen, too, remember!"

When Ardghal slipped into his old way of talking, Fearghus grinned for the first time since Ardghal's capture. "Aye, ye may be at that."

Yet another ember of truth branded itself deep into Ardghal's soul. "And I am Anglo."

Fearghus sobered. "Aye." He returned his attention to his pottage.

While Ardghal waited for the monk's return, he thought more on the holy man's words. He *was* prideful. Taking glory in his prowess of being one of Ballymara's most accomplished knights and in defeating his opponents while giving none of the glory to God. Smug in the fact that the earl had always highly favored him. He'd even borne a prideful attitude that Breanda returned his love and had chosen him above all others. And now all had been stripped from him. His good name, the earl's favor, Breanda. He took a long swig from the chalice set before him.

Aye, he was incensed with the earl for his delay in speaking the truth and in taking advantage of his mother. But his affection for the man had not waned. In the last village he and Fearghus came to, Ardghal surreptitiously heard word that he was suspected of being a threat to the earl. As if he could harm the man who'd once saved his life and reared him! He held back a dry chuckle at the irony. Lord Garland and his men assumed him eager to take the earl's life, thinking that he'd sided with the O'Cullen clan for war. While the chieftain, his grandfather, believed that Ardghal strove for the clan's demise. How fearsome he must seem!

He gave way to a humorless bellow, aware of Fearghus's odd look toward him. The man must deem him as mad as a swineherd. Ardghal merely shook his head and bowed it into his hand.

Although the royal blood of two nations coursed within his veins, he had no home, no family to call his own. He was lost in a web he himself had helped to make.

Almighty Father, I've been brought low by my sinful pride. I humble myself before Thee now and ask Thee to forgive my foolish-ness. A strange calm filtered through Ardghal at the prayer that filled his heart, allowing him to relax and finish his meal.

The monk soon returned, a slip of curled parchment in his hand. His thin lips stretched into a smile as he handed it to Ardghal. "I received this message by pigeon today, which by now most assuredly has been spread throughout the region. Perhaps it will help put your mind at ease over your lady love."

Ardghal knit his brows at the peculiar statement but un-rolled the minute scroll, penned in Latin. His heart leapt with astonished exhilaration at the news then pounded with love for the woman who'd not abandoned him:

Find the man with half an ear. He alone knows who was behind the ambush in Wicklow Mountains. Ardghal is innocent.

Lady Breanda of Ballymara

Chapter 8

M'lady? Ye must dress. Many have gathered for the feast."

Breanda looked with disinterest at the splendid cotehardie of green silk, its sleeves and neckline richly embroidered in gold. She waved her maid away and again scratched words onto the parchment with her pen.

"Ye've grown pale these past days." Elaine's voice quavered. "Ye be slippin' away from us, and that's the truth."

" 'Tis only my heart that's ill. Fear not, I shall play the role of the obedient ward and do as I'm told," Breanda replied in quiet monotone. "Yet how can I be expected to find even a morsel of pleasure in this matter when my heart belongs to Ardghal?"

Elaine broke down, and Breanda swung her gaze to her bowed head in surprise. "Elaine?"

"I beg pardon, m—m'lady. I never woulda done such a thing had I known the trouble it would cause. Despite his threats, I never woulda done it."

"What threats? Who?"

"His lordship, m'lady. He ordered me to spy on you the night Sir Ardghal learned who truly sired him."

Breanda drew in a sharp breath, setting down her quill. "Why would Lord Garland command such a thing?"

"Not himself. 'Twas Lord Cormac gave the order."

So *that* was how Cormac had learned Ardghal was his half brother. Nonetheless, Breanda's mind was weary from lack of sleep and couldn't think past that revelation.

Elaine sniffled. "I heard him gloat to one o' the knights that soon he would control the manor and the lands left ye by yer father."

Faith, she'd been a dullard. Of course that was why Cormac was eager to marry her. His aloof yet victorious glances aimed at her since her rescue had made Breanda wonder what he might be plotting. His first love was power, his second greed. Still, there was little to be done in any case. Many men married for land and, with it, the power they could attain. Such was the way of things; there was no law against it.

Breanda managed a smile for her distraught maid. "Be at peace, Elaine. I do forgive you, though your part in the deception didn't bring me to this moment. And I know how formidable Lord Cormac can be." She looked at the gown laid out on the bed. "Now cease your tears and help me dress. 'Tis time I made my appearance."

Yet Elaine continued to sniffle as she assisted Breanda. Staring into her round mirror of polished steel, Breanda noted the pallor of her own face beneath the complex arrangement of small plaits Elaine had earlier styled around the one thick shank twisted into a braid that traveled down her back. Her appearance was without fault; only her eyes remained haunted. As Elaine fastened a decorative chain of gold around her hips, Breanda felt shackled, a captive to her future.

Lord, grant me the courage to do what I must.

Breanda entered the great hall, well lit with copious candles impaled on iron-spiked stands and a ringed candelabra hanging from the lofty, timbered ceiling. The spacious room was packed with knights and other guests. They sat on benches along the tables, which were lined in rows upon the flagstone floor. These men had come from surrounding estates, accompanying their noble lords, who sat along one side of the high table and would later talk over the matter of war against the clan O'Cullen and anyone who sided with them. Her heart heavy, Breanda stepped onto the dais and took her place at the earl's long table.

"Verily, I am the envy of every man present. On the morrow, lovely Breanda, you shall be my bride." Cormac's eyes were bright. With wine or his victory, she had no way of knowing.

A page poured water from a ewer into a bowl for Breanda to wash her hands. The feast commenced as servants brought in dishes of mutton stew. Breanda had no appetite for what followed. Heaping platters of roasted venison, mutton, and boar, as well as goose, plover, and a fish pie were served to her table of honor on the dais, then to those below. Throughout the feast, she picked at her dish of mushrooms with roasted hazelnuts while watching the men at the low trestle tables as they devoured their meat, throwing their bones and rubbish to the floor, where the hounds bounded over the fresh rushes to gulp down their own feast. The crunching of bones the dogs chewed mingled with the clamor of men's voices in conversation and the sprightly notes the minstrels played in one corner.

Breanda missed the Irish minstrel who'd often visited the

castle. She preferred his poetry and harp to the lute this Anglo played. She failed to understand why the viceroy would deny to the Anglos all things Irish, though the earl once tried to explain to her that the English Crown feared that the Anglos had become more Gaelic than the Irish people themselves, and the king didn't want to lose his power over Ireland.

Power. 'Tis always about power.

Frowning, Breanda quenched her thirst from her silver goblet. Dreading the passage of time that brought her closer to her wedding day, she conversed little with her cousin, the new Lady Barbour, who sat on her right. Nibbling what food she could stomach, Breanda continued her assessment of the guests. Those few ladies in attendance were dressed as splendidly as she, while many noblemen wore the popular counter-changed style of clothing, with heraldic designs and jagged edges in serrated, diverse shapes.

Weary of surveying the nobles, her attention drifted to three monks at a table near the wall. They still wore their hoods, doubtless to dispel the chill. Suddenly her heart seemed to cease beating then hammered within her breast as she briefly caught sight of a face hidden within a brown cowl. As though he felt her intense stare, the monk slowly swung his attention her way. Their eyes met and held.

She dropped her dining dagger. It clattered to her trencher. Cormac looked at her.

"Breanda?"

Realizing the danger, she lowered her gaze but not soon enough. With a loud hiss, Cormac threw down his goblet.

Ardghal realized his folly at allowing his attention to stray and rest on Breanda the moment Cormac glowered his way. Knowing to put off the plan would be madness now, Ardghal shot up from the bench and tore back the hood that disguised him. Running to the dais and the opposite end of the table from Cormac, he further ripped the slit he'd made in the monk's cloak, to free his weapon, and tore his dagger from its scabbard.

The feasting knights, caught unawares, were still scrambling to their feet by the time Ardghal came up behind the earl. He clapped his forearm to the man's thick chest and shoulders, drawing him backward. With his other hand he held his dagger at the earl's throat, careful not to let the blade touch skin. Cormac halted his advance, though he kept his weapon positioned.

"Come no farther," Ardghal warned him and the soldiers, who now circled the high table, their swords also raised to fight.

"You would end my life so easily?" The earl uttered the words as though torn from his heart.

"Nay, my lord," Ardghal responded just as quietly. "I seek not to take your life or your lands or your wealth. I seek only to redeem my good name and that of my clansmen and could think of no other means to gain opportunity to do so." Louder, so all present could hear, he said, "I ask only that you allow me to speak. Afterward, if you wish your guards to clap me in irons, I'll not resist."

He heard Breanda gasp. Under his taut forearm, he felt Lord Garland stiffen then relax. "Lower your swords," the earl ordered his men.

"Father—"

"Be still, my son." Lord Garland halted Cormac's protest. "Let Ardghal have his say."

Ardghal waited until his fellow knights obeyed before lowering his dagger from the earl's throat. The men closest made as if to rush forward and apprehend him, but the earl raised his hand to stop them.

"I stand before you, a man falsely accused," Ardghal began. "If I were guilty of the charges laid upon my head, think me so foolish as to enter your castle with so few men and with so many men-at-arms against me?"

The earl nodded once. "You speak wisely. Continue."

"I searched for Lady Breanda but was weakened from a wound I obtained during the ambush. The O'Cullens found me and tended to me. When I awoke, I learned I'd been blamed for the attack, I and my mother's kinsmen. Later, I came across a message of import, which led me to search for the man I bring before you today. Fearghus," he beckoned. "Bring him forward."

Still wearing the borrowed monk's cloak, with its hood now away from his face, Fearghus gripped the arm of their prisoner. He forced him to walk to the dais then snatched off their captive's hood as well.

"The man with half an ear," Breanda gasped.

Ardghal briefly swung his attention her way, gentling his expression. "Aye. He admitted that an English nobleman hired him to arrange the ambush and abduction. He, in turn, hired a small band of deposed clansmen to do the deed—men who'd been cast from the O'Cullen tribe years ago and had become outlaws."

"Give me the name of this nobleman who instigated such a crime," the earl demanded of Ardghal's prisoner, outraged. "I'll see him punished, and you'll suffer also, if you'll not do as I say."

The man with half an ear lifted his weasel-like face, dark eyes glittering. "The name you seek, my lord, is Lord Cormac of Ballymara. Your son. He arranged the ambush and the lady's abduction to point the finger of blame at Sir Ardghal."

A pall of silence smothered the great hall. Many turned disbelieving eyes toward Cormac.

" 'Tis a lie!" he spat, advancing toward his former conspirator. "I'll slay you where you stand for speaking such a falsehood."

"I'll not suffer alone for your indiscretions," the man shot back. "There are others who saw us meet. Ask them!"

"I've procured the names if you wish them," Ardghal added.

The earl turned dismal eyes his son's way. "Why, Cormac? Why have you done this thing?"

Red suffused Cormac's face. "Always him. You always hold fast to his words—never my own." He lifted bitter eyes to Ardghal. "Well, he'll not again take what's rightfully mine!"

Cormac rushed forward, swinging his blade. Ardghal barely withdrew his sword from its scabbard in time to deflect the powerful blow. Time and again their weapons crashed as Ardghal defended himself and was driven back off the dais. Cormac's rage drove him, and he fought with passion rather than skill. Ardghal gained the initiative, fencing in Cormac. With one leap, Cormac jumped atop a table. Trenchers and goblets flew as he kicked them aside. Men scurried out of the way of the slashing blades.

Ardghal's shoulder throbbed, but he fought as fiercely as Cormac. To do less would mean to die. He could see that truth written in Cormac's eyes. As he parried each blow, the knowledge that Cormac had placed Breanda in peril with his selfish plan of abduction ignited a new blaze within. His thrusts came more swiftly. He took charge of the assault, feinting and thrusting, until Cormac fell back in retreat. Stumbling onto the flagstones, Cormac evaded Ardghal's blow, lifting his weapon high. Ardghal skillfully circled his blade round Cormac's, flinging the sword from his hand. With one step, Ardghal closed in, placing the point of his steel against Cormac's heaving chest.

Ardghal's arm shook with fury as he glared down into his half brother's eyes.

"Go on," Cormac said from between clenched teeth. "Do it."

None would blame him. Cormac had committed treason. He should die.

No, my son, not this way. . . Grant him mercy.

Sensing the still, small voice deep within the center of his being, Ardghal gritted his teeth until his jaw hurt.

"No, Ardghal," Breanda spoke quietly. "Not this way." She stepped up beside him. Her eyes were gentle, beseeching, but understanding, as well. "Not this way."

Ardghal's entire body trembled with fierce emotion; Breanda's words were confirmation to the voice he'd heard within. And yet. . .

He swung his gaze to Cormac, whose eyes defied him, even at the point of death. "I should run you through with my sword for the harm you've caused." Ardghal sucked in a lengthy breath through his teeth. "Yet to do so, I'd be no better than you." He hurled his sword to the flagstones, where it landed with a final clang.

Cormac let out a scoffing laugh. "You're naught but a coward. I should have had them kill you, instead of sparing your life—"

His taunt cut off as he realized what he'd said, and his

gaze pivoted to his father.

"So," the earl boomed, rising from his chair. " 'Tis true! You conspired against me, against all of Ballymara. Your terrible greed and jealousy nearly cost us a war." He straightened, his expression formidable. "Leave my sight; I refuse to look upon your face again. Henceforth, you are exiled to England, nevermore to return to Ballymara—to all of Ireland—for as long as you draw breath. And may God have mercy on your black soul."

Two knights grabbed Cormac's arms and hoisted him to his feet. He shook them off and glared at his father then at Breanda and Ardghal but said not a word.

Once the guards removed Cormac from the hall, the earl sank to his seat, his face gray, twisted in pain. A long moment elapsed before he addressed Ardghal in a low voice.

"I've done you a great disservice, you and your kinsmen." His weary glance took in Fearghus before returning to Ardghal. "Verily, you've shown me nothing but allegiance, and I've repaid your honor by wrongfully hunting you as a criminal. What recompense can I offer to atone for my folly in believing so great a lie?"

"I seek no reward, save one." Ardghal held out his hand to Breanda, and she took it, stepping close to him.

A ghost of a smile lifted the earl's lips. "Ah, yes. However, I can do much better than that. Come hither, both of you."

They did so, and the earl looked out over the great hall, at his guests. "Today, in the presence of all gathered here, I, Frederick Garland, Earl of Ballymara, Baron of Fairway, stand before you and claim Ardghal as my rightful heir. Flesh of my flesh, my son." A loud stir of excited conversation rumbled throughout the hall, but the earl raised his voice to be heard above it.

"Although English law forbids him my title, he shall have my wealth and Ballymara upon my death. Once I laud Ardghal's valor and tell of how he prevented hostilities from rising up against the English Crown within the Pale, I doubt not that the good King Edward will grant his consent."

His father—now proclaimed as such to all of Ballymara—clapped both hands to his shoulders and kissed Ardghal. Stunned, he could only stare. The bitterness he'd carried for the earl had begun to dissolve after his talk with Brother Cleary, and he sensed that their relationship was on its way to being restored.

"My lord?" Breanda asked, as though prompting him.

A trace of amusement flickered across the earl's face. "Patience, lass. I've not forgotten." Again he looked over the crowd. "As a reward for his bravery in preventing what surely would have amounted to dissension and war, I give to Ardghal the hand of my ward, Lady Breanda, in marriage. Since the guests are already assembled here, let the wedding commence on the morrow! I trust there are none to object?"

A thunderous cheer arose from the men gathered. Ardghal clasped Breanda's arms, drawing her close. Her eyes shone with love for him. Suddenly realizing where they stood, Ardghal smiled at his father and said a soft, "I am overwhelmed, my lord. . .Father. Thank you."

The shimmer of moisture in the earl's eyes bespoke his great emotion.

When at last Ardghal and his bride-to-be were done with the congratulations, he led Breanda out of the great hall. Drawing her with him into an alcove, he laid his hands upon her slender waist while she wrapped her arms about his neck. "I cannot begin to tell you how wondrous it is to hold you again," he said.

"You need not tell me. I've dreamt of you here with me endless times this past fortnight." Her expression waxed serious. "I never doubted you, Ardghal. Not for a moment."

"No." He smiled. "You wouldn't. You're my dearest champion, Breanda. A lady of true valor. When I read the message you sent by pigeon, I never realized it more."

Heart overflowing with love for her—this woman he thought he might never again have the right to claim as his own dearest beloved—Ardghal brushed his lips against Breanda's in a tender, lingering kiss.

Epilogue

fifteen years later

Sunlight paled and a delicate mist beaded the air as Breanda commenced a slow, joyful dance near the round tower. Here, in this silent area, she'd often experienced an intimacy with her Creator she felt nowhere else. . . .

Perhaps 'twas because here she and Ardghal were joined as husband and wife. Beside her, on bended knee, he'd spoken his vows before the priest, "I, Ardghal of Ballymara, do vow on my sword and on my name and on my honor to defend the faith and observe all the obligations of holy matrimony." Throughout the years they'd celebrated happiness as well as endured sorrows, growing closer in their union and becoming stronger because of both. Toward Cormac, they practiced forgiveness, daily praying for their childhood companion. Of late, they had heard he'd taken a wife in England, who was sadly as greedy as he. . . .

Perhaps 'twas because here she and Ardghal dedicated their firstborn son, Frederick. At four and ten, he was now a squire to Sir Padrac, who himself once served as Ardghal's squire. Tilting at the quintain was Frederick's favorite exercise as knight-aspirant; indeed, he had grown accomplished at charging with his lance or sword and attacking the dummy of chain mail with shield on its post. Truly, he was his father's son. Now she and Ardghal had a quiver full of children, all with dreams of their own: their three boys to become knights of valor like their father, who'd become a legend in all of eastern Ireland; and their three girls to learn what it meant to be noble ladies of courage like their mother, so they could please the future husbands Ardghal would one day find for them. . . .

Or perhaps 'twas because here, fifteen years ago, Ardghal first pledged his love and wrapped a shamrock around her finger. Breanda laughed and twirled around, lifting her face to the mist.

"My lady fair, what has you so joyful?"

At the long awaited—albeit amused—shout, she spun around and squealed then took off running to greet Ardghal, who galloped on horseback down the hillside toward her. Even after so many years of wedlock, her heart never failed to leap at the sight of her husband. He dismounted and plucked her up in his arms then swung her around and gave her a sound kiss. Pleasure burst like streams of sunshine warming within her.

"Dear wife, I have missed you."

"No more so than I." She pulled his face close again, pressing her lips against his, relishing the kiss that deepened and lengthened and caused her heart to pound with joy.

The mist fell heavier upon them. He ran with her to the stone archway fronting the church. Safely underneath, he set her on her feet and retreated a step until his shoulders hit the arch. "Let me look at you; a fortnight has never seemed so long. . . . Ah, Breanda, you are lovelier than when you were a girl, if that is possible. You are well? You should not be out in such weather."

Breanda knew by his concern that he referred to the babe she now carried. "The sun shone bright when first I came, and the mist approached me unawares, but I am strong. And I shall give you another strong son as willful as his father."

"Or a fetching lass as spirited as her mother," he teased in return.

She brushed back his damp hair that had started to silver. Apart from a few new lines that creased his face, he was the same vigorous man she'd known in spirit and in body. "And would you have me any other way, good sir?"

At her saucy smile, he let out a great bellow of a laugh. He lowered a swift kiss to her lips. "Nay, my fiery wild rose. You are most certainly the woman the Almighty designed for me."

Satisfied with his response, she switched the subject to what she'd prayed about each night since his departure. "All went well? Your grandfather was pleased?"

"Aye. The builder I found to design the stone fortress created a formidable structure. The O'Cullens will hold out well should another clan attack." He grew thoughtful. " 'Twas the first time my grandfather actually smiled at me."

Since the earl's death four years past, Ardghal had become guardian of Ballymara, with the young king Richard's approval, and oversaw improvements to the villages, including the construction of an orphanage nearby. Having been orphans themselves, he and Breanda considered the latter a project of the heart. Using a portion of the wealth left him by the earl, he also helped his mother's clansmen by building them a stronger defense against their enemies.

As a result, the O'Cullens now showed Ardghal respect and no longer presented a problem to the English Crown by refusing to acknowledge the king as their sovereign, though other clans beyond the Pale still resented English control. Fearghus's eldest son had come to Ballymara Castle to serve; he and Niall, Breanda and Ardghal's second son, had become close friends.

Breanda was pleased that the O'Cullens were now allies. The viceroy's edict fifteen years ago amounted to nothing; scarcely any Anglos had observed the law not to marry the Irish and to do away with Irish customs.

"Niall O'Cullen smiled?" She scoffed. "Perhaps when the great falcon makes his home 'neath the Irish Sea. Years ago, when first we met, he looked fierce, as if he would rather see my head on the end of his spear."

"As chieftain, he must show strength. Yet he's had a thorny life, Breanda. All three of his wives and his sons died. My mother and aunt were all he had left. In truth, he holds you in high esteem, and thinks you 'a fine lass.' "

Breanda lifted her eyebrows.

He grinned. "I jest not. He gave me a token to give you, in gratitude for all I've done. It belonged to his head wife." Ardghal pulled something from the pouch at his waist and lifted the hand that contained her wedding band. He pushed a ring onto her forefinger.

'Twas a golden shamrock with an emerald in its center.

"Oh," Breanda murmured. " 'Tis beautiful."

"Remember the words I spoke on the day we first declared our love?" he asked softly. "As sure as the shamrock is green, as sure as Three are in One. . ."

"Our love will be redeemed by the Father, Spirit, and Son," Breanda finished in as sacred a whisper. "And He has redeemed it, Ardghal. He most surely has." They exchanged a kiss, slow and tender. When next they drew apart, she inhaled a wondering breath.

"Ardghal, look."

He turned, and awe slackened his expression.

A many-colored rainbow made a vivid arc in the sky, beginning above lush treetops and ending on a far-off hill. "God's promise to us," Breanda whispered. "He is so faithful. So merciful."

"Aye." Ardghal circled his arm about her waist. "He is at that."

PAMELA GRIFFIN

A native of Texas, Pamela Griffin loves to travel, as does her entire family. Her parents recently returned from a trip to Ireland, chock full of interesting stories and loaded down with Celtic souvenirs. The medieval age is one of Pamela's favorite time periods to write about, and she recently visited Scarborough Faire (a medieval all-day festival) for the first time, and loved every minute of it. She plans to make this an annual event. A best-selling author, she has contracted over twenty books in both contemporary and historical romance, along with one co-written nonfiction book. Writing to her is more ministry than career, and it thrills her to hear evidence of God working in others' lives through her stories.

She loves to hear from her readers at words_of_honey @juno.com, and readers can visit her website: http://users.waymark.net/words_of_honey

A Legend of Love

Part 3

by Linda Windsor

Chapter 10

I f only her faith were as unshakeable as Breanda's and Ardghal's, Moyra thought two days later on the road to Dublin. Raindrops assaulted the windscreen and skidded off the bonnet of her SUV like warriors determined to stop the desecration of her ancestors' legacy. And she felt as helpless as the droplets to defend the legend of the pledging stone.

Now that Jack had taken a day to write up his findings to date from the castle and manor house, they were off to Dublin for the last leg of the investigation. Translated and written from bardic oral history by a sixth-century monk, it was kept in the library at Trinity College. The story of Conn was her last hope for Ballymara's future and her own.

Even if Jack had kissed her. Moyra grew toasty in the dampness of the day and not from her overcoat. Clearly he'd been knocked senseless by someone's elbow or foot as it were, and she'd been rendered senseless afterward. These Americans with their John Wayne notion of what was Irish. If he were really searching for Ireland, he'd stop trying to disprove centuries worth of faith and good will. One might conclude the truth scared him.

"Your cat is sleeping with me."

Jerked back to the present, Moyra spared him a glance as she turned off N11 and followed the signs leading to Trinity College. A campus of nearly forty acres, it was a city in and of itself in downtown Dublin.

"Buttons?"

Jack grimaced. "I think she likes me. All cats like me because I can't stand cats."

"Well, it's a better reception than Tommy O's goat," she reminded him.

Gran's words that cats were good judges of character went against Moyra's impression of Jack, but she hoped, for Ballymara's sake, that Buttons knew something she didn't.

"Least we have some quiet for the day," Jack observed with a wry twist of his lips.

The aliens had invaded that morning, arriving early for the weekend wedding. Ned and Peg, in black and glitter respectively, breakfasted with made-up groomsmen and bridesmaids, who varied in complexion from ethnic shades of pink to a green-brown that the army could use for camouflage. Costume-wise, anything went. And the Klingon language that they mixed with English was more deprived of vowels than ancient Irish.

It seemed strange to travel from Star Trek into the hallowed halls of Trinity College Library with its arched ceilings and walls lined two stories high with Ireland's past and present. Under the watch of the military-like front of white busts standing guard over the treasures, a representative from the library met them and showed them to a table where the collection of the manuscripts containing the legend of the pledging stone of Ballymara had been set aside for them by prearrangement.

"I read through it again last night," the spectacled gent

with a great swirl of gray hair told them. Dr. Terrence Lafferty was a member of the board of directors and had felt obliged to guard the manuscripts himself. "O'Cullen," he mused aloud. After a moment his face brightened. "Not of the same O'Cuilinn in the story?"

"It means holly tree," Jack spoke up, leaving Moyra agape that he'd paid attention to more than just finding something to tease her over.

Lafferty nodded in eagerness. "It's one of the very things young Conn used to win the hearts of his wife's clan. . .after he won her with the shamrock, of course," he said, scowling as he scratched a day-old growth of whiskers. "I didn't set that story out, since you only wanted the story of the stone."

Jack held up his hand. "It's okay. We've only got a few hours to do the stone, much less a tree." The scrape of wood on wood echoed in the cavernous hall as Jack pulled out two chairs and motioned for Moyra to sit down.

"Actually, I could copy that information for you," Lafferty offered. "It's been used time and again. Everyone is interested in how things got started—traditions, word origins, and the like."

"That would be lovely, Dr. Lafferty. And my Gran would be thrilled to learn a little more about her heritage."

Lafferty gave her an enthusiastic nod. "For Gran then."

"She still hasn't smiled at me," Jack said as the man shuffled off.

"Who, Gran?" Moyra asked.

"I even brought her some candies from the castle. Said her own was more tasty."

Without thinking, Moyra put a reassuring arm around Jack. While his suit jacket wasn't an original, his shoulders had been made for Italian tailoring. Startled by her thought, she withdrew.

"If. . .um. . .," she stammered. "If it's any consolation, she's right. . .about the candies."

Thankfully, Jack was already scanning the translation of the ancient manuscript.

Lord, she prayed, leaning in to read the elegant script on the pages before them. *May Conn knock that spiritual chip off Jack's shoulder and show him the Light.*

A Legend of Light

by Tamela Hancock Murray

Blessed are the pure in heart: for they shall see God.
MATTHEW 5:8

Chapter 1

Ballymara, Southeastern Ireland, AD 500

S orcha! Did you hear? Almha was cured of her limp."

Sorcha looked up from sewing the brat she would soon wear. Her sister Niamh stepped on to the balcony, the part of the family lodge where they wove tapestries in abundant sunlight. Niamh swept a straggling piece of red hair from her cheek.

"Healed?" Sorcha asked. " 'Tis not true!"

" 'Tis, too! I just saw Almha for myself. She walks as right as anyone else in the village, all because of the holy man." Niamh sighed and looked skyward. Her green eyes, identical to Sorcha's, took on a light of rapture.

"Holy man? What holy man, Niamh?"

"The one who is camped in the glen near the spring. Conn." Niamh's tongue hugged the sound of his name.

"Oh. That holy man." Sorcha scrunched her nose and flitted her hand at Niamh. "I care not what you saw. I want nothing to do with him, and if you possess more than a swineherd's wit, you will not either. You know how the wise men feel about those who practice such arts—not to mention the man of this house, our own *athair*. I suggest you remove that wistful expression from your countenance."

Niamh pouted and crossed her arms. "Conn has a right to abide in Ballymara. No one claimed that plot of land before now. And since when have we turned out a peaceful man?"

"We are open to those offering no threat to the elders. But I can see by your face he has addled your wits. That is a sign of danger, Niamh. A danger you would be advised to avoid."

"He poses no threat. He will be among us but a short time and will depart as the Lord directs him."

"Directs him?" Sorcha stopped mid-stitch. "His God talks to him?"

Niamh's sideways smile indicated pleasure that she had garnered Sorcha's attention. " 'Tis what he says."

"Strange. We make pleas to our gods, but they do not speak to us except to send a good harvest or a new baby. Is that what he means?" She paused, allowing herself to enjoy a slight breeze against her face.

"I do not think so. He prays for a harvest of souls."

"Souls?" Her sister's veiled speech exasperated Sorcha. "Speak so a body can understand."

"He means the spirit that animates man. At least, that is what I believe he means."

The explanation confounded Sorcha more than it enlightened her. "How can one harvest a spirit?"

"To give one's soul to God determines one's place in the afterlife. Those who believe will find a house in the heavens. That is what Conn preached yesterday."

"The afterlife." Sorcha pondered the elders' belief that a person's spirit lives through death's winter, like the life of a wild rose or evergreen. Yet none knew from this side of the grave.

"Yes." Niamh's voice became dreamy as she clasped both hands to one side of her throat. "Conn says it will be beautiful."

Sorcha wondered how this holy man could declare knowledge of the afterlife that even the most arrogant elder didn't claim. "Pity him who makes his opinions a certainty."

" 'Tis not his opinion but truth Conn speaks. He says *Athair* God is called 'I AM.' "

"I am? I am what?"

Niamh shrugged. "I do not know. But He is the one who created the world."

"Ha!" Sorcha scoffed. "Ballymara's elders will take issue with that, sure as needles stick."

"If they seek knowledge as they claim, they will ponder his words."

Sorcha pulled at a strand of black thread while she watched a shepherd boy chase a stray goat down the path beside the lodge. "Listen to the holy man's strange words all you wish and remember them, for they will be cut short once the council hears of this."

"But the healing—"

"If the healing was not a trick, the council will accept it. But our healer will not like being outwitted by a daft holy man who talks to his God and, worse, hears Him."

"If Dow could have healed Almha, he would have no need to worry." Niamh drew closer and lowered her voice. "No elder is more powerful than this God. Conn says His Son rose from the dead."

"Rose from the dead? Has he proof?"

"Conn says there were hundreds of witnesses."

"Have they risen from the dead so they can come to this time and place and testify?" Sorcha didn't wait for the answer to her sly question. "You will need more than stories to convince *Athair*—or me."

"Think as you will, Sister. I believe He must be God. Consider Almha. None of our healers could make her well. Our gods did not answer the village's pleas for her. Yet as soon as Conn started speaking to his God, she walked!"

"Did you witness this yourself?"

"Nay," Niamh admitted. "Mór told me."

Sorcha noticed that the boy had retrieved his goat, who bleated in objection to the loss of temporary freedom. She nodded as he passed. "Everyone knows Mór is a gossip. Surely you do not believe her," she observed to her sister.

Niamh nodded to the boy but addressed Sorcha. "Think what you like, but Mór is not the only one talking. Over and over I hear that Conn sent a prayer up to the heavens, and a miracle happened."

The heavens. Where the reliable stars are.

Sorcha shook the notion from her mind. It was too much to believe. Too wonderful.

"Still, I would see Almha with my own eyes," Sorcha thought aloud. "Perhaps Mór did not see this holy man slip her a potion to drink or cast a spell unknown to us. Or perhaps Almha was all but healed from our physicians' efforts and the small bit this Conn did finished the work."

"Or perhaps I AM is powerful enough to heal," Niamh reasoned. "If anyone knows about this miracle, it is Almha. Why not ask her yourself?"

The suggestion was intriguing, but Sorcha didn't want to admit to piqued curiosity. She plied her work with renewed vigor, weaving woolen thread into fabric that would make a fine brat to wrap in when the last breath of summer was whooshed away by autumn's chill. Hers would boast three colors to show the family status afforded by *Athair's* place as the king's bard. She stared at her work. "But I am not acquainted with this holy man. Do you expect me to inquire of a stranger?"

From her peripheral vision, Sorcha could see Niamh motioning to her from the door of their lodge.

"Come. He is there, teaching now. Everyone from the village is traveling to Ballymara Glen to see him."

Sorcha secured a thread. "We have our own gods. I have been relying on Brigid, the goddess of light, my whole life. And what about your chosen goddess, Nantosuelta? Do you plan to abandon her?"

"Nay. I can worship them both."

"I see no need for such foolishness. Does our tribe need yet another god—or goddess?" She set her gaze upon her sister's unfinished tapestry. "You would be wiser to tend to your work. Lose an hour in the morning, and you will be looking for it all day."

"But the words of the holy man are never a waste of time." Niamh peered into the distance, as though her thoughts were miles away from the alcove, nestled underneath strong trees that the tribe believed contained divine energy. "He is so different, so mystical. This man talks about someone named Jesus the Christ."

"Christ?" Sorcha dropped her thread and placed her hands in her lap. She fingered the dyed cloth, conscious that its softness bespoke her elevated status.

She eyed her surroundings. The spacious lodge allowed her *athair*, Flann, and the two sisters enough room to pursue their own interests. Because they weren't forced to tend to mundane chores of survival as were women of lesser status, Sorcha and

Niamh had time to weave stunning tapestries and to fashion garments to their pleasure. The gold pendant she wore, with its large, smooth emerald stone that matched her eyes and flattered her golden red hair, rivaled the tribal queen's jewels.

Brigid and the other gods and goddesses had served her well. Why should she devote attention to a rival? The wise men wouldn't like the idea. She had overheard some talking about strange religions in unflattering terms.

A realization struck her. "Is the holy man one of those people they call Christians?"

Niamh responded. "Yea. That is what Mór told me. She and her mother committed last night to become His followers. And there are others from the village willing to do the same."

"Others? But again, what of our ways?"

"Our ways are good, but His way is better."

Sorcha gasped. "Niamh! Do you really believe that?"

"I–I do not know." Niamh cast her glance to the gray stone on which her sandal-clad feet stood.

Fear traveled through Sorcha's stomach. "I do not think going to see this new teacher speak is good. *Athair* will be opposed to us listening to anything contrary to what the Brehon teach. And I am not sure that is my desire." She returned to her sewing.

Niamh hastened to Sorcha's side and tugged at her sleeve. "But this teacher knows things!"

"Sister, be careful. You question *Athair's* position as the king's poet."

"Ha!" Niamh scoffed. "*Athair* is the one who makes the Brehon and every other man in the village quake. You know as well as I that no one wants to be the subject of his poison poetry. And remember how he amused King Festus's court with his verse about Conan the Loud?

> *"Among us all there is a wit,*
> *Or that is how he fancies it.*
> *But knowledge he has not a whit.*
> *Whispers claim him the village idiot."*

Sorcha shrugged. "A verse *Athair* composed with little thought. Not his best, to be sure."

"But laugh they did, and you along with the rest." Niamh tilted her chin and stared intently at Sorcha. "If you do not care to listen to Conn's preaching, just come and see the show. His miracles are amusing, and you would not want to be the only one in the tribe not to witness at least one."

"There will be more?"

"There could be."

Sorcha hesitated.

"Then all is settled. We shall go." Niamh nodded once.

Sorcha didn't want to betray her *athair*, but from Niamh's report, the holy man sounded intriguing. She stared at the pathway, now vacant, that would lead to the glen. She could hear bleating animals along with voices of adults working and children playing. The familiar sounds comforted her, while pursuing strange knowledge seemed risky. "I–I do not know."

Niamh clasped her hands together. "Oh, please! I cannot risk going alone. If *Athair* finds out, he will not punish us both."

Sorcha smirked as she realized Niamh's scheme. She had always been *Athair's* favorite, and if Niamh could convince her to join, *Athair* would turn a blind eye to their mischief. Besides, this new man might speak of more than spiritual matters, but also of the world beyond Ballymara. She'd be foolish to turn down the chance to ply a visitor for news of the rest of Erin. "Oh, all right. I have made progress. He will not scold me if I stop now."

"As if he ever scolds you. Let us not tarry."

Sorcha rose and followed Niamh. Despite her brave words, Sorcha clutched her stomach to soothe its disgruntlement. Yet her dry throat wouldn't have let her eat if she had tried. Surely the gods—and her *athair*—wouldn't mind her efforts to gain as much knowledge of the world and its inhabitants as opportunities allowed.

But no matter how much she learned, she wouldn't abandon the way of the druidic elders. Never.

Chapter 2

As the sisters walked on a narrow passageway taking them through the tribe's rath, which offered the village fortified protection, Sorcha could barely keep up with Niamh's excited step. Sorcha's anxiety grew as large as the mist-cloaked Wicklow Mountains looming beyond dense virgin forest. Yet her curiosity swelled and prodded her to keep moving. As her sleeve brushed against a branch hovering over the path, she wondered about the holy man. How did he survive without tribal support?

Rumor pegged his home as a cave she had explored years before on a dare. She remembered the drone of water dripping from stalactites. Fear of what beast might dwell within its deep crevices had kept her from venturing too far into the blackness. Enduring other children's teasing had been preferable to facing unknown dangers. Admiration at his courage embraced her.

As Conn's glen came in sight, unease set up temporary residence in the pit of her stomach. A crowd had gathered in front of the holy man's abode. She and Niamh were known as the daughters of a powerful poet and sure to be eyed. If only she had brought a shawl to conceal her face. What if her clansmen mistook their presence as *Athair's* endorsement of the stranger's talk?

Accustomed to attention, Sorcha felt strange when no one glanced her way. Men and women alike seemed entranced by the teacher.

"Jesus Christ said that we are to love our neighbors as ourselves." Conn's baritone rang through the air.

"Can we not satirize our neighbors who do not love us, so they may change?" someone asked.

Sorcha looked in the direction of the man's voice, but her gaze rested on Almha. Why, the girl stood to her full height! Her back, once crooked, supported her in a regal manner.

The healing! It must be true!

Conn's voice gained her attention. "With Jehovah God, no one needs satire. Only love."

Love. Athair's *verse would have no place in this religion.*

"But you speak of spirits," another shouted.

"Only the Holy Spirit."

The Holy Spirit? Sorcha wondered what made this spirit different or holier than others. *What strange talk!*

Wanting to see more, Sorcha grabbed Niamh by the hand and pulled her toward the side of the crowd so they could look upon Conn.

Sorcha was dumbstruck. Instead of an aged scholar, this holy man appeared young and strapping. His features were sharp but not gaunt. And his eyes! Green as the grass that covered the land and filled with fire enough to consume it, they revealed a glimpse into a pure soul. Curls black as a raven's feathers glistened. Sunrays peeking through the curtain of tree leaves kissed his hair and face, lending him an ethereal look.

She held back a sigh. The gods had blessed him with undue comeliness. His countenance convinced her that heaven itself had bestowed upon him an otherworldly crown.

And his voice! Perhaps he'd chosen the power and protection of the trees, connecting the earth to the sky, to work his magic upon the crowd. She fingered the stone likeness of Brigid that she wore tied to her girdle for protection. Yet as she listened to the holy man, her hand fell away with her melting doubt, as though his words rang true in her heart and drew her closer. The gods would not allow a deceptive man to be so lyrical and beautiful.

"Why should I care about what you call the Holy Spirit?" a laborer asked. "Do we not enjoy protection enough from our ancestral spirits?"

"Aye, our crops yielded us a good harvest last season. Even better than usual." Sorcha recognized Bryan's voice. He was the man *Athair* wished her to marry. She grimaced. His position as the youngest member of the Brehon expanded his contrary nature. "Our tribe has no need for another god."

Without a hint of distress or intimidation, Conn replied to the challenge. "Your gods are naught but earthly things that change with time. The Lord Jesus asks us not to look to the Father's creation for guidance but instead to Him. Your priests profess that there is more power in the unseen than in what meets the eye."

Bryan hesitated only a moment before trying another tact. "You tell us there is but one God, yet you speak of three."

"Three in one." Conn plucked a shamrock from the grass at his feet and held it high above his head that all might see. "Observe. Three parts, one plant. Three parts, one God. A sacred Trinity comprised of the Father, the Son, and the Holy Spirit."

A Trinity! Sorcha gasped. Surely the Trinity's relation to the sacred number three was no coincidence. This new God of whom Conn spoke was a force not to be ignored.

Though sharp in wit as a dining dagger, Bryan spoke no rebuke. Sorcha felt her lips twitch. He was sure to be in a foul humor when he joined their table in the hall for the evening meal. She could almost hear Bryan boasting to *Athair* about how he challenged Conn, omitting his quick rebuff.

If only she could dismiss the silver-tongued Bryan so easily. Because *Athair* was the king's bard, Sorcha could have her pick of men. But *Athair* wanted her to wed Bryan. Couldn't he see how Bryan used flattery—even asking *Athair* to teach him the finer points of caustic verse—to assure himself an esteemed place among the villagers? Nay, *Athair* was as prideful as his protégé.

As if Bryan could sense she contemplated him, he turned her way, but Sorcha focused on Conn. She couldn't stop Bryan from reporting her presence to *Athair*, but she could remind him of his loss for words to the holy man's statement.

Soon she sensed Bryan close beside her. "Why are you here?" Anger tinged his whisper.

"Niamh asked me to join her. She wanted to see what this man had to say." Sorcha strained to hear Conn.

Bryan glanced at Niamh. "A fool, she is. But that is not news."

"How dare you!" Eyes narrowed, Sorcha spoke with such force that heads turned. She would not allow Bryan or anyone else to cast aspersions on her loved ones.

"I am sorry that I speak the truth," he retorted.

"Then you are not welcome to sup with us this evening."

"Ah, but your *athair* will want to know about this meeting." The gaze he sent Conn's way uglied Bryan's face. "His teachings insult the gods who have treated our people well. He must be stopped before they turn upon us."

"Conn is a free man," she argued. "And not everything he says flies in the face of our beliefs. I am certain our chief and druidic counsel will welcome him with hospitality and show him the error of his ways."

"Ha!" Bryan's scoffing attracted the attention of those nearby, though none was brave enough to suggest that he quiet himself.

Sorcha remained unafraid. Bryan would never unleash fury with *Athair's* favorite daughter, especially in front of witnesses.

"I know the ways of the council better than you, woman." His tone displayed controlled rage. "And rest assured your *athair* will be none too pleased when he discovers you were here."

"I believe otherwise. *Athair* places great value on learning. He will be proud that I sought knowledge. I might even recite what I heard today for his pleasure at dinner."

Eyes hard as flint, Bryan extended his hand to take hold of hers, but she withdrew. "Come along. We have no more to learn."

"Nay. As a free woman, I believe I shall stay." She nudged Niamh, who had been too absorbed in Conn and his message to pay them attention. "We want to learn more, do we not?"

Niamh answered without taking her gaze from Conn. "Aye. Indeed we do."

Conn swept his gaze over the mass of people. When he moved into the glen, he had known of the O'Cuilinn tribe's significance, but they were more numerous than he estimated. Surely God had sent him to Ballymara.

If only the Lord hadn't entrusted him with so many souls! After studying the tenets of the faith at Armagh, the place on the hill that the great teacher Patrick had loved so much in the northern region of Erin, Conn traveled south and sought solitude to contemplate God's purpose for his life. His didn't want to cause a stir. Yet when he saw the little lame girl, the power of the Holy Spirit came over him, and he couldn't fight the urge to ask the Lord to heal her.

That first healing put an end to seclusion. Most who ventured to the glen carried a burden of mere curiosity at best, suspicion at worst. Yet as Conn taught and healed, listeners increased along with requests for healing. Many decided to follow Christ.

The power they marveled over was not his. Conn knew he acted as a mere vessel. The Holy Spirit brought people healing of their bodies—and their souls.

Unlike the peoples of the north, the O'Cuilinn tribe had not been exposed to Christ's teachings before Conn's arrival. Instead they adhered to Brehon Law passed down through a complicated oral tradition, not that which had been revised to comply with biblical truth. While he understood doubts, he couldn't have answered questions without the Lord's help. Once again, he said a silent prayer of thanks and praise to the one true God.

As always when he taught, Conn searched for new faces. A couple of old men in laborers' garb were newcomers, as was a woman wearing the simple dress of a slave. She smiled before averting her eyes to the grass-covered ground as though she'd broken some law for meeting his gaze. Conn suspected the few slaves present would never dare express enthusiasm for his teaching lest they face punishment from their masters. He'd never be comfortable with the common practice of slavery, but Conn was heartened to see that none he saw appeared malnourished or mistreated.

A mane of flaming red hair drew Conn's eye to a pretty lass clad in the fine attire of the upper class. He recognized her from other times, but now she seemed different. Spiritual fire replaced curiosity in her expression. She was at the foot of the cross and needed but to look up and accept the Son.

His glance rested on the woman standing beside her—a woman so stunningly beautiful that he almost tripped over his words. Auburn hair streaked with gold cascaded over her shoulders from under a blue head covering. The color suggested wealth, and the effect of the elaborate wrap put him to mind of a crown. Likewise she wore a finely fashioned frock of blue with a girdle the color of new moss. A large pendant fashioned from gold and set with an emerald stone swung from her girdle. Three gold torcs dangled from her wrist. Surely she was a princess of the tribe.

The woman stared back at him with questions filling her expression. He found himself hoping he could minister to her. Because the wealthy seldom were willing to relinquish their power—or to give all to the poor as Christ instructed—Conn had found them to be among the most difficult to reach.

At that moment he felt led to quote from a letter that Saint Paul had written to the Galatians: " 'There is neither Jew nor Greek, there is neither bond nor free, there is neither male nor female: for ye are all one in Christ Jesus.' "

He looked at his princess, anticipating her expression to tighten and disapproval to light her eyes. Her fine chin tilted upward, and her eyes surveyed him boldly, but not with terseness or disapproval. Her self-assurance was admirable yet offputting. Surely this woman thought herself too good for him—and for the Lord.

So why did he care about this lone woman, when so many

in the crowd wore expressions that revealed their hunger for Christ?

He shook thoughts of the princess out of his head and let his gaze rove over the crowd, knowing each person desired eye contact long enough to feel special. Yet his glance revisited the golden girl, taking in the smooth skin of her face, white as the cream that would rise to the top of a pitcher of milk.

Yes, she was the cream of the crop. Or a rank dangerously close. Too close for him. The religion he taught threatened her husband or *athair*, no doubt. To date, the druids here refused to relinquish power over the people to Christ. Could he drive the serpents of knowledge from Erin's soil as had Patrick? By preaching the Good News in this woman's presence, he tread on perilous ground.

Conn's faith in God was unshakeable, but his confidence in himself was another tale. He never dreamed the Lord would send him prosperous people to convert. Born into wealth himself, he knew the resistance he would face from this new woman and her family. The poor received his message eagerly. If only the Lord would see fit to allow him to remain among them! But the Lord's will, not Conn's, be done.

A glance at the horizon told him that he had another hour or so of light, but he needed time to think and pray alone. "Good friends, the day is long, and the time to rest is upon us. Let us disband for the evening after a moment of prayer."

The atmosphere burned with questions unasked, but he could remain no longer. He consoled himself with the knowledge that even Jesus had taken time to Himself to meditate and pray. Still, Conn never ceased to feel astounded by the hunger of the tribe for the gospel he preached.

"Will you teach on the morrow?" a male voice rang through the sky.

"Nay. I would ask for an evening of solitude. Teaching will resume the night after that." He offered a benediction and had turned toward the seclusion of his cave when someone tapped him on the shoulder.

"Aye?" When he realized his visitor was the girl with the golden and auburn hair and her flame-haired companion, his stomach felt as though it were leaping for joy—and fear.

"I am Sorcha, daughter of Flann, bard to the king," the bolder of the two announced, "and this is my sister, Niamh."

The redhead tilted her face upward as if to show she was just as important as her sibling.

"God bless you both," Conn answered through an uncommon tightness in his throat. "I am Conn, humble servant of the one God." Opportunity stood before him, but whether he was ready to meet it or nay, Conn had no idea.

"Your teachings intrigue me," Sorcha said. "Will you permit my sister and me to linger and learn more?"

His desire for solitude evaporated like dew on a summer morning as Conn stared into her eyes, as green as the Emerald Isle itself. Part of him wanted to let her stay, to talk to her, to answer any question she wished. Another shouted warnings beyond his understanding. But he couldn't let himself differentiate between this woman and the other seekers of the tribe.

"There will be more teaching two days from now. I have requested solitude for prayer until then," he responded.

Her aristocratic features registered a surprise that suggested few ever refused her wishes. "Aye, but I want to know more. Today."

"My lady, I am tired," he said in truthfulness. He knew

better than to venture out on such a proverbial limb without prayer and preparation. He needed the reassurance that this was God's will and that he was ready to follow in the footsteps of men who were much greater spiritually than he. And that God had sent a woman so beautiful, one who offered temptation—this could only be a test. "Another time, perhaps."

"Another time?" Her sweet voice betrayed a mixture of hope and disappointment. "Might I suggest tomorrow? Will you allow me to bring you supper in exchange for knowledge? Surely your God does not require you to stop eating."

"If He does, you shall find few converts here," her sister said, her tone indicating that she jested only in part.

A smile unfolded on the golden girl's lips, riveting Conn's focus. "She speaks the truth."

Conn couldn't resist returning her pleasant expression. "My Lord does not require me to fast for long periods of time. None that I cannot endure with relative ease. I abstained from eating today, which I believe helped me in my teachings."

"Then why do you require solitude?" Curiosity swam in the emerald pool of Sorcha's gaze.

"So I can sense His leading on how to proceed. The magnitude of the crowds my teaching has attracted has surprised me. Pleasantly, I might add."

"The people of our tribe always seek knowledge," Sorcha said. "And to impart knowledge, you need sustenance. At our lodge, we dine on the best food in the village. Just a sample of that fine food is what I will be bringing to you."

Conn noticed dryness in his throat. Though he wasn't sure he wanted to take such a risk, he guessed that refusing an invitation from the daughters of such an influential member of the king's court would be folly. He had no wish to insult the tribe.

He rested in the thought that he would not face his hostesses alone. God was with him.

"It is agreed," he stated. "I shall see you for the evening meal."

Conn watched them depart. At that moment he realized he had never felt so much anticipation—or so much dread.

Chapter 3

Sorcha felt conscious of Conn's gaze burning into her back as she and Niamh walked away from the entrance to his cave. A pleased smile settling on her lips, she squared her shoulders. This wasn't the first time a man had been taken by her appearance. Yet this teacher seemed intent on distancing himself.

Niamh interrupted her inner monologue. "Sorcha, I have never seen you offer such a degree of kindness to a stranger. To walk back all this way on the morrow, to take him a fine meal, asking nothing in return but to speak with him longer. Truly you must believe what the holy man teaches." Niamh's words flowed together in excitement as the sisters walked back to the village.

"I think his words are false. I will never believe them. And I do not see how you can believe them either." Peeved, Sorcha traveled faster, not caring whether Niamh wondered if her ire was building or if she wanted to beat the setting sun home.

Her determined sister lengthened her stride to keep pace, tripping over a root in the path. With a gasp of distress, she regained her footing. "But you said you wanted to learn more." Her breathless challenge ranged an octave higher than her usual voice.

"Only to aggravate Bryan." Dining with the holy man instead of him would certainly put a burr in his bed box.

"Neither give cherries to pigs nor advice to a fool."

"So I am a pig and a fool now?"

Niamh scrunched her nose. "I should have known your motives were not pure. You play a treacherous game to anger a member of the Brehon. You should take care in your actions and speech. Soft words butter no parsnips, but they will not harden the heart of a cabbage either."

"I care neither for buttered parsnips nor cabbage if I must sup with Bryan tonight."

"Tonight! Forever is what *Athair* has in mind. If he had his way, you would be wed tomorrow."

"There will be white blackbirds before an unwilling woman ties the knot."

"If *Athair* hears you say that, 'twill be the last words out of your mouth."

Sorcha didn't want to admit just how much truth Niamh revealed. *Athair* said if she couldn't find a man to suit her before Imbolc, the time of harvest when many weddings were arranged, then she would be wed to Bryan. She held back a shudder.

Niamh wagged her finger at Sorcha. "I will have no part of this business with Conn. No part of it, I tell you."

"Truly I am not as evil as all that."

Just desperate to escape my betrothal to Bryan.

"Nay, but I know you well, Sister. And I can see the workings of your mind."

"You wish you could cast a spell with such power. Then you would be the most popular woman in the tribe."

"I do not need powers. Only eyes. I saw you nearly faint

when you set your greedy eyes upon Conn's handsome face."

Sorcha didn't reply. Approaching the edge of the village, they spied other people. Sorcha smiled and waved at her friends as though she and Niamh were talking about the weather instead of bickering. "Does my interest in the holy man bother you?"

"Nay, I have my beloved Niall. And why should you give up your chance to wed Bryan? He is a wit and comely. And eager to wed you." Niamh smiled at a group of children playing in dirt.

Realizing she could be overheard, Sorcha lowered the volume of her voice. "But the holy man is a challenge. I should enjoy a battle of wits. I am sure I can convince him of his folly. After we speak, he will see that the gods we worship are much better than his God." And spending time with him would get Bryan out of her life. . .or at least any important part of it.

"But our gods make no promise of eternal life," Niamh protested.

Sorcha recalled a verse Conn quoted, a saying that Jesus' disciple John wrote and taught: *For God so loved the world, that he gave his only begotten Son, that whosoever believeth in him should not perish, but have everlasting life.*

"Everlasting life," Sorcha muttered more to herself than her sister.

"So you were listening not just observing his comely face."

Their lodge loomed ahead. Sorcha quickened her step. "I do not know if I wish for everlasting life, but I want Conn."

"You are a charmer, Sorcha, but this time I venture you place too much confidence in your wit to woo. And in spite of his fair face, why waste your time? I heard Conn came here to be alone with his God not seek a wife," Niamh informed her with a prim purse of her mouth. "If you truly do not wish to wed Bryan, you can see for yourself that we have many other hardy men in our tribe. Despite your penchant for mischief, because of our *athair's* position you can make a claim for any man you wish."

"Aye, they all want to marry *Athair's* position through me. I want to marry for love—not because I am the poet's daughter." Sorcha licked her lips at the prospect of the challenge Conn presented. "The holy man has already attracted the love of many."

"The love of words but not of the heart."

Sorcha opened the door to the lodge, a solid structure of appropriate dimensions to house a member of the king's inner circle and his family. "Oh? I am not so certain. I believe there are others who would be glad to call Conn their own." She allowed a sly smile to visit her lips. "In fact, I anticipate a healthy challenge in attracting his attention."

"Then I wish for you to find many four-leaf shamrocks," Niamh remarked as they crossed the threshold. "You will need them all."

The next evening, Sorcha pulled a blue shawl over the bottom portion of her face, clutched a small pot of stew, and slipped out of the lodge after they had their own meal so *Athair* wouldn't miss her. Niamh wouldn't divulge her secret. Sorcha had the rest of the evening to her designs.

As she walked the path, she noticed that the concoction of broth, vegetables, and special herbs—herbs sure to have an effect on Conn—smelled so delicious they tempted her to take a bite. But no, this stew was made just for Conn. Sorcha let a smile of victory settle on her face. She couldn't wait for the comely holy man to partake of the stew. As soon as he did, she would prove irresistible.

She looked up at the trees, with their green leaves that flowed into strong trunks, rooted in grass as green as the emerald stone set in the pendant she customarily wore—the stone as green as Conn's unforgettable eyes. The trees seemed to breathe with her, assuring all was well. Despite the heaviness of the pot she carried, Sorcha nearly danced along the pathway. Certainly the gods were with her.

Conn heard Sorcha's voice from just outside the cave. "I am here with supper."

Under his breath, he whispered one last prayer for strength to resist the temptation of being near to such loveliness. How he wished he hadn't agreed to let her bring him a meal, no matter how much his stomach growled for food. Sorcha's beauty and charm were formidable. Was she a spy for her *athair*, or did she seek knowledge of the one true God? Conn shook thoughts of intrigue out of his head. If she had been a spy, she wouldn't have been forthcoming about her birthright as the bard's daughter. She would have dressed in the lowly garb of a slave woman to trick him. No, Sorcha didn't seem to be a deceiver. She was a genuine seeker.

He hoped.

And he hoped she had brought her sister with her.

He rushed to the cave's opening. Only Sorcha awaited.

"Where is your sister?" Although he realized the question might seem impolite, he had to ask.

Sorcha's eyebrows rose. "Did I promise to bring her?"

Conn recalled their conversation. "No, I cannot say that you did."

"Well, then. As you can see, she is not here. I regret if that is a disappointment to you." Sorcha's tone sounded anything but sorry.

"I seek to counsel only those who wish to hear my teachings. I have no desire to impose Christianity on anyone who is not willing or able to hear the Good News."

"Niamh is willing and able. She is the one who asked me to come last night. I—I can bring her next time."

Conn wondered what tripped the speech of a woman exuding such confidence. Despite her charming and newly revealed vulnerability, Conn wasn't sure there should be a next time. Scripture said to avoid all appearance of evil, yet he was about to share a meal with a beautiful woman—alone.

Heavenly Father, what should I do? He'd asked the same thing over and over between thoughts of Sorcha, yet heard no discernable answer. He could use her to reach the leaders of her people, or she could ruin him.

Sorcha tapped a sandal-clad foot on the ground. "Well, do you plan to let me stand here all evening, or shall I enter?"

Conn considered barring her entry, but the tantalizing scent of herbs and vegetables boiled in broth floated to his nostrils. The odors filled the air with an aroma that promised a quick end to the hunger pangs his stomach sent, a reminder—along with the setting sun—that the evening meal should be taken.

"This pot is heavy, and this clay vessel will hold the heat of the stew only a short time," Sorcha reminded him.

If only Sorcha's own clay vessel—the body that contained her soul—wasn't so lovely! Conn shook his brain of such a notion and nodded. "All right. Come in."

He had made the cave as comfortable as he could, but as he escorted her into his abode, he noticed how she stared at the unadorned wall and squinted in darkness. His cave was lit by a single tallow candle placed on a thin stone ledge and by the cooling embers from his hearth near the entrance.

"Surely this dwelling is mean in comparison to your lodge," he noted.

"It suits you."

"I am a bit rough at the edges, eh?"

"Hardly." He sensed she wished she hadn't blurted out her observation. "I mean it suits your purpose since I understand you will not be living here long." She set the pot on the blanket he had spread on the ground. "Where will you go next?"

"Where the Lord leads." He motioned for her to sit. "I wish I could offer you a fine skin to sit upon. I fear your garment will be spoiled." He had a thought. "Wait."

She stopped mid-motion as he retrieved the only other garment he possessed, a second tunic. He folded it and placed it upon the ground, making the wool as thick as he could to offer her the most amount of comfort.

"Many thanks." Her gratitude sounded sincere. She took the provisional seat, tucking her legs in a sharp angle that caused her feet to touch her backside, a modest and ladylike pose.

"My best is the least I can do for you."

He sat down on the hard ground, ankles crossed. Then he remembered that he didn't possess adequate supplies to host a meal. "I am afraid I only own one conveyance." He dished the herb and vegetable-laden broth into a clay bowl and extended it to her. "Here. Partake of this, and I shall dine after you."

Her face softened. "I brought the stew for your pleasure. I have no desire to partake."

"Are you sure?"

"Aye."

Setting down the bowl, Conn wondered why Sorcha wouldn't wish to eat a meal that promised to be delectable, but her closed expression told him not to press. He shut his eyes, bowed his head, and placed his palms together, letting his first two fingertips touch his chin. "Let us pray." He opened his mouth to begin the blessing, but she interrupted before he could utter the Lord's name.

"Pray? Why?"

He opened his eyes. "For God to bless our meal to the nourishment of our bodies."

"Is this blessing a spell?" To Conn's shock, Sorcha rose to her feet. Her green eyes, soft and inviting before, had taken on a flame of ire. "Do you believe your God must protect you from illness caused by eating my stew?"

He resisted the urge to rise to his feet, not wanting to appear menacing. "Nay. I am eager to partake."

"Then why—"

"I pray a blessing before each meal so the Lord will use its nourishment to give me the strength to do His will."

"Truly?" She seemed too puzzled to speak.

"Truly. Please, sit with me." He motioned toward the rough blanket he had spread out on the floor.

He waited for her to be seated once more, but she hesitated.

"Please. Take your seat, as rough as it is. I beg your pardon that I am not able to be a proper host. I did not always live in a spare manner." He made note of the polished stones set in gold she wore on her fingers and around both wrists, and then observed once again the pendant swinging from her girdle. For the first time, he noticed an image. "What is that carved in the stone?"

Apparently his interest softened her heart. She sat on the tunic. Leaning closer, she pulled the pendant toward him. "It is an image of my goddess, Brigid. Is she not beautiful?" Satisfied that she was, Sorcha turned the pendant toward herself and studied the image. "What does I AM look like?"

"We have no images of Him."

"Then how do you know He is real?"

"How do you know Brigid is real?"

Sorcha sniffed and let go of the pendant so it fell against her tunic. "Your God is for the poor who have little to enjoy here on Earth. I prefer a goddess who blesses me here on Earth."

"God is not just for the poor." He leaned closer to her as though betraying a confidence. "Like you, I was born to wealth."

"You were?" She set her glance on her surroundings until it landed on his bedding made of undyed fabric. "Then where is your thick bedding?" She tugged on the wool under her legs. "Where are your colorful tunics?"

Conn didn't blame her for her disdain. Not long ago, he would have reacted in like manner. He followed her gaze, trying to recall the time he might have seen his humble hut through her eyes. He had constructed a minimal pyre to keep warm and to cook the fish he caught and the occasional rabbit he shot with bow and arrow. He could visualize the fine stone kiln her cooks used.

A small sack of grain and parcel of dried fruits and vegetables rested against the wall next to his bow and quiver, small fishing net, and skin for water. He regarded his stew, served as it was in a sturdy but hardly fine piece of pottery. Sorcha had likely dined sitting at a comfortable table, eating and sipping from bronze implements, and anticipating a soft bed well off her floor, which would not be of dirt but of smooth stone. He wondered why she didn't turn and flee from such a wild place.

"Do you miss fineries?" Her observation sounded more like a statement than a query.

He shrugged. "Not as much as I once believed I would." The temptation to share the description of Jesus' encounter with the rich young ruler crossed his mind, but Sorcha's tightened lips told him she wasn't ready. "I miss my parents and sisters in Britain, but now I travel with what I can carry on my back. I find the lack of possessions freeing."

"As long as you have enough to eat and a place to lie down at night."

"Aye." The stew was growing cold. "And if I may partake—"

"Please."

"Will you bow your head?"

"Bow my head? Is that part of the blessing ritual?"

"Aye. It demonstrates one's humility before God."

"Oh." She hesitated. Conn wondered if perhaps the daughter of a bard didn't want to appear humble. "Your words are sound. I will hear your prayer."

He bowed his head. "God of power and might, humbly we enter Your presence. Holy is Your name. Bless this gift of food to our health and service to Your kingdom, here and in the hereafter. Amen." He felt an unusually strong sense of peace.

Sorcha made no movement.

"Will you not share my bread and drink?"

"Alms from the other villagers?" she guessed.

"Aye."

"I shall not partake of food meant for a holy man's purposes."

"But you are my guest."

"This eve, you are my guest."

Seeing that to insist would be useless, Conn let the vegetables and herbs floating in broth fill his mouth with warmth and leave a pleasant trail of heat as the liquid traveled to his stomach. He fought back a feeling of self-consciousness as she watched him eat, but the stew tasted so good, he didn't hesitate to finish it.

"I see you like my cooking." Triumph colored her voice and expression.

"You made this yourself?"

"Aye. Who else?"

"I—I thought perhaps your cook prepared it."

Sorcha looked down at her tunic. "Several cooks are under our command, but today I prepared this stew with mine own hands, especially for you."

"I am both flattered and honored." Belly full, he felt relaxed. "Since you went to so much trouble, tell me, what questions might I answer for you?"

"Questions?"

"Is that not why you asked to bring me dinner? So we could spend time in learning?" Although he usually washed his bowl after each meal, he decided to set it aside for the time being so he could pay attention to his guest. Remembering how Jesus preached to Mary and Martha, he decided chores could wait as he tried to bring Sorcha closer to a saving knowledge of Him.

"Uh, aye." Her expression reminded him more of a sheep lost in the woods than a woman prepared to learn about Christ. She looked down at her hands and rubbed her thumbs together so hard he almost expected sparks.

Surmising she was nervous, he tried to help. "I noticed you for the first time yester night. Had you seen me teach before then?"

"Nay."

"Then 'tis no wonder you feel uneasy. The gospel is so overpowering with its message that it is not easy to understand at first." He resisted the urge to reach over and pat her tunic-clad knee. "Please. Feel at liberty to pose any question. Perhaps you would like to know the circumstances of the birth of Jesus?"

She shrugged. "Aye."

He retold the account of His birth—how a young woman was visited by an angel and told she would give birth to a savior, and her betrothed's doubts and courage, how Jesus was born in a stable and His family's flight to faraway Egypt to protect their newborn. Yet he didn't feel the energy he usually experienced when he shared the exciting story. Perhaps he didn't discern exhilaration from his student. Sorcha never interrupted, but she stared at him as though she expected something. What? Surely she didn't think he would fall asleep, as his heavy eyelids threatened to force him to do.

To her dismay, Sorcha watched Conn fall asleep. How he slumbered on such a rough floor covering, she didn't know. But the sound of snoring filled the cave.

How had he managed to resist her charms? Sorcha looked her best. When Conn greeted her earlier that evening, his eyes had even held the familiar glimmer of interest she had seen in Bryan's eyes too many times to count. Yet despite Sorcha's charm—and the herbs in her stew—Conn kept his focus on telling her about the birth of his Lord.

She remembered her carefulness in preparing the hearty fare, and the words she said—words that should have guaranteed a successful seduction. Then she recalled that Conn had said an incantation over the stew. Had his words been more powerful than her own?

Could Conn's God be more powerful than Brigid's enchantments?

Sorcha felt grateful that no one had witnessed her abject failure. Sorcha, the most beautiful maiden in the tribe, had failed in her plot to beguile a simple holy man.

Chapter 4

Sorcha's distress grew as she sat on the improvised cushion on the floor of the cave and watched Conn sleep. Now that he offered neither conversation nor protection, she became aware of water dripping in the back of the cave. She shuddered at the thought of what might be waiting in the dark and contemplated awakening her companion. At that moment, he let out a snort and turned onto his side.

Even if she did manage to awaken him, Sorcha imagined he would be in no mood for her seductive ploys. Not that she had cultivated any tricks beyond the herbs sprinkled into his stew and her petition to Brigid. For all her beauty and bluster, Sorcha had lived a life sheltered from aggressive men. *Athair's* power frightened away those who would take advantage, and few men fascinated Sorcha enough to stir her to flirt beyond witty barbs. Sorcha liked it that way.

Disappointed with the failure of her stew yet relieved not to be forced into learning seductive wiles, Sorcha rose and studied Conn's face. Unable to resist the masculine contours and the peaceful beauty of his expression, she bent over and kissed his cheek. His skin felt warm against her lips and rough like a man's but not off-putting as her little experience recalled.

Straightening, she wondered how his lips would feel against hers, certainly not wet and mushy, permeated with foul breath, as had been Bryan's latest advance.

"Curse this stew!" she hissed, astonishing herself with the disappointment that her kiss had failed to rouse Conn.

She bent over and picked up the pot with more energy than needed. After one last look at Conn, she hurried to the entrance of the cave and threw the remaining stew on the ground. The pottage made a plopping sound and seeped into the soil, leaving herbs and vegetables to rot above. Yet its demise failed to quench her anger.

Pot in hand, Sorcha forced a smile to her lips, hoping someone would see her when she emerged from his abode. Despite crowds he had attracted the previous evening, not a soul was nearby. At least, she didn't spy anyone. Then she remembered that Conn had told them he would be teaching again on the morrow. Everyone in the village apparently respected his wishes for an evening of solitude. Such respect foiled her hope for a witness to her plan.

She scowled as a cloud of anger hovered over her head, following her as she strode home. If Conn wasn't willing to pursue her, then she would devise another way to have him for herself.

What had gone wrong? She had made a plea to Brigid, and Conn had partaken of the special brew. He should have been charmed. Yet all he'd done was share his strange teachings with her.

If only he had not said that odd incantation over the meal—the blessing, he called it. Surely those words gave him the strength to resist. But not for long, if she had her way. Sorcha knew she would make Conn hers, and she knew just the falsehood she had to contrive.

He couldn't know that her plans for seduction had failed or that he hadn't even attempted to kiss her. That fact would make it easier to convince him—and everyone else—that he'd wronged her. She assumed he had no memory of their time together in the cave once he fell asleep. So he could not affirm or deny that he'd taken advantage of the daughter of the king's bard. Since Sorcha was the only witness to what really happened, everyone would believe her, perhaps even Conn himself, for she'd seen the light of attraction in his eye. Holy or nay, he was a man.

Once her accusations were made known, *Athair* would demand that Conn marry her or pay her honor price. Since he was already a pauper and had no clan to pay it in his stead, the honor price was out of the question, leaving marriage as the holy man's only option. If he refused to redeem her honor with a wedding, Conn would pay with his life. The thought sent shudders to her body and remorse to her soul.

Conn's teaching about God's commandment not to lie leapt into her mind like a goat, gnawing at her conscience, but Sorcha banished the beast as she passed the deserted wooden village well.

I will do anything to avoid wedding Bryan.

The evening meal completed, most of the villagers were inside their lodges or had gone to the king's hall. Voices could be heard from inside the sod houses of the laborers and the circular lodges of the wealthy as Sorcha made her way to her home near the center of the village, near the king's own abode. Like all the noble homes, her home was white, the result of a generous coating of lime. She could see it on the horizon.

"Sorcha?" a female voice called.

" 'Tis I." She knew without looking that the voice belonged to Mór, a neighbor near her age and one of the town's most vicious gossips.

Perfect.

Mór drew closer, wearing a colorful tunic that revealed her family's elevated status, only one rank below Flann's. Mór's expression twitched with her effort to conceal delight at having found a juicy bit of gossip prancing in her gaze. She waved her hand in the direction of the pot Sorcha held. "What is that you have there?"

"I took supper to the holy man."

Mór's expression twisted as though she was trying to keep from revealing her delight in discovering a secret. "The holy man? But I heard he was not teaching tonight."

"He was not."

"But—"

"We shared a stew alone."

"Did you now?" Mór crossed her arms and hiked a skeptical brow. "I did not know you required healing."

"I do not." Sorcha tapped her foot.

"Then what business did you have with him?"

"Just the meal."

"Just sharing a meal? Every woman in the tribe would give her eyeteeth to share time with him alone. Brigid shines upon you." Envy as green as Sorcha's emerald pendant colored Mór's voice.

"Indeed." Sorcha gave her a coy smile. "Well, now. I must be on my way." She skipped back to her lodge, content that her revised plot was unfolding exactly as she'd intended.

Conn opened his eyes to the dim view of sunrise and a fire long since reduced to embers. Realizing he had somehow slept all night without retreating to his bed, he rubbed his head. Why did it ache so? He stretched and then massaged the back of his neck, where a tributary of pain pulsed.

"What happened to me?"

Then he remembered. He had been dining with the daughter of the king's bard, wolfing down delicious stew and telling her about the Lord and about blessing each meal. He hadn't sensed he was reaching her, yet her expression suggested intense attention. Then nothing.

Fear streaked through his being, and he bolted to an upright position. Had the bard's daughter been stricken as well? "Sorcha! Where are you?" he called.

Only his echo answered.

"Sorcha?"

Still nothing.

Conn took a rush dipped in animal fat and lit it from the left-over embers of his fire then ventured to the far end of the cavern to seek Sorcha. But he found no sign of the young woman. His breath of relief resounded against the cave walls and back. "She must have left. Thank you, Lord, for her sound judgment. I should have sent her away the moment I realized her sister wasn't with her. I pray Your forgiveness for my lack of judgment."

Never could he let anyone think he had entertained Sorcha overnight. His reputation, and hers, would be jeopardized should rumors develop. Her strange attentiveness came back to him, nagging him, as though an answer might lay there to why he'd fallen asleep. She'd refused to eat, he recalled, suspicion mounting. As the daughter of a druid, she'd be privy to the herbs to render sleep. Could she have put such a concoction in the stew? Why?

Thieving? Conn dismissed the thought. She was wealthy. None of his meager belongings would appeal to a lady of her stature. Still, he checked, finding his pouch beneath his rough-hewn blanket and hay-stuffed pillow exactly as he'd left it.

Conn placed his hands on both sides of his head as though to squeeze out the doubt and alarm assailing him. Jesus admonished that worry would not add one cubit to a person's stature. "Lord, protect me from needless anxiety. I pray I have not cause for concern."

"Sorcha!" *Athair's* voice bellowed throughout the lodge.

Sorcha set down the basket of flax she planned to weave into linen for new bedding and tried not to look afraid. A half day had passed since Sorcha had met Mór. Word had spread fast. Too fast. Even though the confrontation was part of her plan, she dreaded speaking to *Athair*.

Sorcha had brought *Athair's* wrath upon herself. She had to face him with courage. Two slaves who had been helping her sort flax quivered and sent Sorcha worried looks.

"Go," she instructed.

They sent her grateful nods and hastened outdoors.

Athair entered. "There you are." Contrary to his usual self, his voice held no regard for her favored position. Sorcha felt grateful that Niamh had already left to join the other women in their sewing tasks.

"Good morning, *Athair*." She hoped her voice sounded normal.

He narrowed his blue eyes until the irises nearly disappeared under massive dark eyebrows. "What is this I hear about you supping alone with the holy man?"

"I–I—"

"You never falter in your speech. 'Tis true, then!" As he wagged his finger, his sleeve waved, reflecting his fury. "Why did you not invite him to sup with us?"

Sorcha stalled at this unexpected reaction. "So you believe that I denied you knowledge? I thought you would want none of his strange teachings shared in this house."

Athair crossed his arms and tilted his head at her. "Truth is great and will win out. Once people discover the folly behind this so-called religion, the holy man will move on." He grimaced. "Christianity. An urban religion to be sure, of little use to us. So why did you seek him out, especially without an escort?"

She hesitated, rethinking the idea of accusing Conn falsely. But he was noble, humble, righteous—everything Bryan was not. And she'd seen admiration in a man's gaze enough to know that she held some attraction for Conn. Once they became man and wife, he would grow to love her. She just knew he would.

She swallowed. " 'Twas folly."

"Aye. In my efforts not to withhold any knowledge—true or false—from you," he continued, "I did not endeavor to put a stop to your attendance of his meetings. But now you must cease. I will not have you getting too close to this holy man."

"But I already have, *Athair*," Sorcha blurted.

Athair's eyes widened. "What?"

"I was alone with him last evening." Her voice sounded weak. She observed the basket of flax on the floor beside her feet. Better to face *Athair's* ire than a lifetime of Bryan's boorishness.

"What?" The rage she anticipated resounded in his voice.

"I should not have done so. He—he was not chaste in the way of a holy man."

Athair loomed large over her, taking her forearms in his clutches with such force she thought they would be crushed. "He took liberties with you?"

"You are hurting me, *Athair*."

He released her arms then took her into an embrace. "Sorcha, my Sorcha. I knew this man was nothing but trouble. Bryan tried to warn me. If only I had insisted that the two of you wed immediately instead of issuing a foolish command that you find someone before Imbolc."

Sorcha shuddered.

Athair broke away and looked into her eyes. "I shall have him killed, I shall!" He called for his closest and most faithful slave. "Bearach!" He paced the room. "Bearach! Now!"

Bearach hurriedly entered. "Aye, my lord."

"Send for our champion Bryan."

The slave nodded.

"Wait! Do not have Conn killed!" Sorcha ran to *Athair* in a panic and grasped at the sleeve of his tunic. "It was not his fault."

Athair held up his hand to instruct Bearach to wait. "Was it not?"

"Yes. . .no. . .I mean would you go against the law and demand death before he is offered the chance to redeem my honor?"

He tapped his foot with one firm motion, his aged face a battleground between fatherly outrage and druidic sensibility. A new guilt fell upon Sorcha's heart at seeing her characteristically collected *athair* so distraught. "*Athair*, if you will allow me to say so, I would consent to a handfasting instead."

"You want to wed this man?" *Athair's* voice sounded confused.

Though she felt far from noble, Sorcha drew herself up to her full height and flooded her voice with conviction. "I will make the sacrifice to save his life."

Two days had passed since Conn had last seen Sorcha. Unable to keep her luminous image and quick wit from his mind, he stirred the fire with a stick. Part of him was relieved, but another part grieved not to have seen her among the crowds who'd gathered since her odd visit to listen to God's Word.

"Conn! Holy man, where are you?" a man shouted in the distance from the cave's mouth.

Placing Sorcha in the back of his mind where she was less worrisome, Conn set down the stick and prepared to greet his visitor. A holy man's time belonged to the people God loved, not whimsy.

Approaching the entrance, he wondered about his visitor. Was he a seeker wanting answers to pressing concerns, or perhaps someone so exuberant about the faith that he wanted immediate baptism? Or was the man seeking another answer, namely Sorcha's whereabouts? What would he say? Conn shook such a thought out of his head. Surely the notion could only be attributed to a guilty conscience. Though innocent of wrongdoing, Conn felt anxiety grip his belly.

Once he arrived at the entrance, Conn saw two men dressed in fine tunics of rich hues that bespoke their high positions. Wrinkles etched on his face announced that the taller of the two, a stranger to Conn, had seen many seasons. Conn recognized the younger, a man of plain face and bright red hair, as a member of the crowds he taught. The young man was prone to argument. Unless God had worked a miracle in his heart, his presence could only mean trouble.

"I greet you a free man. I am Bryan, one of the tribal Brehon," the arguer said.

Bryan was a member of the Brehon—one of the wise men? No wonder he never hesitated to challenge Conn. Undoubtedly his senior companion was of the same order.

Conn acknowledged him with a nod. "Greetings. Peace be with you."

Bryan twitched his lips then nodded to the older man. "This is Flann, the king's bard."

Flann. Sorcha's father!

"Greetings, and may peace be with you as well." Conn straightened his features so as not to show his fear and dread. "Meeting you both is indeed my distinct privilege. And to what do I owe the honor of your visit?"

"Our visit is no honor, sir. Your kind deserves none." Bryan sneered.

The sun shone bright in the sky overhead, but Bryan's answer fell over Conn like a cold, wet cloak. "Then tell me how I might have offended you, that I may ask forgiveness."

"We are told that you entertained a maiden from our tribe this week."

"I did," Conn admitted, the earlier suspicion of Sorcha and the food she would not partake of coming back to haunt him.

"You do not deny it in front of her father?" Bryan's voice was sharp.

"Nay. I do not deny that a young lass brought me a stew two days ago." Conn glanced at Flann and saw his lips tighten.

"And she was known to you?" Hostility seethed beneath the question.

"She is known to me as Sorcha. I have not seen her since."

"What gave you the right to invite her to your abode?" Bryan asked.

Conn returned his gaze to Bryan. He reminded Conn of a wolf pup trying to establish his place in the pack.

"I invited her not," Conn answered. "She asked if she could bring me a meal. Since she was among those who came to listen to my teachings, I assumed that she was a seeker and wanted to learn more about Jesus. She was with her sister, introduced to me as Niamh. I thought she was to bring Niamh with her so that both could learn more from me as we shared a meal."

Bryan didn't stop to contemplate the story. "So you did not object to the fact that you believed the meal came at a price?"

"Nay. I am not ashamed to accept alms in return for my teachings. Such a practice is not against your law. In fact, I believe your law requires hospitality."

"Not for a maiden to serve alone in a pauper's cave!"

Bryan's relentless barrage accompanied by Flann's silence made Conn increasingly ill at ease, but whatever they meant to find out, he preferred that they keep to a familiar setting than to take him before a formal court. "Aye."

"But Sorcha appeared here alone, without her sister, did she not?"

"As I said before, she insisted on bringing stew, and she appeared alone."

"Why did you not send her home immediately?"

Conn could see from the way Bryan's voice took on an accusing tone that tumult awaited. He sent up a silent prayer for guidance and then spoke. "She insisted that we share the stew, and I had not the heart or, I am ashamed to admit, the stomach to send her home."

"Not a fasting day when the company is so beguiling, eh, holy man?" Bryan noted.

"Had it been a day of fasting, I would never have accepted her invitation to bring me supper. But since it was not, I accepted her delicious stew."

"My Sorcha is skilled in cooking." Flann's expression bespoke his pride. "And her wit is sharp as the needle she wields."

"Never have I tasted such sweet broth, laden with ginger, I think."

The sudden exchange of looks between his visitors gave Conn cause for concern. He thought he heard Flann mutter the word "Brigid" beneath his breath, although what Brigid had to do with food eluded Conn.

Flann let out a resigned sigh. "Our Sorcha is quite the mischief-maker, but nevertheless, our tribe cannot allow the daughter of the king's bard to be disgraced."

"Disgraced?" Surprise and anxiety poached themselves in his gut. Their reaction suggested that Sorcha had made it for more than nourishment. "I have done not a thing to disgrace anyone."

"She says you were not chaste with her, and she is to be believed," Bryan said.

Shock jolted Conn from his speculation. "Why, I did nothing of the kind. I would never dishonor any woman in such a way."

"Why should we believe you?" Bryan asked.

"Because immediately after the meal, I fell asleep. I do not even remember when she departed."

Bryan let out an ugly laugh. "You fell asleep in the company of the most beautiful woman in our tribe? Why, if such an opportunity had presented itself to me—"

So Bryan loved Sorcha! Conn took in a breath.

Bryan set his features back into a stern expression and glowered at Conn. "Death is not too lenient a sentence for you."

"Let not hatred taint your thinking, Brehon. I no more deserve death than you, for I have not dishonored your loved one."

Bryan crossed his arms.

Flann spoke. "Bryan, you are a Brehon and entitled to wed an unblemished woman. I regret that my daughter has chosen to make for herself a thorny bed. Now she must lie in it."

"What are you saying?"

"Bryan, you are a Brehon and know well the law. Death is the last resort for such an offense. Instead, Conn must either pay an honor price to our family or take Sorcha as his bride."

"For what?" Conn exclaimed.

"Are you calling my daughter a liar, holy man?" Flann challenged.

"Perhaps she misinterpreted—"

"He is not one of us. He is not subject to the law," Bryan argued.

Flann lost patience with his comrade. "I do not wish to stain my hands with the blood of a holy man, fool. Though I have no use for Christianity, what if Conn's God proves to be more powerful than ours? I will not be responsible for the death of His slave."

"But—"

"I suggest that you wed my daughter Niamh. Surely she has great attributes."

"And what of Sorcha? I have loved her since we were

children. She was promised to me!" Bryan's eyes took on a light of hurt. For the first time, Conn pitied him.

"I surmise that some promises are best broken when circumstances change," Flann said. "I propose a handfasting between Sorcha and Conn."

"A handfasting?" The reality of what they were suggesting sunk into Conn's mind. "Is this a wedding? If it is, then I must decline, even if it means my death. For you see, I can only be wed by a priest of the Christian church."

Flann took a half step toward Conn. "You would choose death over marriage to my daughter?"

"I would choose death over disobeying my Lord."

"An impressive sentiment," Flann admitted. "Then let me elaborate on the conditions of the handfasting. It is a marriage of the fourth degree. If after a year there are no children, the union can be broken without consequence."

Conn reflected upon his words for a moment. Under this arrangement, time would prove his innocence. He had no other choice. "All right, then. I shall agree to the handfasting."

Chapter 5

I shall be wed! I shall be wed!" Sorcha's singing rang throughout the lodge. She waved her arms, sending her sleeves flitting.

"Stand still! I cannot measure your hem with you moving about." Niamh spoke from bended knee. "I wish you had told me about your plans. Then I could have sewn my sister a proper wedding tunic."

"Proper tunic or nay, I shall be wed!"

"And I am stuck with your Bryan." Niamh yanked her needle.

"Worry not. I shall mend all with *Athair* so you, too, can escape marriage to Bryan."

"Just as you fixed your handfasting to Conn, eh?" Niamh rose, accusation in her gaze.

Sorcha's elated spirit evaporated. "So you believe him over me."

"You can keep away from the rogue, but you cannot keep yourself safe from the liar."

" 'Tis afterward that everything is understood," Sorcha countered. "Conn and I will be happy. I just know it."

"You know what the dowagers say. 'Marriages are all

289

happy. It is having breakfast together that causes all the trouble.' "

A slave entered. "I beg pardon for interruptin', but the holy man awaits outdoors." Her voice quaked with awe. "He has asked to see you, milady."

"Conn!" Sorcha blurted. Did he wish to challenge her about the deception? She was sure that confronting *Athair* and Bryan hadn't been easy for him. Bryan hadn't spoken to her since, and *Athair's* attitude remained chilly—and they loved her. How much harder for Conn, a stranger. Had he changed his mind?

She tried to buy time. "Tell him I am busy preparing for the wedding, but I shall see him at the ceremony."

"See him now," Niamh urged. "Whatever he has to say must be important."

Pride wouldn't let Sorcha flee. She addressed the slave. "Help me change back into my tunic, and then you may see him in."

When he entered moments later, Conn's lips were positioned in a straight line. Sorcha greeted him with a smile. She batted her eyelashes and moved closely so he could take in the enticing scent of her wildflower perfume. Yet his stern expression remained unchanged. She braced herself for a lecture as she looked into his eyes. To her surprise, they held sorrow rather than admonishment.

"Our handfasting is on the morrow." Sorcha was unable to conceal her excitement.

"As you wished." He pursed his lips. "I have been in prayer." His expression held no warmth, his voice no emotion—hardly the ways of an eager bridegroom.

"I know our haste is the source of gossip, but do not let

wagging tongues discourage you." Sorcha crushed the material of her skirt with nervous fingers.

"I fear not wagging tongues. But I do have something I feel obligated to say."

His gentle tone urged her to allow her gaze to meet his. "Aye?"

She thought she saw a flicker of interest, a hint of compassion. But if he felt any such emotions, he squelched those sentiments with a stern countenance. "The ceremony binds us for a year and a day."

"Aye." Long enough to rid her of Bryan.

"I have no plans for us to remain together. After the period has expired, I will be moving to another glen to spread my teachings to other tribes."

"Unless love is born."

"My ministry comes ahead of all else."

"As well it should," she said, scrambling for the advantage. "But I am willing and able to travel with you for love's sake."

"Such hardship is too difficult for a tender woman. And there will be no romantic love. After the appointed time, we shall part."

Then I shall have to break my promise to Niamh. I shall never marry Bryan.

Conn's voice broke into her machinations. "Do not question your desirability, but my desire to live for God is stronger." He turned toward the entrance. "I shall depart for now. We shall meet at the appointed time."

Sorcha felt glad that Conn was a Christian. But while his eagerness to break the covenant as soon as was permissible didn't promise an auspicious beginning to their union, at least she had a year and a day to make Conn a part of her eternity.

Despite drizzling rain, the next day the entire tribe attended the handfasting ceremony. Sorcha knew she looked her finest in her beautiful tunic. The sisters' stitchery bespoke their talent, but rich embroidery was not the target of envy with young women. Her groom was.

Only as she walked toward the high priest as the ceremony began did Sorcha realize the seriousness of her vow. Still, she did not delay to promise that she was there of her own accord and felt grateful to the gods that Conn didn't waver. As the ceremony closed, the couple was crowned with garlands with circular forms representing nature's cycles. But when the priest asked that they close with a kiss, the surreal spell holding Sorcha captive burst.

A kiss! No one in the crowd had any idea that the kiss on the lips would be Sorcha's first—from Conn or anyone else. Seeing how nervous Conn appeared, she suspected that he, too, would experience his first kiss in front of the tribe. Nevertheless, they brought their lips toward one another and made sweet contact. Conn's lips were warm and soft—softer than Sorcha dreamed a man's mouth could be. She wanted his touch to linger. Not wishing to control herself, she clutched her arms around his shoulders for an embrace. But he broke free. She studied his expression as long as time permitted. He looked embarrassed but not unhappy amid hoots and applause.

There will be more kisses. Many more.

Their new life together had begun.

Conn wasn't sure what to expect when he brought his beautiful new bride to his cave after the feast. He was a man, and the temptation to claim her physically had not lessened. Though the handfasting gave them the right to live in every way as man and wife under druid law, Conn was bound by the guidelines of Christianity, which forbade him to treat Sorcha as his wife since the ceremony wasn't Christian.

Despite prayer and fasting, Conn possessed strong feelings toward this fiery young woman. Those feelings made him wonder if Sorcha had told the truth. Had he given in to his desires and taken advantage of an innocent, meaning he had created the dilemma?

If Sorcha's belly started to grow soon, all doubts would evaporate. If she was found not to be with child, he still wouldn't be absolved. Perhaps he would go to his grave never knowing if he was a man of honor or a man likely to give in to base wishes when an irresistible chance presented itself.

Remorse overwhelmed him. He had to show his grief.

He looked about the cave, which had taken on a new identity. Slaves from Sorcha's house had brought her possessions to his hovel earlier. Their rich colors and textures looked strange amid his few mean belongings. One was a tapestry she told him she had woven herself. A bright sun shone over emerald green grass and trees with like-colored leaves. People dressed in finery danced in celebration—the festival to the god Lugh, Sorcha explained. Conn found the tapestry beautiful yet disturbing. He didn't like the suggestion implied by the scene. Still, he knew he would be wrong to insist that Sorcha remove the thick weaving. Hanging from the ceiling of the cave, the cloth offered the only shelter between him and Sorcha as she dressed.

Battling over the tapestry would be pointless. Conn wanted

to concentrate on bringing Sorcha to a saving knowledge of the Lord rather than insisting that she adopt Christianity. Conn never wanted to place Sorcha in the position of accepting Christ only to please him or any other man. Conn decided to allow the Holy Spirit to do His work.

Driven to distraction by the movements behind the tapestry, Conn knew what he had to do. He made his way over to the pyre, where ashes remained. He took a generous helping of the dusty gray particles and poured them over his head, making sure they saturated his black locks and smeared his face. In spite of the fact that he owned few clothes, he rent his tunic.

"What was that?" Sorcha asked from behind the tapestry.

"My tunic. It is now ripped."

Sorcha emerged. Conn could smell her delicious fragrance of blossoms. Dressed in a filmy white gown and wearing the wreath of flowers on her head, Sorcha had never looked lovelier.

She opened her pink lips in a gasp of horror. "Conn! What happened?"

"I am showing my Lord how grief stricken I am over my sin that brought you into this circumstance. I shall remain this way for at least seven days, and after I speak this last word, I shall embark upon complete silence during that time. Forgive me, Sorcha, for all that I have done to wrong you."

He had hoped for a word of encouragement, but none was forthcoming. Instead she slid back behind the tapestry, her face grazed with pain.

Forgive me, Father in heaven.

Conn fell to his knees, summoning concentration to pray in silence over Sorcha's sobbing.

"What might I cook you for tonight's meal, Conn?" Sorcha asked a month later.

She was still unaccustomed to preparing food herself. Although *Athair* had allowed her to take two slaves to her new abode, Sorcha discovered that being handfasted to a holy man entailed more work than her former position as the carefree daughter of the king's bard. That day she had seasoned fish to be smoked for winter's preservation and gathered vegetables from the garden. Still, food wasn't as plentiful or luxurious as she remembered at home. Conn's teaching earned alms, but provisions from grateful tribe members were presented at irregular intervals. This was no surprise since Conn's teachings attracted the greater number of converts from lesser tribe members. No new Christians emerged from the powerful Brehon or the king's courtiers. If they wished to maintain their positions of influence, they dared not show interest in Conn's teachings.

"I am thankful for whatever provision you prepare as long as you promise not to enchant it."

Sorcha bristled even though she knew she deserved the barb.

His words wouldn't have been hurtful if she hadn't witnessed pain in his expression. Even though his time of formal mourning had passed and he had long since washed the ashes away and donned mended clothing, pain dwelled in his eyes, and his lips never turned upward into smiles that seemed to appear easily before the handfasting.

Even worse, despite the promise of the first kiss, he had never since tried to touch her. She made a point of drawing near to him often, but he never responded except to pull away from her. Sorcha tried everything—bathing in fragrance, sprinkling the linen bed covering with fragrant dried blooms, and beseeching Brigid's aid as she dosed a few meals with powerful herbs. Nothing worked. The slaves whispered when they noticed her failure.

For an instant, Sorcha almost wished she had never agreed to relinquish Bryan. He would have been glad to treat her as a husband treats a wife.

Just as quickly, the notion left her head. Sorcha didn't want Bryan and neither had Niamh. As it happened, Sorcha's promise to make amends to *Athair* proved needless. Once jilted by Sorcha, Bryan would have nothing more to do with their family. Mór was only too happy to step into Sorcha's place and agree to become Bryan's bride.

Sorcha cut her gaze to her own groom. If only Conn could muster some enthusiasm for her.

Curse that incantation he says over every meal!

"I promise not to charm the meal," she said aloud. "And why would I? 'Twould do no good."

"Have you not learned by now that Brigid's power is naught? There is only one power in this universe, and that is the power of the one true God."

Sorcha recoiled with such force that she nearly burned herself on the pot of boiling stew. "How can you utter such insult! Do you realize how much I will have to grovel to Brigid to make amends, lest she curse us?"

"I have no fear of your gods. Jehovah God is the one who determines whether I live or die in this life and the next."

"Perhaps He is insulted by your foolishness," Sorcha said. "If you continue, your life on the other side might not be a happy one."

Conn laughed, a gratifying emotion in another context. "My destination is paradise. If you will accept Him, you will have a place in heaven, too." He sent her a look that was as close to seduction as she had seen since the way he looked at her during the handfasting. Yet his face showed not mere seduction but an exploration into her soul.

"I do not deserve paradise." She twisted the end of her stick in the ground.

"No one can earn a place in heaven. You only receive the gift if you believe that Jesus is the Son of God."

Sorcha shook her head. "What a wonderful story. If only I could believe it."

Chapter 6

As months passed, Sorcha found no more success in growing close to Conn—at least not physically. She had ceased petitioning Brigid and the fertility goddess Anu. Nothing tempted Conn.

Sorcha stared at the simmering mutton stew, brought as an offering from a grateful convert. She rubbed her flat belly that did nothing to confirm her lie told months ago—but it didn't clear Conn, either. She turned her head so she could glance at him, with his legs crossed and eyes shut, palms facing heavenward.

She suspected he prayed for her. She marveled at his mercy. Trapped into a handfasting, Conn had every right to act in spite. Yet he never did. The kindness in his eyes and gentle tone he used toward her had won her heart. Her desire for physical connection remained unfulfilled. Yet she had to admit that Conn had treated her with more dignity and respect than she could ever have hoped for—or deserved. She couldn't imagine any other man being such a gentleman. Perhaps not taking advantage of the conditions of their handfasting was a way Conn expressed to Sorcha her worth.

Why?

She could only conclude that his faith led him in every

action. She watched him pray each day, seeking the will of his Lord in matters great and small. Even when focused on himself, Conn's prayers were not self-centered. Instead, he prayed for wisdom regarding seekers and resisters. She never heard him ask for his own betterment. Her people usually spoke to their gods only when they wanted something to increase their happiness on earth. The contrast made her want to know more.

Sorcha stirred the stew with firm strokes. She would admit only to herself that she had fallen away from her view of the world since living with Conn. She no longer asked Brigid to grant her wishes, although she couldn't yet bring herself to ask Jesus for anything. Sorcha felt pulled in two directions. She didn't like the feeling. Not one bit.

Frustrated, she left the wooden spoon in the cauldron. "Niamh told me that a handfasting shall be taking place in the village on the morrow. Will you go with me to witness?"

Conn opened his eyes and looked at her, not expressing vexation that she had interrupted. He shook his head as Sorcha expected. She shrugged and signaled her readiness to the slaves to serve dinner. As a daughter of the king's bard, she was expected to attend. At least Conn allowed her to participate without complaint.

She watched him in prayer, marveling at his fortitude and discipline. She had contrived the handfasting so she could escape marriage. Now that she was with Conn, she discovered that she wished nothing more than to be with him.

"Lord," he whispered, "keep Sorcha in Your care."

His voice evaporated as quickly as it had risen. Conn only prayed loudly enough for her to hear when his desire was fervent. She knew him; the prayer wasn't a ploy to get her attention or to gain her favor. She wondered if anyone else had ever prayed for her to any god. She doubted it. She felt her eyes mist.

Her conscience had experienced enough turmoil. She had to set Conn free.

Fear clutching her, she sat beside him. "Conn, I have a confession. If my words mean that you throw me out today, I will go and never return."

Conn didn't seem surprised. Had his God told him this would happen? He leaned close to her. "Sorcha, I do not know why the Lord brought you into my life, but nothing you say will cause me to evict you. Confession is good for the soul. Tell me what you are thinking."

She trembled in spite of his assurances. "I–I mean, you did not," she paused, took in a breath, and let the words flow in a quick stream. "You did not lay a hand on me the night I brought the stew."

His expression didn't register the amount of shock that she had anticipated. "Then I bid you to tell me what happened." His voice held no emotion. Sorcha would have welcomed anger rather than the hurt his green eyes betrayed.

"After you partook of the stew, I watched you sleep."

"Aye." He nodded. "I remember my embarrassment. I ate the stew and woke up to no recollection of the evening. But why did you lie?"

"To escape my betrothal to Bryan. And. . .and I wanted you for myself. When I first laid eyes upon you, I wanted you for my own regardless of the consequences."

"Regardless of the fact that such a lie could ruin us both?" His stare bored into her face, yet his voice still betrayed no anger.

"I knew you would not die. I would not have let the situation play out to such an end. I would have run away with you first. Anywhere." She extended her hand east. "To Rome, even. We

300

could have lived our lives in love without anyone bothering us." Sorcha flinched and aimed her face in the direction of the dirt floor to mitigate the anticipated slap across the cheek.

"Run away to Rome?"

"Aye." She dared to look into his face.

Instead of raising his hand, Conn chortled.

Athair, and certainly Bryan, would have struck her until she saw stars. Sorcha wasn't sure how to react to such a display of mercy. She looked at him in bewildered exasperation. "Are you a fool? I said I lied for my own selfish ends. Why do you laugh?"

He clutched his chest until his chuckling dissipated. "I laugh with relief, Sorcha. All this time, I believed that I had wronged you. To discover that I had not has given me a sense of liberty and righteousness I have not felt in a long time." He stared into her eyes. "Thank you. Thank you for setting me free."

"Free?" Though that had been her thought, she had hoped Conn wouldn't take her up on the bargain. "Then you are angry. You want me to go home."

"I know I should be angry, but the feeling escapes me. I do not know why. But 'tis a blessing."

" 'Tis indeed." Sorcha blinked back tears of relief. "I shall pack my possessions and return to my *athair's* house."

"Wait." He placed his hand on her shoulder. "Now I have a confession."

"You? What could you possibly have to confess?"

He smiled. "I have actually enjoyed our time together."

She thought about his time meditating, praying, and teaching. She was sure he barely noticed her. "You have?"

"Aye. I had settled in for a time of solitude and was wondering how I would muster the courage to face the day-to-day loneliness of a religious recluse."

"Loneliness? But crowds gather to hear you teach."

"They are good to listen to my humble attempt to spread the gospel. But being a friend and sharing my life with them is not possible. God provided for my need by bringing you into my life. Verily, that must be why I feel not a shred of anger."

"You think I am sent from your God?" Her voice betrayed her shock.

"Indeed. And a lovely lass He sent, too. You have proven to possess a sharp wit, and I have learned much about the ways and beliefs of your tribe by spending time in your company. I could not have asked for a more perfect answer to prayer."

Sorcha didn't know how to express her surprise and delight. Perhaps this God of whom Conn spoke lovingly deserved to be worshiped.

Bryan with his superior attitude and cocky ways never would have made such an admission or hinted that she offered him any conversational challenge. And *Athair*, though he loved her, considered her inferior. "But I am just a woman."

"Never say that. Did you know the Lord Jesus while He was with us here on the earth showed great love and respect for women?"

"A male deity showed us love and respect?"

"Listen the next time the crowd gathers, and I will teach with several examples from His life."

No matter how amazing Conn's God proved to be, Sorcha still felt resistance in her heart. "I do not need a male deity," she snapped with more vigor than she intended. "I worship Brigid, the goddess of light."

"Along with other gods and goddesses."

Knowing he was right, she remained silent.

"I found something for you. A simple gift. I feel led to

present it to you now."

"A gift?" Her voice showed surprise. Surely he had not bought her jewelry or imported fabric. Then what?

He withdrew a shamrock from the folds of his tunic, took her hands in his, and placed the fragile stem with its three leaves upon her palm. "See how this shamrock has three leaves?"

"Aye."

"The three leaves represent the Trinity: Father, Son, and Holy Spirit. Remember this each time you see a shamrock. Our heavenly Father watches over you day and night."

He closed her fingers around the little shamrock. Although she had heard him teach in this way before, by giving her the plant, Conn had brought a truth of his faith to her in a personal way. At that moment she realized she was special in his eyes, and the quivering of her heart showed her that she returned his feelings.

She felt compelled to offer a compromise. "If I can worship your God and mine, too, can you find it in your heart to worship both?"

"I am afraid not," Conn answered without hesitation or visible regret. "When Jehovah gave Moses the Ten Commandments, He said that He is a jealous God. As much as I want to please you, I cannot leave room for any other gods in my life."

"I understand," she said, even though she didn't. Why couldn't Conn meet her halfway? Why did this God ask so much?

Later that night as she made her way with the slaves to the handfasting ceremony of her neighbors in the village, Sorcha clutched the decorative bag hung from her waist where she'd placed the shamrock. And she thought of Conn. . .and of his God.

Chapter 7

The shamrock had long since withered, but Sorcha didn't care. She held on to it gently, checking on it from time to time to be sure it was still in place. She thought the shamrock no less valuable than if it had been a precious stone. But unlike the withering stem, her love for Conn grew. And she sensed that he loved her, too.

If only she could convince him to accept her fully as his wife. Though she wished for a physical union, her feelings for Conn had developed beyond bodily desire. She wanted a spiritual, mental, and emotional union, too. She'd come closer to his passions and mind, but his unwillingness to compromise regarding her gods bothered her.

Converts asked him for wisdom. Sometimes married people converted, but their spouses refused. The conflicts they described made the difficulties Conn and Sorcha faced pale in comparison. Conn taught against wedding non-Christians, admonishing against being unequally yoked. That term described their union, held together by the slim thread of handfasting.

At least Conn's teachings grew profitable. When they were handfasted, Conn owned one half-sick goat. Thanks to increased alms and new births, their flock had increased to the point that they required a shepherd. Food was always in such abundance that Sorcha and her slaves were kept busy with preparations.

Sorcha never lacked for exquisite cloth to fashion fine tunics. To her amazement, Conn gave the tunics to commoners. He preferred plain wool, although now at least his tunics weren't patched. He sought to minister as Jesus had, keeping what he required and giving the rest to the needy. But Sorcha understood that Jesus didn't have a wife to make Him fine tunics, and if He had, surely He'd not have given them away and hurt her feelings. Conn answered by telling her that the poor would be grateful to wear such fine garments they otherwise wouldn't have owned. He kept that scratchy, drab tunic.

"I am pleased to see that you have prepared all of the fish," Conn remarked, approaching from the glen after his midday prayers.

Sorcha eyed salted fish, an alm, drying on a rack handcrafted by a grateful convert. "Aye, are they not a fine catch?"

"Indeed, fine enough to share with the poor of the tribe."

Sorcha let out a groan. "But all of our work! Surely the poor can survive without our fish."

"We have an embarrassment of riches in food and in clothing." To demonstrate, Conn tugged on the fur-trimmed concession that kept him warm against the winter chill. "Let us put faith into practice by providing for those less fortunate."

"I know. Do not store up earthly treasures. Pack up the fish," she instructed the slaves. "We shall carry them into the village to share."

Conn rewarded her with a smile then exited the cave. Sorcha supposed he would continue praying.

"This is almost like the miracle of Jesus feeding the five

thousand," a slave girl observed.

She was right. No matter how much they gave to the poor, their goods increased. The development defied all logic, but Sorcha repeated Conn's teaching. "The Lord returns goods to those who provide for His sheep, and many of the poor have agreed to follow Christ."

"What about those who do not? Are we as generous to them?" the girl asked.

"Yes, we are," Sorcha answered.

"In hopes of converting them?"

"In hopes of loving them." Sorcha's response answered many of her own inquiries. For the first time, she realized the impact of God's love and understood why Conn acted the way he did. "Thank You, God."

"You mean, thank you, Brigid?" the slave prompted.

"No. I mean, thank you, God. Conn's God."

The slave's mouth dropped open far enough to catch flies. Sorcha wondered what she must look like, for no one was more surprised by her prayer than she. The petition gave her the realization of how deep her sin toward Conn had been. She knew what she had to do.

She hurried outdoors and found Conn not far from the entrance, standing alone, looking into a small gray cloud in an otherwise blue sky. She tugged on his sleeve. "Conn, we must go into the village. Now."

"Why?"

"We have known each other for three seasons. I ask you to trust me."

Conn didn't wait long to answer. "All right, then. I will trust you."

Sorcha almost wished he hadn't. But if she didn't go forward with her plan now, she might never again find the courage. She rushed back into the cave, slipped behind her tapestry, and donned her finery.

When she emerged, she discovered that Conn had done the same.

On the way to the village, with the slaves behind them carrying the fish, Sorcha wished he would hold her hand. The warmth of his touch would have consoled her. But he didn't offer, and she couldn't ask.

They were greeted by friendly waves and some stares as they headed toward her family lodge. A few people approached Conn to beg healing. Sorcha marveled at how he didn't neglect anyone. She imagined what Jesus must have felt like, and perhaps Patrick, who Conn said had first brought Christianity to Ireland.

Despite interruptions, they reached the lodge. As the slave answered the door, Niamh appeared. "Sorcha! What are you doing here?" She looked at Sorcha's companion. "And with Conn!"

The sisters exchanged an embrace before Sorcha answered. "I need to see *Athair*."

Worry struck her face. "Is everything all right?"

She swallowed a lump of nervousness. "I need *Athair* to call a meeting of the Brehon."

Niamh grasped Sorcha's forearms. "Something is amiss! Tell me what!"

Sorcha shook her head. "I cannot. But you may summon the rest of the tribe. What I have to say must be heard by all."

As they waited for *Athair* to arrive, Conn whispered, "You are going to confess?"

She nodded, looking down at the floor.

"Are you sure this is what you want to do?"

"It is not what I want to do." She returned her gaze to his eyes. "It is what I must do."

Athair entered with familiar bluster. "What is the meaning of this?" He narrowed his eyes at Conn. "I did not give you permission to enter my house."

"A thousand pardons. I shall depart." Conn turned to exit.

Sorcha grabbed him by the forearm. "He is handfasted to me with your full consent, *Athair*. He will remain by my side."

Athair snorted. "As you wish. I know you must be here for a reason, given that you have not entered my house since the ceremony. Tell me your business."

Sorcha obeyed. "We must call a meeting of the tribe."

"The day has begun. How do you expect us to disrupt everyone as they go about their duties?"

"This is urgent, or I would not ask. Summon whoever will come."

Flann tightened his lips, but his voice was gentle. "Though you are no longer a part of my household, you will always be my daughter. I believe that what you have to say warrants a meeting if you proclaim it is so."

"It is so."

A little breath escaped from his lips, and he rubbed his palms together. "Has the holy man decided to pursue the path of the druids?"

Sorcha knew that to answer would be folly. "All will be revealed in good time."

"I will have as many as I can assembled in the center of the village before the sun rises to its utmost in the sky." He departed.

"Do you want me to stay?" Conn asked.

"Of course. Nothing I have to say to my sister is too bold

for your ears." Sorcha eyed Niamh. "Is that not right, Niamh?"

"I have nothing to speak of, except my wedding feast day preparations. The day I wed my beloved Niall will be the best of my life."

Sorcha squeezed her hand. "Your happiness is my own."

"But the months fly quickly, and the time of your hand-fasting to be over is nigh."

Sorcha nodded, wishing Conn would say something to indicate he didn't want the handfasting to end, that he wanted to proceed with a wedding after their year and a day had passed. But he did not.

Athair, please! Give me courage. I do not want to lose Conn, but I cannot keep living my life based on the story of a false witness.

Once more, Sorcha realized the God to whom she sent her silent plea was not her beloved Brigid but Jehovah. Though she remained fearful, the prayer left her with a sense of peace.

If only I could be more like Conn and pray not just when I want something but to seek You, as well.

They were interrupted by Conn's voice. "Sorcha. They are ready to meet with you."

Sorcha took in a breath and tried to not to show her fear.

Most of the tribe, including the king and the full Brehon, awaited in the village square. She searched their faces. Most wore expressions of curiosity. Others saw her, refused to make eye contact, then whispered to the nearest counterpart. A few, mostly the members of the Brehon, wore looks of ill-concealed anger. She knew they felt that, by handfasting with a Christian, she had betrayed them. *Athair* looked the angriest of them all, a thought that unnerved her.

King Fergus opened the meeting. "Flann, my poet, asked us to meet regarding his elder daughter, Sorcha. She has a message of importance. Since there is no other business, I shall allow her to speak."

Sorcha walked to the center of the meeting place, her tribe surrounding her in a circle from all sides. Girded by Conn's look of encouragement, she nevertheless saw that his eyes revealed fear.

I AM, if You want to prove Yourself to me, do it now.

She spoke. "Thank you for respecting my *athair* by meeting here today. I will keep my message brief."

She gave the Brehon a grateful smile. "I have a confession to make. Many here have listened to Conn's teachings and become Christians, so you will understand what I am about to say. As to the rest of you, I ask in advance for your forgiveness. I also want to say that neither my *athair* nor my sister nor Conn knew anything about my schemes before I put them in place. Therefore, I ask that this tribe hold them guiltless in regard to my actions."

Whispers floated around her, speeding her heartbeat and her words.

"When I first saw Conn, like most of you, I doubted his teachings. How could one worship a God who promises eternal life?"

Several people grunted agreement.

"But I did not care about the holy man's teachings. I felt only desire to wed him."

Whispers increased.

"I was expected to wed Bryan." Sorcha looked at her former beau and his betrothed. Bryan's face flamed red while Mór tilted her chin toward Sorcha and took him by the forearm in a possessive manner. "Now that he is betrothed to Mór," Sorcha assured the crowd, "I wish them many blessings."

"Thank you, but your blessings are hardly cause to interrupt everyone's day," Bryan interjected. "I think we can adjourn this meeting."

Realizing that Bryan was reacting to his own hurt pride that he was not able to wed his first love, Sorcha held up her hand. "Wait. That is not all. I must reveal the deception I used to force Conn to join me in a handfasting ceremony."

"Force!" The word rippled through the crowd.

Torloch, the head of the Brehon, stroked his gray beard. "Continue."

"When I saw Conn, I decided I wanted him for myself even though his religion was strange to me. I convinced him to let me bring him a meal. I used special herbs in the stew. But before we ate, he said a blessing over the meal. I thought his words of thanks to God possessed some hidden power, like an incantation. I later learned that they were an expression of gratitude to God for His provision. And now I say a blessing over each meal." Sorcha expected everyone to resume whispering, but she could only conclude that shock had silenced them. "Conn's blessing rendered my powers—and the spell I placed on the food—useless. That was the first time I saw that Jehovah, the one who calls Himself 'I AM,' is greater than my Brigid."

The Brehon murmured. Sorcha could feel the glares of those who clung to druidism boring into her.

"Please do not condemn my daughter," Flann interjected. "She knows not what she says. She has been put under a spell by this...this..." He pointed at Conn. "Christian. Clearly, she needs to return home and let me help her break the bewitchment!"

Scattered shouts of concurrence ripped through the air.

Obviously encouraged by the expressions of support, Flann cried, "I say we should stone this man, Conn!" He directed a livid fist Conn's way.

"No!" Sorcha ran over to Conn and stood in front of him. "If you stone him, you must first stone me."

Conn spoke. "No, Sorcha. I will not permit that. If I must die for my Lord and Savior, so be it." He took Sorcha's hand in his, kissed it, and stepped in front of her.

"No!" Sorcha screamed.

Flann aimed his forefinger at his daughter. "You can see he has beguiled her. Had I known the danger, I never would have agreed to a handfasting." His chest puffed like that of an outraged grouse. "If the elder daughter of the king's bard can fall under the dominance of such a charmer, imagine the destruction he will wreak on the rest of this tribe. Rumor says he has made havoc with his ideas. Sorcha just said that some of our people have agreed to follow this new God. This is an abomination to our gods, the gods of our ancestors who have protected and guided us all these many years. This man must be stopped. Let us make an example of him. Let us begin the stoning now!"

Chapter 8

Following Flann's plea, men stooped to gather stones.

"No!" Sorcha turned to the Brehon, focusing her attention on her former beau. "Bryan, if you have ever cared for me one little bit, I beg of you to stop them."

"I cannot defend what is wrong."

"Conn is not wrong. They must hear the rest of my story. Please! Use all of your influence to stop them. Please!" She threw herself upon his chest and cried into his tunic.

"Make her cease," Mór hissed.

"Stop!" Bryan's voice filled the air. "Stop! There is more!"

Hardly believing her ears, Sorcha looked up at him. Disbelief turned to gratitude upon seeing a flicker of kindness in his gaze. "Thank you, Bryan," she said, realizing yet another of Conn's truths. Hope abounded even for the hardest of hearts. . . and heads.

"Sorcha says there is more to the story. I believe that before we stone a man—any man—we should be willing to consider all points of view and the full accounting of the events." Bryan turned to Torloch. "Do you agree?"

The senior Brehon didn't have to consider the question long. "No punishment shall be executed until all knowledge of the trespass is before the council. Tell us the rest, child."

Although she'd bought Conn time so she might spare him, Sorcha quaked. Her confession would reveal the depth of her cunning and would not be without consequences. Yet she had to confess to save Conn's life—and her soul.

"You believe Conn enchanted me," Sorcha said, "but I am the one who forced Conn into the handfasting ceremony through a lie. I told *Athair* and Bryan that Conn had taken advantage of our time alone together to become familiar with me as a husband knows a wife. But 'tis not true. That evening we were alone, he fell asleep."

The crowd inhaled in a collective gasp. Stones thudded to the ground.

"No, this cannot be!" Flann objected.

Sorcha sobbed. "I am sorry, *Athair*. I should not have borne false witness to you. . .or to Bryan. I was wrong to tell a falsehood, especially to further my own selfish ends."

Torloch intervened. "So you convinced Conn to accept a meal, then you seasoned it with special herbs that failed, but you told your *athair* otherwise?"

Sorcha nodded, tears misting her eyes.

Torloch's gaze set upon Flann. "Everyone in this tribe knows that your daughter is one for mischief. Why did you not consult the Brehon to solve this matter rather than compromising this holy man?"

"I spoke with the member of the Brehon who would be most affected by the outcome of this event, and that is Bryan. He and I approached Conn, who denied nothing."

Torloch looked at Conn. "Is this true?"

Conn answered. "I denied nothing."

"If you are a purported example of holiness, why did you not speak the truth?"

"Because I did not know for certain. I thought perhaps I did not remember what had transpired. I am not known for falling asleep when teaching a seeker; I must confess to not a small bit of embarrassment."

"Then you have been sorely wronged by this maiden and have every right to compensation from her family, who should exile her from Ballymara for her mischief."

Conn shook his head. "Nay, I have no wish for any harm to come to Sorcha. Hers was the impulse of youth, but her heart is good. She did not have to admit her scheming before this tribe and council, but she did."

"But you were dishonored," King Festus objected.

The onlookers stared at Conn. "If I cannot forgive Sorcha for her trespass, then how can I expect forgiveness for any trespass I may have committed at some time in my life, either by design or by negligence?"

Stillness claimed the crowd.

Torloch lifted his arm. "Be that as it may, an honor price is still required. I submit that Sorcha should not live the rest of her days as Conn's wife but as his slave."

Sorcha hurried to Conn in relief. "I will gladly live my life as your slave!" She dropped to her knees and kissed his sandaled feet, her tears leaving trails in the dust that covered them. She wiped them away with her golden auburn hair.

"I would never ask such a thing," Conn whispered.

But Flann wasn't satisfied. "Everyone here can see the humiliation to which my daughter has been reduced!" He shook his fist. "She shall never be a slave to any man! She is the daughter of the king's bard!"

Torloch raised the gray thatch of his brow. "The man is due recompense by law, as you well know, bard. If not your daughter's subjugation to him as a slave, there are two options. You can pay him the price of seven cumals. . .or she faces death."

Sorcha lifted her head. *Death! Surely I do not deserve death!*

"I want neither," Conn protested, but the chief Brehon waved him aside.

"What say you?" Torloch demanded.

"The decision should lie with this community, not with one man."

"Careful, Flann," Fergus warned.

Sorcha could almost hear the sweat rolling down her father's brow as he realized what he'd said in his temper. No one questioned the chief Brehon, not even the king.

" 'Tis not the same when it's your own at the receiving end of the stones, is it, Flann?" Torloch reminded him.

"Halt these proceedings; I implore you," Conn interrupted. "I am proud of Sorcha and the courageous woman she has become. I forgave her long ago."

"But—" Torloch began.

"Hear me, good sir, since I am the one wronged." Conn drew Sorcha to her feet, holding her in the protection of his arm. "Because she has confessed her sin, she has been forgiven by her heavenly Father. Sorcha committed a sin by breaking one of God's commandments. But as I have taught many times, He wrote those commandments in His hand, not man's. If anyone is to punish Sorcha, that one should be God Himself."

"So she should have no punishment whatsoever for lying to you?" Torloch asked, impatient.

"She has lived with fear of discovery and remorse for months. And now she has drawn the strength to face you today and lay her pride down at your feet. She has been punished enough," Conn answered.

"What if I were to say she should be stoned?" an elder challenged.

Conn faced the crowd. "Are any among you innocent of wrongdoing?"

The meeting place fell silent.

"Not one?" Conn persisted.

Still silence.

"Anyone who wants forgiveness need only approach the Lord with a repentant heart."

"But what of a good harvest?" someone asked. "Does your God promise that?"

"Scripture is full of accounts where the Lord blessed those who were faithful to Him. The book of Job describes the abundant blessings of a faithful man—many flocks, a number of children, and a great home—but Job was tested, too, and found dignity in his suffering. He remained faithful to the Lord. After the testing, Job was blessed with more possessions. But forgiveness is even more important. This situation today reminds me of an incident related by the Apostle John."

"The story of the adulteress," a woman guessed.

Conn smiled. "You have been listening to my teachings."

"What about the adulteress?" another asked.

"An adulteress was brought to Jesus to be punished. They were about to stone her when Jesus told them that the innocent one among them should cast the first stone. Just as we found today, no one could." Conn continued, "Jesus said, 'Thou shalt love the Lord thy God with all thy heart, and with all thy soul, and with all thy mind. This is the first and great commandment. And the second is like unto it, Thou shalt love thy neighbour as thyself.'"

Torloch stepped forward, offering his gnarled hand to the

holy man. "Conn, you have just condensed into two simple concepts laws that it took the Brehon twenty years to learn. And since you are the victim of Sorcha's offense and you proclaim your God forgives her, let it be known that this court forgives her as well."

A mingled response rose from the onlookers. Some shook their heads, while others murmured. Almost afraid to accept Torloch's words, Sorcha watched as chief elder conferred with the other members of the Brehon, King Festus among them. Soon Torloch turned back toward the crowd and lifted both arms to summon their attention.

"Years ago, our ancestors recorded a great star that marked the birth of a great King, as well as the darkness on the day of this King's death." Torloch nodded in Conn's direction. "And now His holy man tells us Jesus condensed all of man's laws into two." The old man scratched his head. "Who better to teach us than He who was proclaimed by the heavens themselves?" Torloch reached out for Conn. "And so I invite His servant Conn to teach us, that we might make his Master our Master as well."

"I humbly accept your grace and that of the one God." Conn's voice tightened with emotion.

King Festus lifted his sepulcher and brandished it over them. "Then let it be so. From this moment, the O'Cuilinn tribe of Ballymara will know this Christ as our teacher."

Sorcha couldn't believe what she was hearing. *Christ, the tribe's master and teacher? Surely Jehovah God and His Son Jesus are greater than all the Irish deities put together. Who else could have delivered such undeserved pardon for me?*

The day after the handfasting expired, Sorcha's fantasies came true. She was committing to Conn for life, in the midst of true love. Matthew, a Christian hermit priest whom Conn had taken a month to locate in another rath, had agreed to perform a ceremony accepted and approved by the church.

Flann walked with her down the pathway leading her to love. Her arm linked in his, she realized such a miracle could only be of God—the one true God that Conn, and now she, worshiped.

In remembrance of what Conn had taught her, Sorcha wove shamrocks into her wedding wreath, a floral ring that included a ribbon of red for the blood of Christ, black for His Crucifixion, and white for His resurrection.

When Matthew asked Sorcha if she would pledge to live with and to love Conn not for a year and a day, but until death, she could hardly speak, her happiness was so great. When Conn vowed to do the same, the glimmer in his eyes told her that his joy was no less. Finally he belonged to her, and she belonged to him—no deception, no falsehood, no herbs needed.

If only I had been honest from the start. I could have saved everyone strife and unhappiness. But I did not know I AM then. I know Him now.

The couple exchanged rings and said in unison, "As sure as the shamrock is green, as sure as Three are in One, our love will be redeemed by the Father, Spirit, and Son."

"Let this stone where we pledge our love always be known as the pledging stone," Conn added. "No promise made here shall ever be broken."

Conn drew near to kiss Sorcha. The kiss she always dreamed of—so warm, so willing. As they embraced, uncaring of the tribe's presence, they found true happiness in a love that would endure beyond the ages.

TAMELA HANCOCK MURRAY

Tamela is an award-winning, best-selling author of twenty Christian romance novels and novellas and seven Bible trivia books. She lives in Northern Virginia with her godly husband and beautiful daughters who keep her busy with church and school activities. When she and her husband married over twenty years ago, the bottom layer of their wedding cake was baked into the shape of a three-leaf clover.

Tamela loves to hear from her readers! Visit her Web site at www.tamelahancockmurray.com, or e-mail Tamela at Tamela@tamelahancockmurray.com.

A Legend of Love

Part 4

by Linda Windsor

Chapter 11

Maybe it was the exposure to the aged books or simply tension and worry as Moyra tried to absorb the story of Conn and Sorcha and read Jack's notes on the sly, but she had a banger of a headache by the time they'd finished. Instead of the hot meal he'd promised to treat her to, he offered her two aspirin and the option of grabbing some takeaway from a Chinese restaurant on the way out of town. It sounded heavenly to Moyra, who soon found her headache was soothed by the scent and warmth of the hot and sour soup. And the pullover where Jack, who'd insisted on driving, had chosen to share the meal presented a lovely view of the Irish Sea.

"I can't do the holy man bit," he quipped, "but consider me your knight in shining armor."

Okay, so she'd cried when Sorcha and Conn were willing to put their lives on the line for each other and how God rewarded them. And the pledge meant so much more now.

They'd been so interested in the story that lunch hadn't crossed their minds until it was too late. "Perhaps skipping lunch was the cause of my headache," she said as she stuffed the paper soup cup into the carryout bag. "I'm feeling much better."

"And you're ready to wrestle the car keys back?" Jack's face was a mirror of mischief.

"If you'd like." He could be so charming when he wanted to be. "Otherwise, I'll read about my family or rather about the holly tree roots."

"You read; I'll drive."

Contented to be spoiled for a while, Moyra picked up the photocopy of the legends associated with the tree. She'd known of the one where, after allegedly being used for the cross, the tree's berries turned from white to scarlet to reflect Christ's blood. Because of that, the holly was frequently associated with the Passion. The story of the shepherd boy who could only make a crown of holly as a gift for the Holy Infant and how it grew beautiful red berries in baby Jesus' presence was also familiar.

But the use of the tree by Conn and ancient holy men like him spoke to her battered spirit. The ancient druids had always held the tree sacred for its symbolism of everlasting life. They considered the tree the lord of the winter, bearing fruit in the midst of the season's lifelessness. So when the holy men brought the news of Christ, they proclaimed him Lord over death, Creator of the creation—the holly—and used the tree as a symbol of the Passion with yet another perspective.

"When all appears lost," Moyra read from the page, "and winter surrounds us, lose not your hope. Look to the holly tree and remember the Christ, the true Lord over winter and death."

"Cute," Jack observed, more tolerant than interested. But then Moyra preferred his full attention remain on the traffic.

Despite the spring wildflowers growing on the hills they passed, winter surely surrounded her and her hopes for Ballymara. The Christ who created the holly tree, the *cuileann*, renewed them. It was a tailor-made message of hope just for her through her family namesake.

Father, I claim the blood symbolized by those berries and the Christ who shed it, my Lord, over this wintry darkness.

Enveloped in a peace beyond her ken, Moyra wasn't aware that she'd drifted off to sleep until she was jerked from her nap by a sudden swerve of the car and the loud honk of the horn. She popped open her eyes in time to see an equally startled cow trotting down the road. The SUV leaped, or so it felt, off the paving and landed with a disheartening splat in a roadside bog.

"What kind of place is this with animals running about at will?" Jack fumed at her side. "Are you okay?"

Aside from her heart wedged somewhere in her throat? Moyra nodded. "Seat belts work wonders."

"Good thing we have an SUV." Jack shoved the gear into reverse but to no avail. They swished a bit in the muck, remaining as entrenched as ever.

Moyra couldn't make out the words he ground between his teeth and was content to leave it that way. She looked around them, recognizing they weren't that far from the Lafferty land. "I'm thinking there's a farm not far from here."

Jack cut her a sharp look. "Don't tell me, follow the cow?"

A grin crept to her lips, despite the fact that she'd ordinarily be blowing smoke out both ears by now. The same calm that had lulled her to sleep filled her voice. "Now, now, don't throw a wobbler. I imagine the dear is on her way home. Twilight isn't all that far away." Soft and gray as the day had been, darker clouds now churned from the northwest where they'd just been. "I think we'd best hurry."

Clearly unwilling to chase the creature that he held responsible for his predicament, Jack shifted the gears back and forth. "Drive all the way from Dublin on the wrong side of the road and a. . ." He gunned the engine, groping for a decent word. "A moon-eyed cow runs me off the road."

Moyra unfastened her seat belt. "Be a dear and hand me that umbrella in the door pocket."

"Where do you think you're going?" he asked as she slipped out of her practical pumps and reached behind the front seats for her Wellies. Boots were a staple in her car, given the wet climate.

"I'm going to hike up my skirt and wade to the road, where I intend to tear off for the farm beyond that rise before the bottom drops out of the sky."

Jack slammed his head against the headrest. "Some SUV."

"It's an SUV, not an amphibious vehicle," Moyra pointed out, pulling first one boot on then the other. "I'm sure the farmer has a tractor or Mr. Lafferty does. We're near his place, so we'll be out in a jiff. . .and with tea, no doubt."

"And he's going to come out in what looks like a building thunder buster to get us out of this?"

"Why wouldn't he?"

Lips thinned, Jack cut off the engine and pocketed the keys. "I keep forgetting that I'm in some Brigadoon-ish dimension."

"Do you think someone will make off with the car while we're gone?" Moyra couldn't help tugging at his deteriorating humor. She thought her knight would boil in his armor from exasperation. And it felt wonderful not to be the one about to pop a clog.

"Stay put," he ordered, throwing the door open and getting out of the car. "Aw man," she heard him groan as he sloshed his way around to her side. "I lost a shoe," he told her upon reaching her side and opening her door.

"What *are* you doing?"

Instead of answering, Jack slipped his arms beneath her and lifted her from the car. "Hold on to your umbrella, Moyra Rose," he said in a John Wayne voice. "No sense in both of us freezing our knee caps off."

Jack was as strong as his broad shoulders suggested. But not even John Wayne could wade out of this bog with double the weight on his feet. Undaunted, Jack struggled with his first step—

"Honestly, Jack, I have my Wellies—"

And stumbled.

With a shriek, Moyra landed flat on her back in the water. Jack pitched over her. The icy water rushed up her skirt and through her clothes. "Get off me," she shouted, pushing him away before her hair was soaked as well. "Your gallantry is about to drown me."

Chapter 12

"Great day in the mornin', what happened to the two of you?" Katie exclaimed as Moyra led the way into the house. "You look like that pair in the American Gothic painting. . .minus the pitchfork."

Ordinarily Jack might have laughed at her accurate assessment, but he still suffered pangs of humiliation.

Tired and likely still chilled to the bone as he, in spite of the dry borrowed farm clothing, Moyra swept bedraggled, rain-kinked curls from her face and gave her sister a steely look. "We went for a swim." She raised her hands like a preacher reaching for God's help. "What does it look like, Katie? Jack ran off the road, and we landed in a bog. But for these borrowed togs, we'd be dripping where we stand."

"Humph, no small wonder," Polly snorted from her living room rocker. "Never give an American your car keys, Moyra Rose."

"It was the Murphys' cow, Gran," Moyra replied in his defense.

She had taken his dumping her in the water better than he had, and Jack intended to thank her for tolerating his little stockinged-foot rant afterward. In fact, for tolerating the entire episode. He had been driving faster than prudent, which only added to his ire—at himself.

"Oh dear. I'll put on some hot tea and coffee," Katie said, trundling off for the loft kitchen as he took to the stairs.

"Taking a hot shower and getting into my own clothes would be heaven," Moyra said, walking past Jack, who stood back so that she might precede him.

"Milady, your soggy knight is with you all the way. Figuratively speaking," he added at her sharp swivel and glance.

Don't even go there, he told himself, looking down at the mini-braided rugs covering each step. Still, the suggestion warmed him from the inside out. "And thanks for not taking my head off when I not only ran your car into the bog but dumped you, as well. That's the last time I try playing hero."

Moyra opened the door to her bedroom. "There's many a man wouldn't try." She attempted a smile and closed the door behind her.

The woman was an enigma. In the beginning, she'd given him the scorched earth treatment. After nearly drowning her in a bog, she'd given him—what was the word?

Opening the door to his own quarters, Jack stopped short. His newly laundered shirts were scattered on the floor and his bed a tangle of covers, not made with the usual tidy, almost military precision. More startling, the blankets moved.

"Moy—"

Jack broke off at the sound of a pitiful mew. With a growing mingle of suspicion and dread, he strode over to the bed and carefully lifted away the covers.

"Well, hello, Buttons. Look what you've brought me." What was it with him and cats?

Kittens, to be exact. Three black with white socks like their mother and one orange tabby, all squirmed in a pile, blindly looking for their bedraggled mother's nourishment.

The mother cat looked up at him as if to say, *You wouldn't believe the day I've had.*

With a sigh, Jack answered, "Trust me, Buttons, I've got an idea."

"Aliens." Gran raised her eyes to the ceiling the following morning as if God might explain her granddaughter's loss of sanity. "And Buttons havin' her babes in the American's bed instead of the nice little basket I made for her in the furnace room. What is the world comin' to, Moyra Rose?"

Moyra smiled up from her tea and toast, trying not to wince at Gran's fire red hair. The girls had done it last night, just as Gran's former pitch black had softened to a more natural shade.

"And me, lookin' like I ought to be singin' on stage with that John fella with the funny glasses," the older woman snorted. "I've lived too long."

Gran left the Loft kitchen with a plate stacked high with pancakes for Ned and Peg's wedding party, who now gathered in the Mugger's Loft, making plans for the rehearsal dinner Saturday after the game.

"Put on your sweet face, Gran," Moyra called after her.

At that moment, Jack peeked around the doorjamb. "Fierce as a toothless hound, eh?"

"You're catching on." Moyra motioned him in. "Sit down. . . unless you want to dine with the Trekkies in the Loft."

"How's the new mother this morning?" he asked, helping himself to a cup of coffee from the commercial pot.

"Wishing she could send the kittens back to where they came from, I'd think." Moyra chuckled. "But to answer your question, mama and kits are fine. Have a look in the furnace room when you take a notion." She pointed across the hall to a door next to the family kitchen and living room, a pet door installed in one of its panels.

She could still see Jack sitting on the edge of his bed in a jogging suit, hair wet and uncombed, watching a nest of mewing fur with the most befuddled expression. One would have thought he considered sharing his bed, the way he ever so gently stroked Buttons's fur. More the wonder, the mother cat, who never took kindly to strangers, allowed it.

After cleaning the bed and room to a fare-thee-well, Moyra and Gran had moved Buttons and brood to the furnace room.

"So what's on the agenda for today?" Moyra asked as Jack sat down. He hadn't mentioned any plans the night before.

"I want to go over my notes. . .and that stuff you have on the holly. Could be a nice touch," he said, lifting the cup to his lips. "Readers like that sort of thing."

"Don't we all like an affirmation of our faith, one way or another?" Moyra got up and opened the fridge door. "Would you like some eggs? Or there's hot cereal on the stove."

"Don't bother. This toast is fine. And I won't be mentioning the holly in a religious context."

Not in a religious context? "Let me fix fresh," she said, snatching up the platter of cold toast that she and the family had shared earlier. "The birds have to eat, you know. Gran loves walking down to the river and feeding the ducks and birds with the leftover bread."

"I meant to ask," Jack said. "What happened to her hair?"

Moyra popped more bread in the toaster and set it before joining her companion at the table. "If Peg said jump in the river, Gran would at least consider it. Although if my niece doesn't stop using Gran for a guinea pig, the poor dear'll have no hair to color. You saw she wears a hat when she goes out."

Jack grinned. "I don't remember my grandparents."

"And your parents?"

"Divorced. Mom lives in LA with her second husband, and I haven't heard from my father since he moved to Key West. . .has a fishing boat there, but I've never been invited."

Despite Jack's shrug of indifference, Moyra sensed a core of bitter resignation. "Were you young when they divorced?"

"In college." He jumped to his feet to get the toast before Moyra could respond. "Guess they'd done their duty by me. . . staying together for my sake and fighting like pit bulls till I was out of the house. What about you?"

Moyra fetched him a clean plate. "A car crash took them to heaven when I was twelve. Gran's raised me here at the public house."

While Jack buttered his toast and slathered homemade marmalade over it, Moyra refreshed her tea from a thermal carafe.

"I gotta ask," he said at last.

She lifted her brow. "Ask what?"

"Why is everyone so obliging when I intend to show how the pledging stone is a fraud?"

Why indeed? She'd wondered that herself and came to only one conclusion. "Because you are our guest and a fellow-man. . .no matter how misguided you might be," she added, unable to let the point slide. "And while we are a small village, Jack, we're large on faith and do our best to live it. Some are better at it than others, grant you, but we try."

"So faith is why you stopped short of biting off my head and spitting down my neck?"

Moyra weighed her response as it gathered. Right off, her boss had threatened her into tolerating Jack. But somehow, digging into Ballymara's past had underscored the need to give him a chance to see the truth on his own.

"In the end, yes. I saw that you were not the ogre I'd first thought. And as a decent man, given the chance, you might come to see the truth about the pledging stone of Ballymara."

She slid into her chair, placing her hand on his arm. If ever her heart was on her sleeve, it was now. "Have you seen it, Jack?"

He covered her hand with his, entwining her soul with his gaze. "I mean this with all my heart, Moyra Rose O'Cullen. There is a part of me that wants to believe in that stone. But to date, I haven't read anything to substantiate its power."

"It's not the power of the stone, Jack." Moyra groaned. " 'Tis the power of love. . .God's love. Can't you see that?"

As though a curtain dropped over it, Jack's gaze became veiled. Back stiffening, he withdrew from their contact. "God hasn't been as generous with His love in my life, Moyra, so I hope you'll understand when I say no."

Numb with disbelief, Moyra hardly flinched when he pushed away his half-finished coffee and rose. In heart and soul, she'd known Jack had been changed. After all, she'd changed. So Jack *had* to.

"I'm spending tomorrow with John and late afternoon with the football club."

She nodded. *Is this it, God?*

As Jack's retreating steps echoed in the hall, a knock

sounded on the door. It was Ned, evidently done with his chores and ready to join the fun. At Moyra's invitation, he stepped through the door.

"I just dropped off the wedding programs at the chapel, and look at this." He tossed a sprig of holly on the table. "Got it from the holly in the churchyard. Did you ever see so many berries in a cluster this time of year? You'd think it was Christmas."

Chapter 13

The Mugger's Loft was a riot of celebrating football players, while aliens from galaxies Moyra had never heard of filled the dining room for the rehearsal dinner. Gran ran the kitchen with some temp help from the golf-and-country club, producing a sumptuous Celtic meal of fillet of trout with a warm goat cheese tart, baby leaf salad with pine kernels, and a basil pesto. The alternate was rack of lamb with a turnip and nutmeg au gratin. No one made lamb like Gran. The country club had been after her recipe for years. *Chranachan*, a spirited pudding borrowed from the Scots of raspberries, toasted oats, and soft cheese and vanilla ice cream, served as dessert.

Yet Moyra's appetite was as scant as the meal was abundant. Since their talk the morning after the bog debacle, Jack had maintained a distance. A loud roar of laughter drew her attention to the doublewide entrance separating the rooms where Jellybean, the newly appointed mascot of the Ballymara Rams skittered into the dining room, the fake ram's horns banded with elastic to his head making the animal fit right in with the majority of the rehearsal dinner guests.

Before Moyra could react, Gran burst into the dining

room, brandishing a broom with a vengeance. At the sight of the old woman with hair as unnatural as its horns, the startled goat decided to take its chances with fifteen or so football players and scampered back into the cheering throng.

"I let ye bring that animal into the Loft, lads," Gran hollered, moving after Jellybean with a surprising speed for her age. "But I'll not have it in me dining room. Someone take it over to Tommy O' at the pub across the street."

Jack appeared for a second, looking grander than a soul ought in the Ballymara Rams shorts and shirt. Many was the game she'd watched without getting distracted by sturdy legs and broad shoulders. . .until that afternoon.

"I'll do it, Gran," he said. "And thanks for being such a good sport." With that, he bussed the older woman on the cheek. For the first time since Moyra could remember, Gran was at a loss for words. With a nod and a righteous sniff, she walked back through the dining room and through the kitchen doors to the huzzahs of the alien guests.

Not so much as a glance at her, Moyra thought, stabbing at a piece of the delicious fish with her fork. Just when she'd thought there was a chance—she'd seen Ned's berry-laden holly hadn't she?—it felt as though she were back to the square-one standoff. And Monday he flew home to the States.

It was the faith issue, she thought the following afternoon as she examined the deep purple maid-of-honor dress in the mirror with a look of utter dismay. All she needed was a mask, and she could trick-or-treat with the best of them. She heaved a sigh, watching the artificially plumped globe cinched beneath her bodice and at her knees rise and drop with it. Jack Andrews would as soon believe in the stone as love, and even if she were practiced at the art of flirtation, or inclined to flirt, his mind would hardly be changed by an eggplant with arms and legs.

Not that Moyra would ever have the chance, but if she ever did have a wedding of her own, her niece Peg was going to pay dearly for this.

The wedding was a circus straight from the Starship Enterprise. Surely Conn and Sorcha, Breanda and Ardghal, and Nick and Keely watched dumbstruck from heaven as a pointy-eared Ned, clad in a red shirt with black pants, and Peg, looking like a white eggplant with pointy ears, exchanged their vows. After passing through the bell-ringing congregation at the end of the ceremony, they stopped beneath the arched entrance containing the pledging stone and sealed their union with the ancient pledge.

"As sure as the shamrock is green, as sure as Three are in One, our love shall be redeemed by the Father, Spirit, and Son."

Padrac snapped pictures, both for the wedding and for Jack's article. Once the after-wedding photos had been taken, he called out to Jack. "How about one with you and Moyra Rose in the entrance?"

Moyra felt the color seep from her face. The whole world would see her in this dress.

"You know, a follow-up on the article," Padrac finished.

She sought Jack with a plaintive gaze.

Jack shook his head. "Forget that, Padrac. I want this to be a credible article. One look at that dress, and my reading audience would toss the magazine without reading it."

Moyra let out her breath in relief.

"Not that you aren't the loveliest plum I've ever seen," Jack added, offering his arm. "Ride with me and Padrac to the country club?"

"Too big for a plum," Moyra amended. "I'm an eggplant. . . and I promised to drive Gran, Katie, and Patrick over. But we could toss you in the back or strap you to the roof."

Jack smiled at her paltry attempt at humor. "You know, there was a time when I'd have thought you really meant that. But I'll ride with Padrac, thank you. Gran might be packing her broom."

There was a time I'd have thought you really meant that.

Jack's words trickled through her mind later at the golf-and-country club, as, seated at the head table next to the radiant bride, Moyra picked at her share of the galactic, gray-iced wedding cake. Ned and Peg had already hacked a chunk of the Enterprise-shaped confection with a sinister-looking dagger and smeared it on each other's face to cheers in English, Irish, and alien-ese.

Now the DJ resumed his music while Gran sliced and served dessert with a skill that suggested all her cakes were shaped like spacecraft. Clad in a shimmering, pearl gray dress-robe, Polly O'Cullen was quite the Vulcan grandmother, her thankfully thick and healthy hair once again pitch black.

The bridesmaids in their collective universal knowledge had decided the night before that there were no scarlet-haired Vulcans. But Gran drew the line on the pointy ears, covering them with her hair, which was pulled back in her classic knot and porcupined with little silver sparkling sticks.

Try as she might, Moyra couldn't get into the celebration. Jack Andrews dominated her thoughts. That first day or so, she *would* have meant her offer to strap Jack to the rack, especially if torture was involved. Today, she didn't know how she felt. . .aside from miserable. Miserable that she hadn't changed Jack's mind and miserable that he was going away before—

"Excuse me, Lady Eggplant, but would you give this knight in *rusted* armor a second chance and dance?" Jack's emphasis on *rusted* made Moyra grin.

She pushed away from the table and fought to straighten the stays that held her skirt ballooned about her waist, hips, and legs. "If we fall in the pool, at least I'll float."

A mini pool had been brought in and adorned with plants in one corner of the room. Floating candles cast a glow upon the tiled ceiling, lending a romantic light to the hearts of Ballymaran and visiting alien alike.

"I just wanted to tell you that I'm catching a ride tonight to Dublin, so you won't have to worry about driving me to the airport tomorrow."

The news pitched Moyra's mind into a bog, chilling and scattering thought. "It would have been no trouble," she heard herself say. What had she done? Why did men bolt from her, even when she made an effort to be nice?

"One of the team players is headed there to drop his son off at the university tonight, so I'm going with him."

"But. . .did. . ." She stammered like her heart.

"You are one special lady, Moyra Rose O'Cullen." Jack's voice grew husky as he continued. "This has been a memorable assignment."

Assignment. Her chest clenched. That was all it was. Distracted by a tide of despair, Moyra hardly noticed that they'd stopped dancing while the music played on. His embrace tightened about her, overcoming the stays that had maintained a distance between them. His gaze smoldered as she met it with her curious one. Or was it the glow of the floating candles near their feet?

Jack kissed her. Not the stolen kind, but one that declared *I don't care who sees us*—and more. More than his lips spoke. This was a melding of the hearts beating in counterpoint to each other's drum. It was sweet, yet dizzying. It spoke of passion enough to melt her stays, yet respect. And when he drew away, a part of Moyra went with him.

"Thank you, Moyra Rose. Never lose that beguiling combination of fire and innocence."

With a wink, Jack turned and left through a side entrance. Moyra wanted to run after him, but her feet refused to move from the spot where his kiss had welded them. Unshed tears brimmed in her eyes, stinging, mosquito-like compared to the pain assailing her heart.

"He'll be back, Moyra Rose." At the touch of a frail hand on her arm, Moyra turned to see Gran standing beside her. "Now dry your eyes and get out there with the unmarried girls to catch the bouquet." She pointed to where a group of giggling hopefuls gathered behind the bride. "And this time, darlin', be sure to catch it."

Chapter 14

Moyra tucked the ad copy that she'd prepared for a Dublin-area circular about sights to see in Ballymara under her arm and headed down the hall from her town-center office to meet Mayor Creegan. Two months since Jack had left, and she still had her job. But then, Jack's article in *World Travelogue* hadn't come out yet.

"Moyra, glad you could come on such short notice," Creegan said when she knocked on the jamb of his open door. "Come in. Have a seat."

The way he talked, one would think Ballymara was a hotbed of activity. The room still held the faint scent of cigars from the days when smoking hadn't been banned in public places.

"I brought the Dublin ad you were in such a rush—" Moyra broke off. There it was, sitting on Creegan's desk as if it had materialized from her earlier thought—the quarterly issue of *World Travelogue* in all its shining glory. Featured on the cover, no less, was picturesque Ballymara Chapel with the caption THE PLEDGING STONE OF BALLYMARA—LEGEND OR LARK by Jack Andrews.

Moyra dropped into the leather chair across from Creegan

to catch up with her sinking heart.

"I marked the article." Unsmiling, he motioned for her to pick the issue up.

Father in heaven, hear my plea. "Did we come out alright?" she asked, leaving it to God to figure out exactly what that was. To salvage Ballymara's past and future. To bring Jack back, her heart chimed in with logic.

"Go on, read it. He covered everything, your family past, the whole shebang."

Padrac should be proud of his work, she thought, opening to the marked spot. She'd heard he'd been paid very well for his photos.

"Just the highlighted parts for now," Creegan prompted with his usual impatience. "You can take it with you for the details."

Moyra searched the glossy pages for the yellow high-lighted print. She groaned upon reading how Jack challenged the stone and repeated the words from the plaque. If she were uninvolved, the hook was excellent. She'd have to read until the end. Flipping from page to page, past the stained-glass peacemaker window with the lariat-toting shepherd and the mercy representation of the patrons of the orphanage-turned-almshouse-turned-church-hall; past the panoramic shot of Ballymara Castle and photos of the Brennans in costume.

There was even a shot of Jellybean prancing back and forth between the field and stands at the football game where the Rams battled in yellow and red against the blue and black clad opponents. The heart of Ballymara was all there in photos—Gran's Publick House, a long shot of High Street, and the early morning view of the chapel, graveyard, and round tower ruins with the sun-dashed sparkle of the river beyond.

"The last page, Moyra Rose," Creegan said, nostrils flaring with exasperation. "Read that. . .aloud, if you please."

Aloud did not please her, but the mayor's *if you please* meant *do it*.

"And so I left Ballymara, mission nearly accomplished. I could find no historical record of any broken vows or contracts made at the famous pledging stone. But I can tell what I did find. I found a place that opened its arms and heart to me, a stranger out to possibly rob many of them of their livelihoods with this article.

"There was the couple who offered me a king's hospitality and tour, allowing me to research at the table where Lady Breanda and Ardghal might have decided to build an orphanage because of the mercy they'd been shown. While I'm not into wedding planning, I don't think I've ever seen a more perfect place for a wedding party to stay and have a reception.

"And I can't say enough about the people of the village: the football team who plays something like soccer to us Americans but with more kick, hands, and elbows; the farm couple, who provided dry clothes and hot tea and pulled my vehicle out of a bog after a cow ran me off the road—my fault, not the cow's; and Polly O'Cullen, a sprite of an elderly woman who runs Gran's Publick House and serves home-cooked food that will make a guy swallow his tongue. A better sport, you'll never find. Then there was Father Mackenna, who went out of his way to provide me information about the peacemaking cowboy who rode into Ballymara and stayed.

"With each day that passed, I understood my nineteenth-century countryman's decision more and more. In retrospect,

I came to understand the legend of the pledging stone. You see, fellow travelers, the power is not in the stone itself, but in the heart and soul that it represents. It lives in the people of Ballymara. It's not something you can measure or quantify. It's meant to be felt.

"And so, I saved the one who most impressed me to the last—the pretty Irish colleen who showed me Ballymara. Moyra Rose O'Cullen said many wise things that escaped me at the time, for I was looking for the obvious, that which can be detected by the standard five senses, not the more powerful things in this world that can only be *known*.

"But I recall vividly the proverb Moyra Rose O'Cullen quoted me on the day I insulted both her and the spirit of Ballymara. 'The only cure for love is marriage.'"

Moyra looked up from her reading. "I did tell him that. I thought we'd use it as a theme when we do a new brochure." When Creegan flicked his fingers at her to read on, she did:

"After much deliberation and the worst case of melancholy I've ever had, I've come to the conclusion that I am smitten."

Moyra gasped, driving her heart to the back of her throat. "Smitten, he says."

"Read, Moyra Rose, read," her employer insisted through clenched teeth, as though in pain.

"So I leave it to the reader to judge on his or her own the merit of the pledging stone legend. As for me, by the time she reads this, I will be waiting, in the arch of Pledging Stone Chapel, ready to eat the proverbial crow and recite Conn's ancient vow, because this misguided, cynical writer needs relief from this thing called *love*."

The road from High Street to the river was lined with familiar faces, but Moyra raced down the hill toward the church afoot, her SUV still parked in the town-center lot. She was breathless when she spied Gran, Katie, and Peg holding open the iron gate to the churchyard. And as she drew close enough to see beneath the berry-laden branches of the holly trees, there was Jack, grinning like he was standing barefoot on a bed of their sharp, pointed leaves.

"Go on, Moyra Rose. Catch him good this time," Gran called out as Moyra rushed by her and into Jack's open arms.

"Jack, I read—"

Jack cut her off with kiss. Breathing heavily through her nostrils, Moyra gave back as good as she got, not about to let a little thing like asphyxiation come between her and the man who'd won her heart. Camera flashes and clicks confirmed that everyone in Ballymara knew of Jack's return except her.

"I love you, Moyra Rose O'Cullen," Jack growled, drawing no more than a breath away from her lips. "You've given new life to my heart and my faith."

"I. . .love you, too," she said in a rush, reaching to brush her hair off her face. Somewhere along the way, the band that secured it at her neck had been lost. "I must look like a wild woman after my dash down the hill."

"Aye, that you do, lass. My wild Irish rose," he said, drawing her over to the plaque. Trapping her between his arms, with both hands now on Conn's ancient vow, he arched his brow at her. "Care to join me, or do I have to do all the work alone?"

With a dazzle of a smile, Moyra turned so that her hands

were on the stone, too.

"Say it so's we all can hear ye, darlin' girl," Gran instructed from the foot of the steps.

"I'm thinkin' she wants to make sure this takes." Moyra giggled, for Jack's ear only.

"Ready?" he asked.

She nodded.

"Did you ever see a holly bear all through summer?" someone remarked in the background.

Myra's heart smiled as she and Jack began in concert. "As sure as the shamrock is green, as sure as Three are in One, our love shall be redeemed by the Father, Spirit, and Son."

Epilogue

The crescendo of the organ music signaled the guests to stand in Pledging Stone Chapel as Mayor Creegan escorted his daughter down the aisle. Padrac, back from university for the summer, took pictures, moving about the church quick as a leprechaun to get the best angle. Next to Moyra in the pew, her husband, freelancing for the *Ballymara Tribune* between his writing assignments from the New York office of *World Travelogue*, jotted down notes.

"Wish I'd been doing this when Peg got married," he grumbled beneath his breath. "It'd be a lot more to write about than white lace and roses."

"*We* had white lace and roses," she reminded him as Mary Creegan walked by, a light unto herself with happiness. The mayor looked as though he were about to faint.

"And sprigs of trimmed holly, don't forget that," Jack said of their Christmas wedding.

Moyra hardly heard the ceremony. Prayer consumed her consciousness, prayer to the Lord of winter, the Christ of her heart, who carried her through the dark time, when she felt stripped of life and hope, and answered her petitions beyond her expectations. She'd prayed for a good article about Ballymara but hadn't prayed for Jack's return, even though she secretly longed for it.

But God knew her heart's desire better than she. Now she was happily married to a man who, in finding his love for her, had found Christ once again.

The gentle touch of Jack's hand on her swollen belly brought Moyra back to the church where the bride and groom now approached the arch as husband and wife. As they began to recite Conn's pledge, Jack mouthed the words to her.

"As sure as the shamrock is green, as sure as Three are in One, our love shall be redeemed by the Father, Spirit. . ."

Jack gave her an impish wink and improvised, "And little one."

LINDA WINDSOR

Linda Windsor is the author of sixteen secular and ten-plus inspirational historical novels and modern romantic comedies. Inspired by Irish ancestry, she wrote *The Fires of Gleannmara* Irish historical trilogy, with *Riona* finaling for the 2002 Christy Award, while her trademark humor shines in her award-winning contemporary romances. The Eastern Shore of Maryland author lives in a big, family-restored eighteenth-century farmhouse with her husband (with whom she shares a music ministry), two children, and mom—shades of the Waltons and loving it.

Visit Linda's website at www.LindaWindsor.com.